RUBBLE

SKYE MCNEIL

HOT TREE PUBLISHING

ALSO BY SKYE MCNEIL

APPOINTED BY FATE TRILOGY

APPOINTED BY FATE

EXONERATED WITH LOVE

CREDENCE

ATLAS SERIES

HEARTS ABROAD

OCEANS AWAY

MACHA MC SERIES

DOC T

KEVLAR

RUBBLE

BREWER

FOR INFORMATION, CONTACT THE PUBLISHER, HOT TREE PUBLISHING.

WWW.HOTTREEPUBLISHING.COM

EDITING: HOT TREE EDITING

COVER DESIGNER: BOOKSMITH DESIGN

E-BOOK: 979-1-922359-84-1

PAPERBACK: 978-1-922359-86-5

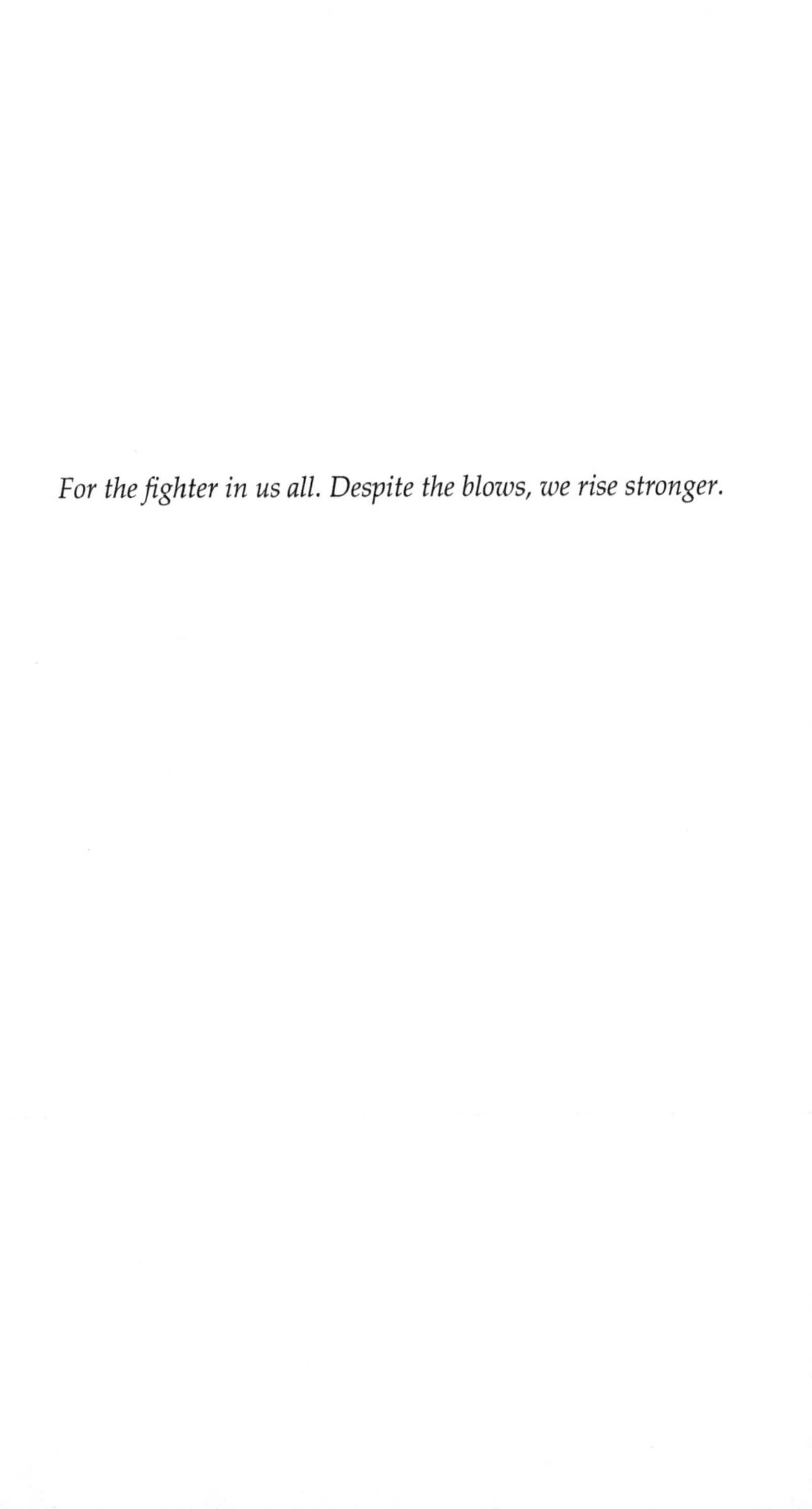

For the fighter in us all. Despite the blows, we rise stronger.

PROLOGUE

KASSIAN

Kassian Hardy slowly lifted his head, eyes no longer focused on his raw bloodstained knuckles.

The bars of the jail cell clanged noisily, and the door slid open. He stood, making sure to give the other occupants a steely glare before favoring his left leg on his way through the barred exit. There was no way in hell he could take on the five men he shared a cell with only moments earlier. Though he walked away the victor in his recent MMA fight, there was a cost to his unscathed record. He clenched his jaw, pain shooting through his muscles with every step he took.

It's worth it. A small part of his subconscious disagreed. Even if he kept up his winning streak, the damage to his body would eventually take its toll. He shook his head and straightened his back. No, he wasn't about to give up the one thing that made him feel alive, wanted, needed... even if only for a few rounds.

The hallway widened to the entrance and Kassian glanced around the nearly vacant room. The stench of bleach, vomit, and piss caused his nose to wrinkle. They were scents he knew all too well. Memories of his past life flooded him, but he swallowed, pushing them down yet again.

He paused at the front desk, the thick plexiglass streaked with fingerprints and a red lipstick smear. "Who paid the bond?"

The jailer shoved Kassian's personal belongings through the small hole at the bottom of the glass and jutted his chin to the right.

Following the direction, Kassian narrowed his swollen eyes at the man in a leather cut signing discharge paperwork at the other desk. He snorted. *A biker, great.* His trainer usually posted the bond when a fight went rogue, but that wasn't him.

Curling his hands into fists hurt, but he didn't give a damn. Owing anyone wasn't his style if he could help it. He could pay the guy. Once he collected the winnings from the previous night's fight, that is.

"Who the hell are you?"

His voice echoed over the puke-green covered walls. All eyes immediately snapped to his six-foot-six-inch frame. Every eye but his bond benefactor's. The man with bright red hair speckled with a touch of white just kept sliding his pen across the forms.

"Are you deaf, old man?" Kassian crossed the space in a mere four steps, his long legs eating up the flimsy laminate flooring. He towered above the biker, the emblem on the back of the leather cut one he'd never seen around town. He couldn't deny the goddess-like creature it depicted was intimidating and fascinating at the same time.

Finally, the man stopped, nodded at the woman behind the window, and turned toward him.

"Nah, not deaf. A little selective in my hearing." He smirked. "Or so says my old lady."

Kassian's head pounded from the wallops he took the night before, but the casual words with an Irish accent only made it worse. He glowered at the shorter man, but the biker didn't react or even twitch. He merely stared right back into the mismatched eyes that stunned every girl Kassian met.

"Cut the shit. Who are you?"

"Lorcan O'Grady to you, but my club calls me Reaper."

Kassian glanced at the name on Lorcan's vest, then to the patch on the opposite side. "President, huh? That supposed to mean something?"

Lorcan shrugged and leaned against the counter. "Is

Rubble supposed to mean something to me?" Before Kassian could reply, the other man continued. "Because I saw your fight. You're good, sure, but you don't live up to your name, boyo."

A shot of adrenaline coursed through his veins. He never watched the crowd before, during or after a fight. It'd only throw him off. Still, it surprised him that a biker from God knew where came to see him demolish another fighter.

"Old man, I'm tired, bleeding, and sore, and you're barking up the wrong tree if you think I'll join whatever misfit gang you got." He slid on his jacket, bruised arms screaming at his jerky movements. "I don't join clubs, so you can fuck off."

Chuckling, Lorcan started walking toward the door. "Oh, I'm not here to recruit you. My club doesn't need a hothead."

Despite the truthful barb, he had to know. "Then why'd you pay to get me out? My trainer is probably on his way right now to do the exact same thing."

The biker slipped on his sunglasses, his blue eyes now hidden from the world. "Because I'm hoping that somewhere beneath all your bullshit is a man I *do* want in my MC."

"Don't count on it."

Lorcan glanced to the window then back. "So, I shouldn't tell the Feds where you're at?"

Ice filtered through Kassian's veins. No one knew about the warrant except his trainer. He closed the distance between them and gripped a fistful of Lorcan's cut. "Who the hell told you about that?" he seethed between his teeth.

"Boyo, not much happens in my town without me hearing about it."

"I'm not from your town."

"No, but your parents were." In one quick move, Lorcan escaped Kassian's grip and shoved him off balance. "And I swore I'd find you and look out for you. I'm a man of my word."

Kassian chuckled darkly. "My parents were addicted to any drug they could get their hands on. No way they cared even a lick about me."

Lorcan removed the sunglasses, the concern evident in his eyes. "Your mum died after you were born, Kassian. And your da… sure, he had his demons, but he loved you. They both did."

This wasn't the story his child protective services handler spewed every chance she got. Not to mention every foster mom who took him in over the years. Women abandoned and mistreated him for as long as he could remember. He wasn't sure if he should or even could believe what this stranger said.

"Doesn't matter. I have a life here." He brushed past Lorcan and into the streaming sunlight.

"Aye, but for how much longer? Your body will give up long before your mind with each fight. Then what will you have? Memories of winning?"

Kassian kept his eyes trained on the horizon. A city bus would be along soon enough. *Since apparently my trainer forgot.*

"I'm offering you a family. One that won't give up on you."

It sounded too good to be true. It was all he wanted growing up. After being tossed from group home to foster family on repeat, the desire to have some good in his life remained the same. He eyed Lorcan. The man looked decent enough.

"I'll be eighteen in three months. You lost your chance."

A police siren blared on the street, passing the jail quickly, the city bus not far behind. This was his chance to escape. Run before anyone knew where he was. He could start over. Again. He'd done it ten times before.

"You don't need a judge to say you're family." Lorcan smiled up at him. "Just somebody who wants to take care of you. Macha can do that."

"And I'm just supposed to believe this?" Kassian scoffed, wincing when the cut on his lip cracked open and the metallic taste of blood hit his tongue.

The city bus neared, its engine huffing noisily

under the day's heat. But it was the dark sedan behind it that gave Kassian a moment of pause. There weren't any lights, but he had been able to spot an undercover car from miles away ever since he was eight years old.

Running a hand over his bald head, he let out a breath. His past had caught up to him and he could either run or face it.

"What's it going to be, boyo?"

Kassian swung his gaze to the Irishman. To his surprise the man wasn't leering. He was merely lighting up a smoke.

"You, I guess." He shrugged. "So, what do I have to do? Take somebody out? Toss a few fights? What? There's always something." Being indebted to anyone felt like shit, but prison would be worse.

Lorcan took a long drag from the cigarette. "None of the above." He waved to Kassian and started walking toward an early 2000s model pickup truck.

For a moment, the world stood still. The city bus chugged away, and the patrol car shut off. Kassian couldn't tell if this biker was loony or legit, but he'd take his chances. He'd never give up MMA. Not for this guy or any other. He was a fighter and he'd never hang up that role.

He moved toward the truck, giving the county jail one last glance over his shoulder. A new start was exactly what he needed.

"So, that's the cost?" he asked, safely stowed in the truck.

Lorcan handed him a stack of brochures. "You've been on your own too long. You need structure before I'll even consider letting you in my club." He started the truck, '70s rock music filling the cab. "Pick one of those and I'll do the rest."

Kassian rifled through the pamphlets and snorted. Every subject from counseling to joining the Armed Forces stared back at him. "Why should I?"

Lorcan pulled out of the parking lot, the cigarette resting in his left hand making Kassian itch for one. "Nobody's given you a fighting chance, Kassian. I want to. Macha wants to give you an opportunity for a better life. If you decide later you don't want our help, we'll accept it. Until then, consider our club your last foster home."

Kassian kept staring at the Irishman, waiting for him to take back the words. It didn't make sense. He was nobody except to the state. The alternative was to go back to a foster home that didn't want him. The club didn't sound appealing, but neither did a foster home. *I guess the club's better than being on the run.*

"What about my warrant?"

"Taken care of. Your underground fighting days are over." Lorcan flicked on his blinker. "Macha does things above board whenever possible. Fighting included."

"And my trainer? I owe him."

"Done as well. You're free and clear to do whatever you want. Your case worker won't give us any hassle since you're aging out of the system soon anyhow." Lorcan smirked. "Guess you're quite the handful."

Sitting back, Kassian shuffled through the brochures again. None appealed to him directly, so he placed the one that promised he could toss a punch or two and not get into too much trouble on top.

"Marines. Good choice."

"I won't be joining your club. You can bank on it."

Lorcan chuckled but didn't reply. Kassian stared out the window at the passing scenery. He'd bail as soon as he could. Macha wasn't in his future. Fighting was. He could never be at home in a club.

CHAPTER 1
RUBBLE

THE DATE FLASHED ON HIS PHONE. *Seventeen years. Has it really been that long?* Kassian "Rubble" Hardy carefully slid the razor over his tattooed head. *Yep, seventeen years since I was a dumbass kid.* He watched in the mirror, careful not to nick his skin. Normally, he'd let one of the MC's nymphs help him shave. Since most of the nymphs were preparing for the winter games at Snowshoe Lodge, he was on his own.

Hearty laughter echoed from the clubhouse's den. Well, mostly on his own. He was never quite alone with thirty brothers coming and going from Macha's main clubhouse at any given time. That didn't include the nymphs, old ladies, or club hoppers either.

Sliding one hand over his head, Rubble felt for any stubble. Finding none, he wiped off the shaving cream and took one final glance in the mirror. The tattoos on his body told stories, but the ones on his skull told myths. Celtic and American myths alike. The MC's patron, Macha, was the dominant figure on his body, always looking out for him. His artwork had attracted plenty of attention over the years, but that wasn't the point. People could look all they wanted. His life was Macha. There was no room for anything but the club.

He chuckled softly, recalling a time when he swore the opposite. Becoming the club's sergeant at arms took more than years of military training. It also included growing the hell up and no longer being a hothead. Years overseas knocked that out of him. He smirked. *For the most part.*

He ran his fingers over his long beard as he searched for a clean shirt. Finally finding a new design by Doc's old lady, he pulled on the long-sleeved T-shirt and buckled his jeans. Movement from his bed caught his attention and he lazily eyed the nymph from the night before. She was pretty, sure, but that was as involved as he got with women. He snagged his leather jacket complete with Macha's emblem and swatted the nymph's ass for good measure. She'd done her job. It was all he desired.

Closing the door behind him, Rubble inhaled the heady scent of coffee laced with cinnamon, a hint of icing, and curls of cigarette smoke. A nymph darted out of Brewer's room ahead of him, naked except for a blanket around her shoulders. He rolled back his broad shoulders. This was why he loved the MC so much. From FBI agents to Irish princesses, the club was always full of surprises. *You never know what Macha will bring.*

He reached the kitchen in time to see Doc adding icing to his famous cinnamon twists. Grabbing one, Rubble bit into the warm roll. "Damn, you've gotten so domesticated lately. That old lady of yours sure knows how to crack a whip."

"You just wish you had a woman as kickass as my Isa," Doc said, flipping up his middle finger.

He stuffed the rest of the pastry in his mouth and talked around it. "Yeah, cuz that's what I need… to be pussy whipped."

Before he could pour coffee into the mug on the counter, the scent of jasmine filled his nostrils. He didn't even need to turn around to know Kevlar's old lady, Nikita, joined them.

"Don't forget to bring a few of those to my appointment today," Isa said, catching the corner of his eye.

Rubble leaned against the counter, slowly sipping the hot coffee, and merely watched the scene unfurl in front of him. The kitchen, once too large in his opinion, kept shrinking with every new member and their significant other.

Doc tossed his oven mitts onto the counter and

kissed Isa's cheek, then stooped low to kiss her swollen belly. "Don't worry, I won't." He tucked her scarf into her coat. "Meet you there at three."

Isa nodded at Rubble, grabbed three cinnamon twists, and waddled toward the front door. A gust of cold Colorado air trickled down the hallway, bringing Kevlar and Hawk with it.

"Hey, guys. Snoopy mentioned something about doing a lotto-style tattoo sale. He say anything like that to you?" Hawk asked, sitting on one of the barstools.

Kevlar shook his head. "Nah, but it sounds like Snoop. Always trying to bring in more cash to the parlor."

"We'll discuss it at church," Rubble added, stealing another pastry from the counter. He gave Doc shit about domestication, but the man could bake, and nobody complained about it.

"Gotta run to Denver today. Be back after dinner," Nikita said, zipping up her leather jacket. It didn't have Macha on it, but FBI instead. It still baffled Rubble how Kevlar's old lady was a Fed. He swallowed his bite. She was the only Fed he didn't mind.

Kevlar laced his arm around Nikita's waist, kissed her hard, then squeezed her ass. "I'll be handcuffed to the bed waiting for you."

Nikita rolled her eyes, Rubble grunted, and Doc chuckled. They all knew the man wasn't teasing.

They'd all experienced a taste of the kinky couple, mostly under accidental and hilarious circumstances.

"Kevlar, you done working on that '69 Camaro? The client called about it last night." Rubble held up his finger when the clubhouse landline rang. "Hang on. Macha clubhouse, what's your pleasure?"

"Is Queenie there?"

He glanced around the kitchen and down the hall. "Nah, she's not in yet."

"Damn, okay, um—can you have her call me?"

The woman was barely audible given the noisy clubhouse and what sounded like traffic on the other end. Rubble snapped his fingers to silence the others. "Sure. What's your info?"

"Jupiter. She'll have my number."

"Jupiter? Like the planet?"

"Last I checked."

"All right, I'll let her know." He hung up before Jupiter could say anything else.

"Everything all right, Sarge? You got a weird look on your face." Hawk pointed a cinnamon twist toward him.

Rubble sent a text message to Queenie, then shrugged. "Just a message for Queenie, that's all."

His brothers seemed to accept that, so he started toward the front door, ruminating on the recent phone conversation in his mind. Jupiter hadn't sounded familiar and there was a hint of fear in her voice. It was never a good combination in his experience.

Just as he stepped outside, Queenie responded that she'd take care of it. Over the years, Rubble had slowly learned to trust women again, all thanks to the woman he saw as his adoptive mother, Queenie. Only a select few women earned the right to be in his circle of trust.

The weather in Snowshoe, Colorado was mild at this point in the week. Horns blared and brakes screeched in the not so far distance. Snowshoe was abuzz, preparing for the next set of events that'd make club life more colorful. With the Xtreme Winter Games beginning the next week, the town would be overrun with new business, strangers, and trouble.

He pulled his hood up, shielding his tattooed head from the falling snow. More than snow was brewing in the town. This was a constant for Snowshoe and for Macha, which was why he kept up with his mixed martial arts. After defeating two MCs last year, he hoped the winter months would bring peace.

A distant police siren caught his attention, reminding Rubble that tranquility wasn't his lot in life. From foster care to the MMA ring to the Marines to Macha, he didn't need peace to be happy. He just needed his MC. His family.

CHAPTER 2
JUPITER

Eight hours to go. Jupiter Jones blotted the greasy gas station pizza with a napkin. There were only three pepperonis on the large piece, but it was no matter. Her stomach could barely handle anything, let alone the "spicy pepperoni" advertised on the sign in the window. It was the only place she could find off the beaten path. She knew no one would recognize her as the wife of one of the largest cattle ranch owners in Texas.

She shivered, but not from the rain pelting the windshield. Her soon-to-be-ex-husband, Lyle Jones, was the reason she drained the one bank account he never knew existed, purchased a beat-up Honda Civic, and split eleven months ago. Staying at the small ranch house outside Carlsbad wasn't an option anymore. *Gotta keep moving before Lyle's goons find me again.*

A semitruck rumbled into the parking lot, the bright beams lighting up the car interior long enough for Jupiter to catch the reflection in the rearview mirror. She clenched her teeth and hand simultaneously, the cold pizza now smashed. The bruises around her eyes had faded some, but the swelling of her jaw couldn't be hidden, no matter how many pounds of makeup she applied.

Her olive-green eyes dipped to the neckline of the hooded sweatshirt she purchased outside Waco last month. Perfect fingermarks encircled her neck. Those weren't from Lyle, though. Those were what happened when she escaped one of the men hired to capture her. The marks Lyle left were worse, much worse. Jupiter blinked away the horrors from months on the run and shifted the car, ready to put miles under her belt.

She should've left when Lyle first started hitting her.

"Stop it, Jupiter. You left when you could. That's what's important." She turned on the radio. A country ballad streamed into the small car that was filled with the bare necessities. There'd been no time for her to pack all her possessions. She'd left when Lyle had been on a business trip. Bouncing from state to state was difficult, but she'd made do. She didn't need much to survive. Now it was time to go somewhere unexpected. She'd exhausted the Southern states and was headed north. *Next up, Colorado.*

Switching lanes, Jupiter gripped the steering wheel tighter. Ironically, it was her mother-in-law who told her to leave. *Flee* was her exact word. Evidently, the Jones men tended to be less than loving toward their trophy wives. *Would've been nice to know when I met him.* But Lyle held even more over her head than the threat of violence. She never wanted to be involved in his shady international dealings, but he hadn't given her much of a choice. He'd forged her signature, making her as liable as he was.

Her phone lit up and she sighed at Queenie's name on the caller ID. Picking it up, she felt herself relax just a little. "Hey, I wasn't sure if you'd call."

"Of course I would, sweetheart. I haven't heard from you in, well damn, over five years. How are you? How's your mother?"

Tears pricked Jupiter's eyes. Queenie was like a second mother. One she hadn't seen in too many years. "Mom died last year."

Jupiter's father had also died unexpectedly of a heart attack. She let out a breath, heart clenching at the knowledge that she was parentless. She hadn't gone to her mother's funeral. Lyle wouldn't allow it. As badly as she wanted to drive to Iowa and visit her mother's grave, it'd be the first place he'd look for her.

"Oh, honey, I'm so sorry."

"It's okay, I'm fine." She sniffled and cursed herself for losing control. "I actually wanted to see if I could stay with you for a while."

"Oh?"

"I'm, uh, in a bit of trouble."

"What do you mean? What's wrong? Where are you?"

"I'm on my way to Colorado." She quickly filled Queenie in on the assorted details of the last five years. When she was done, Jupiter held her breath, hoping her best chance of surviving wouldn't refuse to help.

"That bastard. I'll cut his dick off myself and shove it up his—"

"I just need somewhere to lie low for a bit. I can work for you, or for the club, even."

Queenie tsked and papers shuffled on the other end. "There's this cute little bakery I bought a few months back. They're nearly done with the renovations, so it's perfect timing. I remember all those yummy treats you used to make. Will you help me open it?"

"You mean I can stay with you?"

"Lord, yes, girl! Get your ass up here and we'll sort out everything after you've rested."

Relief washed over Jupiter. Suddenly, hiding in the

Colorado Rockies didn't sound so crazy. "Thank you so much."

"I can send a few of the boys to meet you at the Colorado border, if you'd like, for your protection."

"I can handle myself." She slid her gaze to the .45 pistol and box of ammo in the passenger seat she'd swiped from Lyle's safe. "Be there soon."

After hanging up, she let out a steadying breath. Soon she'd be far from her battered past and looking forward to her future without checking over her shoulder at every corner.

CHAPTER 3
RUBBLE

"Don't forget to tighten that gasket or this whole thing will fall apart on ya." Rubble patted the prospect's shoulder and made his way through the maze of cars in the shop. The scent of oil and grease only made the sunny afternoon better. Fresh snow had given the club's garage, Speedy's Repair, plenty of new clients thanks to the visitors for the winter games. Macha's ski lodge was at capacity too, another bonus for the club.

"I'm gonna grab a sandwich from the clubhouse. Rosa mentioned she was making meatball subs today," Kevlar called from the door. "Want anything?"

"Same sounds good, thanks."

Rubble walked back to the office and was greeted by the sight of paperwork tossed here and there. He had a system that worked, even if it was a little messy.

His commanding officer in the Marines would kick his ass all the way to Tuesday if he ever stepped foot in the small space, but Rubble had been perfecting the place since he returned after serving his time overseas.

The shop phone rang, and he eyed the mass of paperwork, searching for the old receiver. Finally finding it under a quote, he answered. "Speedy's Repair, how can I help?"

"My car slid into the embankment outside town."

"Sorry to hear that, but we can help. I'll get my tow guys on the road." After getting the rest of the man's information and exact location, he hung up and sent two prospects out.

Loading the computer's emails, Rubble scanned the overnight parts requests. Since they were one of the largest shops in a fifty-mile radius, many of the smaller repair garages called in requests when needed. It wasn't his favorite part of running the garage, but it kept him busy.

The scent of tangy marinara wafted toward Rubble, and he whipped his head up to see Kevlar enter the office and plop a sandwich wrapped in foil on his desk before taking the chair across from him.

"Holy hell, Rosa knows how to make a sub." Kevlar bit into his own and made a satisfied face. "Oh, God, this is better than sex."

Rubble smirked, unwrapping the foil. "Don't let

your old lady hear you say that. She'll probably—on second thought, tell her, but do it in public so we can watch her kick your ass."

Kevlar flipped him the bird, and they ate in nominal silence, impact guns and clattering tools the only sounds coming from the shop. It was their normal routine outside of working on cars and one Rubble didn't mind one bit. He didn't take the simplest pleasures in life for granted. Not after his rough childhood.

"Think the club's ready for the games?"

Crumpling the foil, Rubble tossed it in the nearby trash can. "As ready as we can be. Queenie and the old ladies have been doing quite a bit, and so have Dolly and her nymphs."

"Yeah, Kita helps when she can. The FBI keeps her pretty busy." He wiped his mouth with a paper towel. "You gonna participate at all or are you too old for that shit?"

Rubble leaned back and smoothed his beard. "Not too old, but other than being a club volunteer, I'm not joining the amateur competition."

"So, too old?" Kevlar stood, a knowing smirk on his face. "Just like you were in Jalalabad?"

"We both know I would've made that jump if the damn camel didn't move."

They chuckled at the memory of one of their few days off. They'd been through hell together overseas, and Rubble was glad the man made his way back to the club after his tour ended. Brotherhood was the key to Macha's success.

"But I don't blame you. Kita would kill me herself if I got hurt in general, let alone at an extreme winter sports venue." He stood and threw his trash away. "I'm gonna work on that engine block this afternoon. You have anything on tap?"

Standing, Rubble joined Kevlar at the door. "Yeah, I'm kind of behind on that rebuild Hawk and I talked about, but since it's cold weather now, I can wait a bit."

"The Mustang?"

"Yep." Rubble eyed the powder blue 1965 Shelby GTO350 sitting under a tarp. "She'll be a beauty once we're done."

"Boys, I'm taking the second tow," Queenie called from the bay doors.

Both Rubble and Kevlar swiveled toward the president's old lady. She was decked out in denim today. Even her bedazzled jacket matched.

"You need help?" Rubble asked when she neared.

Queenie shook her head, her hair covered in a jean cap. "Nah, just picking up an old friend who had some car troubles."

Rubble fished out the keys and handed them to her. "You're sure? It's no problem. I have some time."

The willowy woman cocked her head and gave him

a once over. "Sweetheart, don't take this the wrong way, but if my friend saw you, she'd probably be more frightened than she already is."

Furrowing his brows, Rubble wanted to argue. There was something that didn't feel right about the situation.

Kevlar pointed to the snow falling steadily. "Drive safe. Call us if you need help."

Queenie's booted feet hustled her to the old tow truck and within moments, she had driven it free of the garage parking lot.

"What'd ya think about that?" Kevlar asked, leaning his forearm on the door frame.

Rubble watched the truck disappear down the street, a knot forming in his stomach. "Not sure. Let's hope it's not another damn woman bringing trouble," he mumbled, recalling the recent firefights when Isa and Nikita joined Macha. "We have enough of those around here."

Kevlar's hearty laugh filled the garage. "Aw, come on. Macha women are worth the trouble."

"That's yet to be determined for me." Glancing to the clubhouse then back to the prospects working in the garage, a knot filled Rubble's gut. Something wasn't right about how easily Queenie disappeared without one of the club members. Sure, Queenie was as headstrong as the rest, but she always took a prospect with her when the weather was dicey. He'd never let anyone give him shit about protecting Queenie. She was his family and if she thought a woman needed help, he wouldn't argue with it.

He eyed Kevlar who had a shit-eating grin on his face. "What?"

Kevlar smirked. "Nothing."

Annoyed, Rubble walked past him, back to the car he was reconstructing. He needed to keep his hands busy and try not to think about the woman Queenie was on her way to rescue. Easier said than done.

CHAPTER 4
JUPITER

The snow swirling outside the Civic looked more gray than white thanks to the road slush. The wind howled more now than it had when the fifteen-year-old car broke down for a reason Jupiter couldn't decipher. She tapped the dash, the angry orange lights blinking furiously. "If I'd paid more attention to Levi when he talked about cars, I'd know what's wrong," she mumbled, opening her burner flip phone. She couldn't think about her brother right then. It'd only remind her that he would've helped if she'd asked. *He's got enough on his plate.*

Twenty minutes had passed since she called Queenie. Her long fingers were beginning to grow stiff. Gloves weren't necessary in Texas, so she hadn't owned a pair since leaving Iowa. *Should've planned better.* She shook her head, thoughts muddled. The problem was that she'd barely had time to plan at all. Hiding out in the warmer states seemed like a good idea until Lyle picked up on her trail time after time.

A knock on the window frightened her away from the past. Queenie's worried face shone from the other side and Jupiter felt her heart lighten. Climbing out of the small car, she was taken aback by the bear hug.

"You're a sight for sore eyes." Queenie held her at arm's length and scanned Jupiter's face. She didn't mention the discolorations, but Jupiter noticed how the older woman's face clouded slightly, nevertheless. "Come on, this storm is getting worse."

"But my car."

"I'll have one of the boys pick it up later." Queenie nodded toward the big truck idling behind them. "It's cozy and warm, I promise," she said, opening the passenger door.

Anything sounded better than staying in the cold Civic on the side of the road where anyone could stop and hassle her. Jupiter grabbed her purse and backpack, safely stowing the gun in the small of her back before hurrying to the truck. Once inside, she shivered at the drastic change in temperatures. Sure enough, it was a balmy seventy-eight degrees in the cab. She rubbed her hands together in front of a vent and Queenie shifted into gear.

They drove in silence, Queenie casting a glance her

way every now and again. She'd have to say some-thing eventually, but Jupiter hoped she wouldn't. As badly as she wanted to tell Queenie everything, a small part of her wanted to recoup then disappear again without sharing her story.

A large sign for Snowshoe whizzed by along with more snowdrifts. They pulled into a large parking lot just inside city limits, a neon sign blinking nearby above a bar and tattoo parlor combination.

Queenie shut off the engine and turned toward her. "You'll need to change your hair and your name. You don't want Lyle sniffing around and finding anything."

Jupiter unbuckled her seatbelt. She considered buying a box of cheap hair color from a gas station but couldn't bring herself to lose her blonde curls. Tucking back her hair, she worried her bottom lip. "The hair and last name I can do, but not my first name."

"Honey, it's a unique name." Queenie's brows furrowed. "One people around here will remember."

For a split second, she almost agreed. It'd be easier to start fresh.

"Ah, but with the winter games, there will be a ton of new faces and names." The older woman leaned over and cupped Jupiter's cheek. "You'll be all right. Macha will keep you safe until you decide what to do next."

"Thank you," she managed, voice wavering. Tears

threatened to spill now that she was safe. *Safe for a while.* She couldn't stay in Snowshoe forever. Eventually, she'd have to face her past.

"THIS ROOM WILL BE YOURS FOR HOWEVER LONG YOU NEED it. Only visitors are on this floor, so no one should bother you."

Queenie opened a door at the end of a long hallway on the second floor of the clubhouse. The scent of stale smoke and perfume wafted from every corridor, but Jupiter wasn't about to complain. She had limited funds, and the last time she slept through the night was too long ago for her to remember.

Stepping inside, Jupiter watched the room come to life at the touch of a light switch. The bedding was simple, a single quilt over a full-sized bed. Other than a small dresser to the right of the bed, the room was empty.

"You can see the garage from here. Hope you don't mind the view or the boys." Queenie chuckled, pulling back the curtain. "They can be loud assholes at times, but they have hearts of gold."

Jupiter set her bags on the end of the bed. "This is perfect, thank you."

"Oh, stop thankin' me and get some rest. I'll grab

you something from the kitchen. I bet you're famished."

She smiled sleepily, the lure of food the only thing keeping her eyelids open. "Don't go to any trouble."

Queenie chuckled. "You're no trouble, sweetheart."

Alone at last, Jupiter scanned the room again. She didn't have much to unpack, so she didn't. Getting too comfortable wasn't a good idea anyhow. Lyle's men were on her tail whether she admitted it or not. Despite taking backroads and keeping her head down, hiding in this sleepy snow town wouldn't last long. She'd have to leave soon. Putting down roots anywhere wasn't happening. *Not for a while.*

A clatter from outside caught her ear and she crossed to the window. The snowstorm had all but paused since she arrived, giving her a clear view of the garage below. Three men in leather jackets stood outside the bay doors, cigarettes in hand, smoke drifting alongside their breaths on the cold air.

She started to move away, but her attention was pulled back when one of the men started laughing. Curious now, she peeked out from behind the curtain. The man in the middle of the group was at least a head taller than the others, his frame dwarfing the two bikers. But it was his laugh that made a smile sneak across her lips. A combination of hearty and deep, the sound sent a tickle down Jupiter's spine. She shivered at the notion that a laugh could make her feel anything after years of avoiding emotions when it came to men.

Trying to make out his features, she huffed. The window needed to be cleaned and she couldn't see the man's face clearly. Using her sleeve, she attempted to wipe away the grime.

"Och, I told Dolly her nymphs forgot this room," a voice said, startling Jupiter away from the window.

"Sorry, love, didn't mean to startle you."

Jupiter straightened and pushed back her hair. "No problem. I was just being nosy."

"As you rightly should be." The woman held out a plate with a sandwich on top. "I'm Isa, by the way. Doc is my old man." Her face suddenly scrunched, and she rested a hand on her belly. "And this stubborn lad or lass won't give me a day of rest. I'll be glad when it's over and I'm not being kicked from the inside out." She smiled secretively. "Somewhat."

The strong Irish accent made Jupiter wonder how she settled in Colorado. "Jupiter J—Quinn. Jupiter Quinn."

"Nice to meet you, Jupiter." Isa grinned. "Queenie sent me up. Apparently, she had to check on Reaper or she'd have come up herself."

Stomach growling, Jupiter sat on the edge of the bed and took a bite. The turkey and cheddar could've been savory steak with how quickly she devoured it.

Isa chuckled. "Guess I should've brought two."

"Isa, are you in there?"

Jupiter's eyes swung to the door that seemed to be attracting everyone's attention ever since her arrival.

"Aye, Dolly, what now?" Isa opened the door, one hand on her hip. "If that nymph said I pulled her hair, it's because I did. That sprite shouldn't have taken the last cookie. I'm pregnant, not a saint."

Dolly snorted. "Yes, because we all thought you were a saint before Doc knocked you up." She rolled her eyes before her gaze settled on Jupiter. "Oh, hello. I didn't realize we had someone staying up here. I'll have Cherie clean tomorrow."

"I don't know how long I'm staying," Jupiter said, getting to her feet. She couldn't help but gawk at the woman who wore a tank top despite the frigid temperature outside. She was covered in tattoos with a piercing in her nose, and her black hair was pulled into a ponytail. In her own way, she was stunning, gorgeous even.

"That's all right. You stay as long as you need." Dolly held out her hand. "I'm the nymph wrangler, as the boys call it."

"What's a nymph?" The image of a fairytale creature came to mind, but Jupiter doubted it was accurate.

Isa blew out a breath. "And with that, I'm off to the doctor." She smirked. "The actual doctor, not mine." She waved at Jupiter. "I'll see you around, yeah?"

"Sure. Good luck."

More ruckus came from the window and Dolly snorted. "Those damn bastards will keep you up at all hours." She pushed the window up and yelled, "Hey, some people are trying to rest!"

"Who? You? We all know that's not true," a teasing voice called back.

Curiosity getting the better of her, Jupiter joined Dolly at the window. The same three bikers were there, cigarettes in hand.

Dolly lifted her middle finger nonchalantly, which got a chuckle out of the men. "Don't make me come down there and kick your ass, Kevlar. You know I can."

Jupiter stood to the side and watched the man called Kevlar shake his head, eyes rolling. The shorter man nodded toward her.

"And who's your friend? A new nymph, eh, Dolly? You said you'd give me first dibs on new girls."

Heat flooded Jupiter's face and she suddenly understood what a nymph was in the club. "Nymphs are club girls, aren't they?" she whispered.

Dolly offered her an apologetic smile. "Yeah, they are." She whipped her head back out the window. "Dammit, Cueball, she's not a new girl. This is one of Queenie's friends. God, you're a jackass sometimes."

"Aw, shit. Sorry, lady. Didn't mean no harm."

Jupiter wasn't sure she could look out the window again, but then she heard the last man's voice.

"A friend of Queenie's? Is that who she left to pick up?"

The deep timbre of his voice sent sultry shivers across her skin. Never had a man's tone done that to her. She peered cautiously around Dolly and took in the hulking man. Without the dirty window contorting him, she could finally see his features. A black beanie covered his head, and a pair of curious eyes prodded her. His dark beard was expertly trimmed and groomed, but it was his stature that made her breath catch. Even her five-foot-ten-inch frame would be small next to him. Under his jacket and dark denim jeans, she knew there were chords of muscles merely waiting to spring into action. He was the epitome of a bad boy biker, and that sent her pulse into overdrive.

"What's your name?" he called, taking a step closer.

She noticed his unique set of eyes then, one green and one blue. "Jupiter Quinn."

He reached up and smoothed his beard, tattoos prevalent on his hand and fingers. "That's a nice name."

Jupiter licked her suddenly dry lip. She wasn't even face-to-face with the man and her palms were sweating. From fear or attraction, she couldn't tell. "What's yours?"

"Rubble." He cocked his head to the right, studying her the same way she did him.

"There you are, Dolly. Jupiter, why're you hanging your head out the window?"

At the sound of Queenie's voice, Jupiter jumped, hitting the back of her head in the process. Rubbing it, she tried to ignore the chuckles from below.

"We were…." She couldn't find any words that sounded right.

"The boys were being loud, so I kindly asked them to keep it down," Dolly said, walking to the door. "I'll catch up with you later, Jupiter." She offered her a broad smile. "Oh, and welcome to Macha."

Queenie shut the window and clucked her tongue. "Reaper, er, my old man, needed me to sign some paperwork for the bakery. We already bought it, but your phone call made me hurry the renovators. I already have another girl who can help you. She worked at a bakery in Europe, so between the two of you, you'll have it bursting with delicious treats."

Jupiter glanced to the window then the door. "Is everyone here involved in each other's lives?"

Laughing, Queenie sat on the bed and patted the spot next to her. "Yes, very much so. It's all part of being a big, happy, noisy family. I wouldn't trade it for the world."

A yawn took over Jupiter's reply and she rubbed her eyes.

"Sleep's the only remedy for that." Queenie pulled back the quilt and Jupiter kicked off her shoes. "We'll catch up later. Get some rest. No one will hurt you here."

Jupiter nodded, not fully believing those words. An echo of Rubble's laugh came from the garage and this time, she smiled at the sound. *Maybe I am safe here.*

CHAPTER 5
RUBBLE

"All those in favor of implementing a random tattoo generator at the shop for a flat price, say 'aye.'"

Rubble watched several club members shake their heads while Hawk, Snoopy, Klink, and three new members voiced their support. He was all for making money, but a scheme like this could leave customers upset at their random tattoo, and that was never good for business. *Especially during peak season with the winter games.*

Reaper, the club president, pounded his small gavel on the solid wood table. "Motion shelved until the next meeting."

He nodded to the treasurer, Boulder, and the man quickly went over the cost breakdown of the club and the revenues they brought in from their various businesses in Snowshoe. So far, Snowshoe Lodge brought in the most, but that was no surprise. Anything snow related made the club money. It was always their biggest source of income, with the rest of their enterprises filling in when the weather was fair.

"Sergeant, you have anything to add before church ends?" Reaper asked, cutting into Rubble's thoughts.

As sergeant at arms, he was responsible for any scuffle the club or its members got into. It was a badge he wore with pride that he'd only relinquish upon death. He checked his cell phone for any updates from local law enforcement and shook his head. "Calm waters currently, Prez."

Reaper harrumphed. "Good. After two skirmishes last year, let's hope we get to take this year off."

Several members chuckled. The sting from bullets still resonated in Doc, Kevlar, and other Macha members, but it was a risk they took in club life.

"Brewer, you're working closely with the city council. Is the town ready for the games?"

All eyes turned to the lanky redhead who had a beard to match. "Yes, sir. We had a meeting this morning. The projections are twenty-five percent higher than they were last year." He glanced down at his notepad filled with scribbles. "So far, every hotel in Snowshoe is booked solid, including our very own

Snowshoe Lodge. We've hired ten additional staff and our volunteers will be part of every event." He grinned. "Isa and Queenie are determined to sell out of our merchandise, and with these numbers, we just may do that."

Reaper pushed up his small glasses, leaning back in his giant chair. "Good, good. We have two weeks until the opening, gentlemen. Enjoy the free time while it lasts. I expect full cooperation the moment the games begin." He smirked. "In other words, stay out of trouble, please." He banged the gavel. "May the goddess ride with you."

The members disbursed after that, conversations beginning or picking up where they left off before church started. Rubble lagged along with Brewer, Doc, and Kevlar.

"Ah, damn, I forgot to mention the bakery," Reaper mumbled, taking off his glasses and rubbing his temples.

Kevlar exchanged a glance with Rubble. They were both thinking the same thing. The club was already down a VP and their president was closer to retirement every day.

"What bakery?" Doc asked.

"Queenie purchased it a while ago, but we hadn't done any renovations to it yet. She found a couple girls to run it. Apparently, they have baking in their blood." Reaper sighed. "The renos should be done this week, but I'm sure the girls will be behind the moment they open because of all the tourists."

"Where's the shop located?" Rubble asked, more curious than before about the girls Queenie found to run the place. Ever since seeing the gorgeous blonde in the window the other day, he couldn't help but wonder who she was and why he hadn't spotted her around the clubhouse since. Queenie was keeping her under lock and key, and he wanted to know the reason. After all, security was his primary role in the MC.

"Downtown. Just down and across the street from the boutique. It's a sweet little spot on the corner."

"Pastries and coffee during a winter event? Yeah, they'll be busy all right," Kevlar added.

Reaper turned to him. "What's the garage schedule like? Busy?"

Rubble toggled his head. "Steady."

"Can you spare a man or two to help the ladies out until they're on their feet?"

Doc coughed. "Sounds a bit like a protection detail. Nope, I'm out." He stood. "It worked well for me last time, but I think it's somebody else's turn."

Brewer shook his head. "No can do. I'm up to my eyeballs in running the community outreach shit during the event, plus the bar."

Reaper's ice blue eyes swiveled between Kevlar and Rubble. "Down to two."

Just as Kevlar opened his mouth, Rubble interrupted, "I'll do it."

Kevlar's eyes bugged and Doc laughed himself out of the room.

"You sure?" Reaper asked, eyeing him warily. "It won't be any fun. Being bossed around isn't your thing."

He shrugged. "The club needs my help, and unless somebody throws a punch at the Cutthroats, we should be quiet for a while. Kevlar can man the garage in my absence, and I'll check on the projects at night."

Pulling out a pack of cigarettes, Reaper lit one. "I'll double-check with Queenie, but it should be fine. The two women are a mite skittish around men, but one has backbone. Least that's what my old lady says." He inhaled the smoke and chuckled. "Hell, you may turn out to be a better baker than Doc."

Rubble stood, not sure if he'd made the right decision. He scratched his forehead, pushing the beanie up slightly on his bald head. Queenie's untimely visitor had something to do with the new bakery. He felt it in his bones. And there was something off about the girl. He needed to learn more, and there was only one way to do that. *Get close.*

PUSHING THE LAST BIT OF SNOW WITH THE PLOW attached to the front of the old truck to the larger pile, Rubble backed up and parked. The lots were finally clear. He hopped down and grunted. *But not for long.* More snow fell from the dark sky above him. It was a constant for Colorado. Normally, he didn't mind tending to the sidewalks and parking lots. It was a mundane and brainless task he could do. Lately, though, he couldn't get Jupiter off his mind. His once boring task now gave him more than ample time to think about Jupiter. She was pretty, sure, but the mystery surrounding her was the reason she kept popping to the front of his thoughts.

He walked to the garage and scowled, seeing a prospect fucking a nymph against the workbench through the window. The only part that bothered him was that the young kid didn't lock the front door and any Jack, Jill, or Stanley could waltz right in and steal tools.

Wrenching open the door, he flicked the light off and on, which made the nymph gasp and the prospect turn red. He'd walked in on plenty of his brothers with women. The act itself wasn't the problem.

"I told you five times before to lock the goddamn front door, dumbass," Rubble said, walking to the door and locking it. "Before that, you undercharged a lady cuz she was hot, and before that, you were caught loafing around the bar when you should've been working." He turned toward the prospect and clenched his hands into fists. He was sick of playing babysitter to these idiots all the time. "If you fuck up again, your ass is out."

"Rubble, I swear—"

The glare Rubble tossed the prospect's way was dark enough to shut the shorter man's lips. The prospect nodded, pulling up his pants. "It won't happen again."

The nymph giggled, smoothing her skirt and tugging her red bra back in place. She winked at Rubble and sashayed to the back door, the prospect hurriedly in tow.

Rubble ran a hand over his head, the gesture pushing his beanie off. Normally, shit like that wouldn't bother him. He blew out a noisy breath and finished closing the garage. His stomach grumbled and the late time reminded him he'd missed dinner.

Knowing Queenie always put leftovers in the fridge, he stomped over to the clubhouse, eager to grab a plate and relax. Kevlar nodded when he entered the clubhouse, his old lady throwing darts in front of him. Rubble returned the gesture and maneuvered through the busy room until he made it to the kitchen. Rifling through the food, he finally spotted a generous slice of meatloaf alongside a serving of mashed potatoes and green beans. After warming up the plate, he grabbed a chair and positioned it so he could see all exits. It was something foster care and the military taught him, and it was the one thing he couldn't forget.

Country music droned in the background, laughter mingling with the twang of the old song. Snoopy and Legs played cards with Dolly, Brewer, and Hawk. Dolly laid a royal flush, taking the pot of poker chips. Legs started cursing in Spanish and Rubble smirked. He was ninety percent sure the siblings were cheating somehow. Proving it was another matter.

Doc and Isa were nowhere to be found, but that wasn't new. The expectant couple didn't stay up late nowadays. He couldn't blame them for getting a little peace and quiet. It was nearly impossible with this lot.

He scraped the last bit of mashed potatoes onto his fork and lifted it to his mouth. Before he could finish them off, he caught sight of Queenie and Jupiter coming out of the communal bathrooms on the first floor. He leaned back in his chair to get a better view. Sure enough, a towel was wrapped around Jupiter's torso and she had another one on her head, her olive-green eyes wide and filled with uncertainty.

Rubble stood and placed the plate on the counter, his curiosity getting the better of him. He casually walked down the hall—his room was there, after all—and peeked through the open door.

"Now, rinse it out and you'll be good to go," Queenie said, motioning to the shower stall where water was already running. "Go on now, girl."

Jupiter sighed and did as she was instructed. The towel tucked at her breast fell to the floor and Rubble blinked hard at what he saw. Her skin was milk-white with a splattering of freckles on her shoulders, but the scars made his stomach pitch. They weren't long and jagged like his war wounds. Hers were perfectly placed and precise in nature. For a moment, all he could see was the discolored flesh. His mind wouldn't allow him to appreciate her plump ass or even the tribal tattoo along her spine.

She disappeared into the stall and Rubble took a step backwards. He'd seen his fair share of naked women, but none that stunned him like Jupiter. *And I've only seen the back half.* He ran a rough hand over his beard, tugging on it to snap him out of the trance she unknowingly put him under.

From that second forward, he had to know everything about her. Had to understand why she was in Snowshoe. Had to learn why she hadn't come earlier. Scars like hers were made over years of abuse. He winced at the memory of one foster family who'd dished out similar wounds to naughty children, him being the forerunner.

Her hair. His brain finally caught up to his eyes and he glanced into the bathroom again. Sure enough, Jupiter's once formerly long blonde locks were now short and brown. He balled his hands into fists. She needed help and he'd make sure she got it.

CHAPTER 6
JUPITER

Three days had passed since she arrived in Snowshoe. She'd done little else but catch up on sleep. Jupiter reviewed her reflection in the mirror. Brown hair stared back at her and she reminded herself it was for the best. Avoiding the club members was partly due to her healing bruises. The less questions to answer, the better. Thankfully, the makeup was finally covering up the purple and green on her face and a comfy hooded sweatshirt hid the rest. It was time to meet Macha.

Jovial voices drifted up from the floor below, seeping into her very soul. It just felt right to be down there. She descended the small staircase and wound through the hallways until she found the kitchen. The granite countertop and top-of-the-line appliances came as a surprise, as did the man with bright red hair currently dicing vegetables.

"Hey, you must be Queenie's friend." He grabbed a celery stalk. "Jupiter, right?"

"Yeah." She took a seat on a barstool and surveyed the kitchen. It opened to a spacious dining room with a long wood table and matching chairs. She'd heard the bikers during mealtimes, their joking and voices always sounding so pleasant.

"I'm Brewer." He jerked a thumb over his shoulder. "I run the club bar, Booze & Tattoos."

"And do meal prep?"

He chuckled and added the celery to a growing pile of vegetables. "If the club needs it. We rotate making dinners when the nymphs are busy. With the upcoming Xtreme Winter Games, they've been very busy."

He said the last part with a slight smile and Jupiter immediately wanted to hear a biker's perspective of the women. "Nymphs are… uh… club girls, right?"

Brewer's light blue eyes danced merrily. "Yes, ma'am." He walked to the fridge and pulled out a bag of bell peppers. "My sister, Dolly—I think you met her already— takes care of the nymphs, and the nymphs take care of Macha's bikers."

Jupiter nibbled on her right thumbnail, trying to piece together this biker club. Other than what was portrayed on television, she was clueless when it came to their inner workings.

"You have questions." It was a statement, and one Brewer didn't seem to mind saying.

She nodded. "A lot of them, actually."

"I'm not sure I'm the right person to tell you." Brewer dug out a plastic Tupperware. "But I've been in Macha since the day I was conceived, so I suppose I'm as good as anybody." He quickly put the assortment of diced vegetables in the container and grabbed the peppers. "Hit me with what you got."

"What is Macha? Is it a person?"

Brewer retrieved a ceramic mug and filled it with black coffee. "Sugar or cream?"

"Cream, please."

After he handed her the coffee and creamer, he started dicing the yellow peppers. "Coffee first is what I always say. Now, back to the subject at hand. Macha was a Celtic goddess of war, life, and death. She was as badass as they came and men both feared and worshipped her. She was a protectress in battle and peace."

Jupiter blew on the coffee then took a small sip. "How does she fit into a biker club?"

He finished the yellow peppers and moved on to the red. "Our club is quite different when it comes to women. We treat women with respect and as equals which isn't the biker norm."

Jupiter took another drink, hints of butterscotch infusing the brew. "But why? Aren't women possessions to MCs?"

"Yeah, usually." Brewer rinsed off the cutting board before placing it in the dishwasher and took the seat next to her. "If you're a Macha old lady, you put up with a bunch of bullshit from the club. It's why women deserve our respect and devotion. Any woman can satisfy, but a Macha old lady knows what it means to be truly loyal to her Macha man."

"Are you saying cheating doesn't happen?" Jupiter knit her brows. That wasn't normal in many relationships, let alone one in a motorcycle club.

"Oh, no, I'm not saying that. I'm just saying, if it does happen, the members have a safe outlet for it." He scratched at his neatly trimmed beard. The only unruly thing about him was his wavy red hair. "Enter nymphs. Macha nymphs have more than one job in the club. The main one is personal satisfaction."

"Sex."

He smirked. "Yeah, sex. But they also help us run our businesses, take care of club members' kids, cook, clean, and a lot more."

"What do they get out of this arrangement?"

"Our protection and opportunities." Brewer leaned

over and grabbed the pot of coffee, refilling her cup. "Macha doesn't treat nymphs any different. Any violence toward a woman could result in being thrown out of the club. If a nymph no longer wants to be here, they can leave with our full support."

After receiving both violence and disloyalty from a man, Jupiter found it difficult to believe. "Someone mentioned that Dolly is the nymph wrangler. What does that mean?"

"Ah, yes. So, Dolly is the madame of the nymphs, which means she makes sure they're taken care of, they get to work on time, and have chances at a life outside the club should they choose it." He nodded at a woman passing through to the den. "Dolly has set up many nymphs over the years with spouses, colleges, jobs, the works, and Macha supports this."

The notion that women were revered struck Jupiter's heart. It was precisely what she'd hoped to find in a man, and instead, she found it in a motorcycle club. *Of all places.*

"Sounds too good to be true."

Brewer shrugged. "It may be. Nobody's perfect. We all slip up sometimes, but Macha doesn't give up on someone until they give up on us." His blue gaze darted to her jaw. "And whoever did that to you shouldn't be walking this earth without a broken limb or two."

Jupiter swallowed hard. Coming downstairs was a risk but one she was slowly beginning to accept. She couldn't live in that tiny bedroom the rest of her stay.

Queenie sailed in, hair in a messy bun on top of her head. "Oh, good, you're finding your way around the clubhouse. Come with me. I've got something to show you."

Standing, Jupiter smiled at Brewer. "Thanks for chatting with me. See you around."

Brewer waved just as a group of bikers burst into the kitchen from the back door. Following Queenie, Jupiter glanced over her shoulder and latched eyes with the tallest biker in the group. It was the same bearded man she met the other day. He didn't say anything or even smile. He merely watched her carefully until her cheeks flushed and she hurried to keep up with Queenie.

Hours later, Jupiter sat in the clubhouse's den. It was covered in dark paneling like she'd seen in log cabins. Photos, mostly of club members, littered the walls. A roaring fire sat beneath a large screen television. The oversized recliner was the ideal location for a long cuddle. Not too close to the television but close enough to snag some of the heat radiating from the crackling wood. Thinking back over the day, she smiled absently at where she'd spend most of her time. Macha's bakery. The bakery was nearly done with construction. Just the finishing touches which Queenie promised would be perfect.

Jupiter set aside the bowl once filled to the brim with chicken dumpling soup. With a full belly and heavy eyelids, she yawned and adjusted the neck of her hooded sweatshirt. The bruises faded slowly, but enough club members had seen them. They didn't ask questions, a fact she was grateful for since she didn't want to explain. Already, she was less self-conscious about the healing bruises. Most she could hide with clothes and makeup, but she didn't feel the need. Not when this group of people accepted her as she was.

Being hidden by Macha felt wrong but also gave her a sense of anonymity. She didn't like calling in favors with Queenie, but she was exhausted from trying to outsmart Lyle. The warmth of the room quickly lulled her to sleep and she woke three hours later to a loud thud on the floor. Sitting up, Jupiter noticed the room was darker than before. Her eyes swept to the fireplace where a large man was hunched over the hearth, tossing chunks of wood into the dwindling fire.

She recognized the bald head covered in ornate tattoos before he even faced her. From her position, she could see them clearly. They all depicted fantasy scenes related to the goddess Macha. A black bird perched behind his left ear, and Macha's form encompassed most of the top of his head. A dagger and bow stood out near the goddess, her blue eyes haunting whoever dared look upon her.

"They're beautiful," she said quietly.

Rubble swiveled from his crouched position, lips a straight line. The fire behind him caused a halo effect, his mismatched eyes stunning in their separate ways, but together they stole her breath. "Hurt like hell but was worth it."

He turned back toward the fire, adding three more logs before replacing the screen in front of the hearth. "I saw you sleeping and figured I'd add a few more wood blocks before bed." His gaze moved to the clock. "You slept through a crazy game of pool down the hall."

Jupiter caught the time and stifled a yawn. It was the first time in years she felt safe enough to not worry. "I guess I needed to catch up on some sleep."

Rubble studied her face, the intensity in his eyes unnerving. She tried to move further into the chair but couldn't. Finally, his brows relaxed, and he offered her an apologetic smile. "Sorry, I'm a bit precautious with people who abruptly show up on our doorstep. The two before you brought trouble."

Catching her bottom lip between her teeth, Jupiter turned her eyes to the fire. "The last thing I want is trouble."

"What do you want then?"

"Safety." A weary smile crossed her lips. "And freedom."

"From whom?"

He took a step closer and Jupiter sat up. There was nothing menacing about his tone or even his hulking stature like she'd expect. He was curious and she couldn't blame him.

"Why do you think it's a person?"

Rubble crouched down next to her chair and scanned her eyes. She couldn't look away if she tried. The longer she kept his gaze, the more she wanted to open completely to him.

"I just do."

Jupiter swallowed the urge to lean forward and touch his full beard. It was wild and unruly, and her fingers itched to feel it.

"Hey, Jupiter, do you want some homemade ice—" Dolly paused mid step. Her eyes quickly took in the scene she unexpectedly interrupted, and Jupiter blushed at the sly grin on the other woman's face. "You know what? I think you're good on sweets for the night."

Dolly turned and left the den before either of them

could utter a breath. Rubble didn't smile, but he did stand to his staggering height and look down at her.

"Don't stay here too long. After being downstairs with the nymphs, the prospects tend to be overly friendly."

Jupiter held her breath until his boots echoed in the hallway. She waited a full minute before standing and hurrying up the stairs to her bedroom. Suddenly, the urge to explore the MC clubhouse became high on her list of activities for the next day. *Along with steering clear of Rubble.* He sent a tingling through her body that was a combination of sensual and intimidating. Both frightened her, but one did so more than the other.

CHAPTER 7
RUBBLE

Keeping himself busy wasn't hard at the clubhouse. Between Cueball egging on a pool tournament and the nymphs eager to please the bikers before the winter games began, Rubble had his hands full.

"Your shot," Hawk called, finishing off his Guinness.

Lining up his cue stick, Rubble easily sunk the six ball in the left corner. Hawk snorted when the four ball followed next. He missed the last one, giving Hawk a chance to come back. Grabbing his beer, Rubble finished it off and watched a prospect leave with a nymph in tow. His dick jumped with the need for attention. *Calm down, you'll get some.* He refilled his glass with the tapped beer and returned in time for Hawk to hit the eight ball in by accident.

"Damn, just can't sink the right ball," he heckled good-naturedly.

Hawk fished out a twenty-dollar bill and slapped it in Rubble's hand. "Yeah, yeah, I need to take tips from Cue."

"Like that'd help."

They racked up the balls again and turned the table over to Snoopy and his girl, Legs.

Finding a pair of chairs, Rubble and Hawk sat, each nursing their beer and watching the rest of the bikers. In the far right corner, Doc was whispering something to his old lady that caused Isa's eyes to widen and cheeks to flush. A pair of nymphs were giving Boulder a lap dance. Dolly sat on Klink's lap, leisurely surveying the room while the man all but drooled on the back of her neck.

"Sometimes, I really wish my sister wasn't in the club," Brewer said, pulling up a spare chair next to them. He sank into it and rolled his eyes when Dolly flipped him the bird.

Rubble sipped his beer, eyes always alert. He rarely drank to excess, never one to like being too intoxicated to make rational decisions. He'd learned the hard way when he was a dumbass kid. Ever since his one MMA loss, he'd never been drunk. Buzzed, sure, but not drunk.

"I chatted up that Jupiter chick yesterday," Brewer said, leaning back in the chair.

This got Rubble's attention. He'd volunteered to help at the bakery, but Queenie kept putting him off for one reason or another. Jupiter managed to stay out of sight too often and he couldn't very well tromp up the stairs and ask the questions he needed answers to without drawing attention.

"What's her deal?" He watched Brewer's face for a tell. Everyone had one. Brewer usually bunched up his nose when he was lying.

"Not my place to say."

He wasn't lying, but he was holding back. Rubble tossed back the last of the beer, the alcohol barely influencing his nearly three hundred pounds of solid muscle.

Hawk catcalled one of the nymphs nearby, who in turn flashed him. "Well, that's my cue." He hopped to his feet, girl in tow.

"Why do you care about Jupiter? Is it because she'll be working at the bakery?" Brewer asked, nudging Rubble and watching him closely.

Thankfully, Rubble had plenty of practice holding a bluff. "She's new to Macha, and I'm in charge of our security. I don't know her background so I can't assess if she'll be a threat. We don't need any more MCs pounding at our door because of a woman."

Brewer let out a bark of laughter. "Damn, Rubble. That's cold."

"No, it's accurate. First there was Isa, then Nikita. They both brought a shitstorm of bullets to our door. I don't mind a good fight here or there, but we nearly lost a few men." Rubble narrowed his gaze. "I can't keep you all safe if you keep bringing in nonmembers."

"Marines to the core, aren't ya?" Brewer rolled his eyes. "Loosen up. Go hit something at that gym of yours. Get some pussy. Sleep in until noon. You'll feel better and won't give a damn about this new girl." He patted Rubble's back then stood. "Trust me."

"I do, brother." He waited until Brewer left to add, "But I don't trust her. Not yet at least."

SNOWFLAKES HIT RUBBLE'S FACE, MELTING ON IMPACT. HE lifted his gaze and noticed the light gray clouds overwhelming the sky in every direction. Stepping over a slushy puddle, he pulled out his keys and opened the door to the small warehouse that had been rebuilt as a club gym. He flipped on the lights, the fluorescents slowly coming to life to illuminate the space. It was mostly free weights, but a large boxing ring sat in the middle, the focal point for anyone who entered. *Hard*

Hitter flashed in neon across the back wall. It'd been Reaper's idea to name the makeshift gym after its founder, Rubble himself. Initially, he didn't want the reminder of his MMA days, but after a few weeks back in the states, daily workouts in the ring became mandatory.

Rubble shrugged off his leather jacket. He had on a green long-sleeved shirt underneath. Quickly switching from boots to athletic shoes, he walked over to the raised ring and ducked underneath the ropes. Rubble cracked his neck from left to right before beginning his usual regime of jabs and swings.

Jupiter's face popped up after two swings. That sweet, secretive smile of hers was dangerous. Finding out why wasn't easy. The few times they'd interacted, they were around others. Getting her to himself was the only way he'd uncover the true reason she was in Snowshoe.

"Need a sparring partner?"

Rubble glanced toward the door as Brewer came into view. Over the last few years, they'd ruled the gym. The club hosted a handful of fighting events and the duo always finished at the top.

"You bet."

Brewer hustled to the ring, workout gear in place. Snagging a roll of tape from the side, he ducked under and started wrapping his wrists. "I tried getting Doc here the other day. You should've seen Isa freak out." He chuckled. "Woman thought he was gonna die. It's a workout, not a death sentence."

Rubble pounded his gloves together. "I've seen one too many men go down and not get up, so I understand her angst."

"You and your fancy words." Brewer pulled on his gloves. "Let's get at it. I have a full day's worth of bitchy customers to punch out."

For the next twenty minutes, the two grappled amid swings. Brewer managed to get a good jab in to Rubble's side, but Rubble ended up pinning him between his legs until he tapped out.

Grabbing Brewer's hand, Rubble helped him up, patting him on the back. "Good few rounds there."

Brewer spit out his mouthguard and nodded. "I'll get you one of these days. You can't remain undefeated in Macha forever." He grinned. "Somebody will lay you out and I hope to hell I'm there to see it."

Rolling his eyes, Rubble tossed him a bottle of water and chugged his own. "Yeah, right."

"Maybe Jupiter can get you to submit."

"I don't submit, brother. If someone beats me, it's because they're a far superior fighter." He pointed at Brewer. "And no woman but Macha gets my submission."

Brewer wiped his face with a towel then chucked it at him. "If you say so."

They moved toward the standalone punching bags. Rubble took the larger one to practice his kicks while Brewer opted for the smaller one at eye level. The rhythmic sound of gloves against the bags calmed Rubble. For the first time since Jupiter arrived, he focused entirely on his workout routine, not once wondering why she chose to come to Macha now instead of another time.

After ten minutes, Brewer slowed his punches. "Have you heard anything about Shovelhead?"

Rubble's fist tightened and he kicked high before turning slightly. "We lost him in Dublin. I caught wind that he may've returned to the States, but nothing's verified."

Brewer plopped to the floor and started doing pushups. "Damn, I'd like to see him behind bars or better."

"Like to see who behind bars?"

Both men glanced up to see Kevlar closing the side door, his hat covered in snow.

"Shovelhead."

Kevlar exchanged a glance with Rubble. "Ah. I'm still catching up on everything that went down. I never thought Shovelhead would betray Macha." He moved to the weight machine and started pulling reps. "I was kinda in my own Kita-induced coma the last few months."

Brewer snorted. "Pussy will do that to a man."

Kevlar paused his rep and flipped him the bird. "Just wait. You'll get your just desserts, don't worry."

"Nah, I'm not big on relationships." Brewer stood and started in on jump squats. "Somebody always gets hurt."

Rubble watched the two men he saw as brothers. Both had their reasons for avoiding relationships. *And somehow Kev got over his.* He moved to a smaller punching bag, working on his arm strength. *Could I?* Years of abuse by his foster moms left a bad taste in his mouth for the opposite gender. Since being in Macha, he'd learned to respect women even if he'd never let himself love one. Queenie was the sole exception. She was his mom. And a few other women wormed their way into his heart, but only in a sisterly fashion. Letting himself be vulnerable to a woman was more dangerous than any war he'd fought in.

"Hey, you see the bakery yet?" Rubble asked, hoping to shift his mind from Jupiter.

Brewer grinned. "Yup. My parents would love it if they were still around."

Kevlar cleared his throat, clearly forgetting the bakery Macha had years ago before Brewer and Dolly's parents died. "Kita showed me the other day. I guess her friend Yasmina is going to run it alongside Jupiter and a handful of nymphs. Should be a good money maker for the club."

Pausing his punches, Rubble's mind was suddenly thrust back into a Jupiter fog. Keeping an eye on the mystery woman wouldn't be difficult. The urge to pass the job off on some prospect tempted him, but he couldn't. Jupiter needed someone to protect her. He sensed it the moment he heard her voice. He had mixed feelings about the shy woman. He was drawn to protect her, yet still felt the need to protect the club from her. Rubble couldn't put his finger on his hesitation. One thing he knew for certain, he wanted to talk to Jupiter and see just exactly what Macha was in for while she stayed under their roof.

CHAPTER 8
JUPITER

"This is stunning."

Jupiter ran her fingers along the counter as she scanned the small lobby area where customers would wait for tasty treats. She could almost smell the chocolate croissants and cherry crisp bites. The shop was located next to an insurance broker with a dry cleaner two doors down, and she couldn't help but notice the Macha emblem on the door of the cute boutique within shouting distance.

She slowly walked around the space. The bakery's interior was painted a sky blue, decorated with the surrounding mountains and wild streams in mind. Faint pink made appearances in the display case. A ghostly figure was stenciled on the load-bearing wall above the front counter, her mesmerizing blue eyes and pitch-black hair friendly instead of overpowering.

Jupiter immediately knew who it was. The sketch was similar to the emblem she'd seen on the MC cuts and in Rubble's tattoos. *Macha.*

"When can we start?" she asked.

Queenie beamed a smile. "I'm glad you like it. Yasmina will be back from Denver tomorrow, and she's excited to meet you." She hugged Jupiter. "I'm happy you're here. Your mother would be proud of you for leaving that bastard."

For the first time in years, Jupiter realized she hadn't been thinking about Lyle. That simple fact encouraged her. She was doing the right thing. The attorney she hired in Dallas told her as much, but the man also received a significant chunk of cash to make her divorce as quick as possible. Eleven months in, she was losing faith on the fast guarantee. She just wanted to be done with Lyle and live her own life.

"I think she would've liked this bakery." Jupiter traced the decal in the window with her eyes. "Heaven's Treats suits it."

"Trust me, you'll have a line out the door." Queenie looped an arm around Jupiter's shoulders. "But don't worry, you have a couple days to prep and dust off those recipes. One of the boys will be around in case you need help."

Jupiter's pulse quickened. "Which one?"

"Rubble."

The thought of the large man in the small space should've scared her. Instead, it sent a warm flutter to her stomach. *Stop it. You aren't even divorced yet.*

"Great. I'm sure he'll be very, um, helpful."

Queenie chuckled. "As helpful as a big guy like him can be. He means well, but he's just so gruff. Sometimes, I wonder what his life would be if he hadn't joined Macha." She dug the keys out of her purse. "Come on, girl. We could use your expertise in the kitchen tonight. Reaper has gumbo on his mind, and I have no idea how to make it."

After locking up the shop, they drove the ten minutes to the clubhouse. The parking lot to the tattoo and bar was bustling thanks to the tourists. Jupiter made a mental note to check both out before she was overwhelmed with the new bakery.

They hurried inside from the steadily falling snow, stomping their boots on the rug.

"You're not supposed to bring the snow inside," an accented voice teased.

Jupiter worked on sliding off her boots while Queenie scolded her old man, a smile on her lips. It was sweet how the two always seemed so in love even after years of being together.

"I don't think I've ever seen them fight."

Looking up, Jupiter was face-to-face with a pair of

eyes that bolted her feet to the floor. Goose bumps tickled her arms and she suddenly felt cold and warm all at once. Rubble. "How long have you known them?"

"Since I was seventeen." He steadied her when she lost balance pulling off the last boot.

Jupiter froze at their contact. His strong yet gentle touch made her pulse quicken. For a long moment, she held her breath. He hadn't pulled away yet and she suddenly didn't want him to. Meeting his eyes, she felt her body tremble, but it wasn't from fear.

Rubble's gaze darted to her arm then he quickly let go. She wanted to explain, but she wasn't even sure how.

"You've been in the MC that long?" she finally asked, trying to keep the conversation afloat.

He shook his head. "No, but just about. Reaper pulled me out of a dead end when I was almost eighteen. Been with them ever since. They're the closest thing I have to parents."

Jupiter instantly wanted to hear more. "What were you doing before? Where were your parents?"

Rubble's gaze drifted from her eyes to her lips then back. "I guess we'll be seeing quite a bit of each other soon."

Disappointed he sidestepped her questions and dropped his gentle hold on her arm, Jupiter started toward the kitchen where the most noise was emitting. "Guess so. Hope you like being bossed around."

"Not usually. I like to be the one in charge."

The way he said that simple phrase in his deep voice made Jupiter pick up her pace. The man was causing new and dangerous sensations in her body. Her mind lingered over the memory of him touching her, and she swallowed hard when it didn't scare her.

To her relief, they reached the kitchen, and Dolly linked her arm to pull her toward the giant pot on the stove.

"So, I asked Doc for some tips, but he doesn't know how to make gumbo either. I heard you spent some time in Louisiana, so you may have a few tricks up your sleeve."

Jupiter took the offered spoon and sipped the soup. She tried not to make a face but judging from the giggle from Dolly, she failed. "Needs more garlic to start."

Dolly held up her hands. "Hey, this kitchen is all yours. I don't even know why they let me in here except to eat. I'm a shit cook."

Focusing on the task of fixing the gumbo, Jupiter didn't notice Rubble sit on a stool across from her.

"Louisiana, huh? Are you from there?"

She looked up. "No. I'm originally from Iowa."

"Like Doc and Kevlar."

"I didn't realize they were from there." She found the garlic and fresh parsley leaves.

"Yep. Doc used to be a paramedic until Reaper, his uncle, called him home. And Kevlar's got a sister living in Des Moines. She's a lawyer married to some ex-mobster turned cop."

The skillet in her hand slipped and clattered to the floor. "Shit." She quickly picked it up and set it on the stove.

"Which part of that scared you? The lawyer or cop?"

Jupiter narrowed her green eyes to slits. "Neither. My brother's a cop and lawyers have helped me in the past."

"Never been too fond of lawyers myself." Rubble leaned forward, resting his forearms on the counter. She couldn't help but stare at the tattoos peppered over his exposed skin. Without a doubt there were more beneath his clothes. She swallowed hard at the realization that she even wanted to see them.

"Why are you hiding here? Why not call your cop brother?" Rubble asked.

"I don't want to involve him." She chewed her bottom lip. "It's embarrassing and there's nothing Levi can do."

Rubble reached out and covered her hand. Jupiter lowered her gaze to their connection and quickly pulled away. He almost seemed hurt by her reaction. "Tell me about it, and maybe I can."

When she retreated to the stove, he stood and made his way around the counter, leaning his back against it. "How do you know your brother won't help unless you ask?"

Curling her hand around a bunch of green onions, she started chopping. "I'm handling the situation."

"Why don't I believe you?"

Jupiter looked up and gasped at how close he was to her. His stern eyes were scanning her face, looking for answers she wouldn't relinquish. "Because you don't want to."

Rubble moved back slightly, and she unexpectedly caught herself moving toward him. "Better watch where you put that thing." His eyes dropped to the knife still in her hand. It was dangerously close to his gut. "I'm not gonna hurt you, Jupiter. Nobody here will."

Recognizing her stance, she quickly set down the knife, hands shaking. "I need to finish this and you interrogating me isn't helping."

He nodded and offered an unconvincing smile. "Holler if you need me. I'll be in the den."

Once he cleared the room, Jupiter let out an audible groan. He got under her skin so quickly and intensely her instinct was to go on the defense. Thinking back, she cursed herself for not controlling her tongue more.

"God, that smells fifty times better already!" Dolly came up behind her and sampled the gumbo. "Shit, you're gonna give Kevlar a run for his status as best cook here."

Jupiter didn't hear the rest of Dolly's praise. She couldn't get her mind off Rubble. In the space of one conversation, she was torn between wanting to spill her secrets and wanting to run away from his inquisition. Queenie was a second mother to her, so it was simple to confide in her. But Rubble. She shook her head. He kept popping up wherever she went. *And it's only going to get worse when he's with me at the bakery.*

She groaned again, but this time for a whole new set of reasons.

CHAPTER 9
JUPITER

Jupiter glanced uneasily at Dolly. "Wait, you train here?"

The shorter woman pulled her ponytail tight and nodded. "Yes, ma'am. For as long as it's been open." Dolly fished out a pair of boxing gloves. "Which was… hmm… How long has it been?" She turned and shouted, "Yo, Rubble. When'd you open this place?"

"This is Rubble's gym?" Jupiter crossed her arms over her chest, not sure where the man in question was until he slowly walked into view. Sweat beaded on his forehead, a cutoff T-shirt showing his muscular arms covered in tattoos. He was a mess, a beautiful hulking mess of masculinity. Desire flamed low in her gut at the sight of him.

Rubble glanced over her then settled on Dolly. "Ten years give or take."

Dolly grabbed Jupiter's hand and started wrapping tape around each one. "Old man over there was fresh out of the Marines when Reaper gave him the place. Rubble turned it around too. Used to be kinda crappy."

Jupiter watched Rubble's lithe movements at the weight machine. Her eyes widened at the stack he free lifted. The muscles in his neck strained, making his snake tattoo bulge.

"Focus, girl."

She returned her gaze to Dolly and noticed the conniving grin. "What?"

"If you're gonna go after that beast of a man, you better learn about what he loves." Dolly strapped the gloves on Jupiter's hands and took a step back. "We'll go over some self-defense moves first."

"I already know self-defense."

Dolly's brow quirked and Jupiter heard the weights clink in place. "Oh, do you?"

She nodded. "Over the last eleven months, I've stopped in gyms for simple instructions." She knocked the gloves together. "They've helped me escape a few close calls."

"I'm impressed." Dolly grabbed another set of gloves and donned them. "Show me what you got, girlfriend."

Staying on the balls of her feet, Jupiter slowly circled Dolly. "I've never used gloves like this before."

"It's more or less the same. No head shots if you're playing by MMA rules." Dolly lunged forward and Jupiter easily escaped the strike. "All right, very nice."

Narrowing her eyes, Dolly kicked, and Jupiter cringed at the impact. Legs were her weakest point in fighting. She'd nailed a guy in the balls before, but it was one lucky shot.

The space around Jupiter seemed to hush. She focused on her footwork, arms following suit. For a solid twenty minutes, they exchanged blows, each one getting minimal contact with the other.

When Dolly moved for her again, Jupiter stepped forward and jammed at Dolly's face. Shoving aside the strike, Dolly went for a side blow, and Jupiter stuck out her arms to block Dolly's and then threw a punch at her exposed neck.

Stepping backwards, Dolly coughed at the unexpected jab. "Damn, Jupiter, you and Nikita just might get along better than I thought."

Jupiter paused her circling and smiled. "Nikita would kick my ass."

Dolly laughed. "Yeah, she would, but it'd be fun to watch, wouldn't it, Rubble?"

Swiveling toward the weights, Jupiter met Rubble's curious gaze. He'd been watching the whole thing. Suddenly nervous, she pulled the glove strap with her teeth, freeing her hand to get bottles of water.

"She's got potential, that's for sure." Rubble's low voice echoed in the open space, sending delightful chills up Jupiter's spine.

Returning with the water, she noticed Rubble moving toward the punching bags. "It's been forever since I've hit one of those." She handed Dolly the water and wiped the sweat off her forehead.

"I think you have a fan."

Jupiter eyed Rubble as he hit the bags with alternating kicks and jabs. "Most guys think women who fight are intimidating."

"Fuck yes, we are." Dolly capped the water and tossed the bottle to the side of the ring. "It also makes us harder to get."

"I don't need any man to catch me, thank you very much." She ducked under the ropes and headed toward the weights.

Dolly caught up to her as Jupiter selected the weight limit. "A strong, independent woman doesn't need a man." She leaned against the wall. "But it's okay to want one."

Settling on the seat, Jupiter grabbed the bar, pulling her arms forward to meet in front of her face. "I don't think it'll ever be okay for me. Too much shit's happened for me to rely on a man."

Crouching beside her, Dolly started stretching her hamstring. Neither one spoke for a long minute. The only sounds filling the gym were her weights clinking and Rubble's fists pounding into the punching bag.

"When you're ready, I'll show you some Krav Maga I learned from a guy I met in Israel. He was special ops there, so don't tell." Dolly lifted a finger to her lips and Jupiter noticed the small ink pen tattooed on the digit. "It's pretty useful, if I'm being honest."

Jupiter finished her set. "I'm all for learning more."

She grabbed Dolly's hand and helped her off the floor. They walked in the opposite direction until they could hear Rubble's noises only faintly at the other end of the building.

"What'd you mean about Rubble being a beast?"

Handing her a fighting helmet, Dolly grinned. "Rubble was an amateur MMA fighter when Reaper found him. He only had one loss but was undefeated in competitions."

Jupiter glanced across the gym, but Rubble wasn't in sight. "That's where he got his name?"

"They called him that in the ring because everything he touched turned to rubble." Dolly pushed up her sleeves. "I've seen him fight. He's ruthless, calculating every move and anticipating the next one. Honestly, he's as badass as they come. Macha needed his kind of strength for getting jobs done. The Marines turned his MMA fighting into something ten times deadlier."

A chill swept across Jupiter and she saw Brewer entering the side door, bringing snow in with him. "Is he dangerous?"

"Only as dangerous as he wants to be." Dolly pulled on a helmet. "Rubble is a beast no woman can tame."

"Why tame him when you can unleash him?" Jupiter watched Rubble laugh with Brewer. The camaraderie between the two reminded her of her own brother. "Isn't that what Macha wants to do with him?"

Dolly slowly nodded, but her blue eyes told a different story. "You're something else, Jupiter Quinn." She grinned. "Now, you ready to get your ass kicked?"

"Bring it on."

***

Lyle: How are you, pet?

JUPITER BLINKED FAST AT THE MESSAGE ON THE BURNER phone. Hands trembling, she turned on the light next to the bed. She'd sent her iPhone to her lawyer in Dallas, but requested they forward any messages from Lyle so she could stay ahead of him.

Jupiter: Be better if you'd sign the papers.

She waited anxiously for the reply. Over the last months, she feared his daily harassment. She shivered despite the warm quilt.

Lyle: Business is boring, thanks for asking, but they're keeping me entertained. Too bad you're not here, you little scamp. If I could only catch you, we'd have so much fun together.

Swallowing at the insinuation, Jupiter tried not to think about who or what he was doing in Europe. She honestly didn't care about his sexual exploits. He'd cheated on her ever since they were in college and she forgave him every time. *Not anymore.* She gripped the phone tighter and checked the time. *It's late. Too late.*

Jupiter: Never happening again. Sign the papers.
Lyle: It will and not until I see you again. I miss your pretty face, my pet.

She shuddered at his term of endearment. It wasn't meant as one. She was his *possession*, and that was her reminder. He didn't message her again, and she turned off the light. Lying on her back, she stared at the ceiling fan slowly oscillating. She couldn't sleep without one on, no matter the temperature outside.

"You can do this, Jupiter. You have a plan. Your

lawyer helped you come up with it," she said to the empty room. The wind howled outside her window and she tugged the quilt up higher. If she was anywhere but the Macha clubhouse, those words would've meant nothing. Somehow, between these walls, she was safe. Safe from the elements. Safe from Lyle. Safe from being hurt. She just hoped it stayed that way.

CHAPTER 10

RUBBLE

Bewitching green eyes swarmed his vision. Those damn eyes of Jupiter Quinn's haunted Rubble the rest of the night. They haunted him when he played pool with Kevlar and Cueball. They haunted him when he ate the best gumbo in the world. *And of course, she made it.* They haunted him when she sat across the table from him at dinner. But the worst was when they haunted him during sex with a nymph.

Rubble tossed the used condom in the trash while the nymph was already pulling on her clothes. She left without a word, and he was grateful for that. He didn't feel like chatting. *Fucking Jupiter Quinn and her perfect ass.* He grabbed the pillow next to him and held it over his face, grunting at the thought. He barely knew the girl and she somehow wiggled under his skin and tore it up.

Chucking the pillow to the side, he stared at the ceiling. She was somewhere up there. *Is she still up, unable to sleep because I'm on her mind?* He let out a breath. *Not likely.*

He'd first seen Jupiter through the second-floor window, and from that day forward, he wanted to know more. Queenie was as tight-lipped as a monk, which meant he had to figure Jupiter out on his own. It wouldn't be an issue if the woman didn't spit fire whenever a man challenged her.

He tapped his bare chest with his fingers, coming up with an idea to disarm Jupiter carefully. The way he originally wanted to do that was out of the question. As badly as he longed to fuck that pretty body until she screamed his name, he was positive she wasn't of the same mind. *Not yet at least.*

Standing, he grabbed his jeans and pulled them up. He slid on his shirt, then boots and wrapped his leather jacket over his shoulders, fishing out the pack of cigarettes as he headed out of his room and toward the front door. Kevlar nodded at him from the pool table where he and Cueball were having a game. Rubble jutted his chin back and rounded the group of nymphs fawning over the prospects recently back from the shooting range. He rolled his eyes at the boasts the newbies were saying just to get in the nymphs' panties. They didn't have to lie. The club girls would treat them right even if they couldn't shoot worth a damn.

Rubble paused at the front door, Isa waddling in from the parking lot, a cute scowl on her face. Doc wasn't far behind her, an exasperated expression on his face. No doubt, Doc's old lady was overexerting herself again and refused to listen to her man.

Chuckling, Rubble couldn't help the pang in his chest at the thought of his own old lady being a sassy know-it-all who he'd have to punish in his own special way. If he let down the walls around his heart, he wasn't sure he'd survive. Rubble exited the clubhouse and lit a cigarette, the frigid breeze taking his mind away from whatever happily ever after he refused to admit he wanted.

Stepping under the awning, he inhaled and let the nicotine calm his nerves. It wasn't working tonight.

"What the hell are you doin', boy?"

Glancing over at Reaper, who was walking up from the tattoo parlor, he held up his hand. "Gotta smoke, Prez."

"In this shit?" He coughed, years of nicotine lingering in his lungs. "Can't blame ya. Every now and then I get jittery and a good light is all I need."

Rubble handed him one and the club president inhaled a moment later. "That's the stuff." He checked over his shoulder. "Don't tell Queenie, yeah?"

Rubble flicked ash into the snowdrift. "Tell her what?"

"Good man."

They stood in the cold another minute before Reaper spoke.

"You gotta be careful with Jupiter. She's had it rough lately. Don't think she's ready for any kind of romance."

Cocking his brow, Rubble laughed. "I don't do romance, Prez. You know that."

"No man does romance until he meets the right woman."

The door squeaked open behind them as Hawk and Cueball came out for their own smoke break.

"Later, boys," Reaper called, patting Rubble's shoulder.

The cold finally catching up to his fingers, Rubble tossed the butt to the snow, hearing the small sizzle before he reentered the clubhouse's warmth. He ran a hand over his beard then his head. He needed a cold shower and sleep before seeing Jupiter Quinn again.

THE SHOOTING RANGE OUTSIDE SNOWSHOE WAS FOR Macha club members only. Locals tried to pay their way into the range, but the club wouldn't allow it.

There was just something about the wooded space that was sacred, untouched by the rest of the town. It was the main reason Rubble tromped out there no matter what the weather to clear his mind. Ever since seeing Jupiter's bruised face, he'd been itching to let off a few rounds into the nearest target.

Loading the black 9mm, Rubble made sure no one had walked into the area before he aimed at the large target downwind. He squeezed the trigger, expiring the entire magazine. Despite his ear protection, he could almost hear the dull thud each bullet made in the hay bale. The range had plenty of different targets to choose from, and he typically started with the larger ones and digressed to the smaller, more difficult ones in order to hone his aim.

He put the safety back on the gun and placed it on the tree stump next to him. Pulling out his safety earplugs, Rubble started walking toward the hay bale. His phone starting ringing just as he arrived in front of it.

"What's good?"

"I'm bringing Jupiter out to the range in a few."

Rubble scowled at Dolly's matter-of-fact tone. "Why? She doesn't need a gun to work in a bakery."

"You don't know that. Don't leave until we get there."

He crouched down and examined his marksmanship. "How do you know I'm even there?"

"Cuz one of the nymphs told me, duh. Honestly, Rubble, you should know better than to tell a nymph where you're going. The girls tell me everything." Her voice lowered. "Everything."

Holding in a growl, Rubble stood and stalked toward the gun stand. He needed to shoot a few more things before the nosy madam got there. "I'm leaving in twenty minutes."

"We're pulling in now." Dolly disconnected before he could respond.

Reaching his gun, he didn't hesitate before adding another magazine and firing. Joshing with Dolly was one thing, but being around Jupiter put him on edge. He wanted to kiss her and shake her at the same time. Neither one seemed fitting for the gun range. *Though it would be fun to fuck her behind the—*

"Walking on." Dolly's voice sounded over the hum of his gun and interrupted his train of thought.

Clicking the safety in place, he placed the gun in its holder and turned to face the two women walking his direction. Both were bundled up thanks to the cold weather. He couldn't help but notice Jupiter's slender legs sheathed in black leggings, her feet covered in thick boots. The puffy pale gray coat hit her mid-thigh, hiding her ample breasts and equally squeezable ass.

He rubbed a hand over his beard, tugging on it to remind himself he couldn't think of her in that way. He couldn't imagine bending Jupiter over and smacking her ass until it was as red as a cherry. She was Queenie's friend and a Macha employee. He had self-control. Or at least he hoped he did.

Jupiter's dazzling green eyes met his and he couldn't stop his inadvertent inhale. Without a doubt, hers were the most alluring he'd ever seen.

They stopped shy of his location, Dolly toting two guns in each hand. "Don't mind us. We're going to let off a little steam."

Rubble tried not to think of the steam his and Jupiter's bodies could make in the snow beneath their feet. He nodded and turned back to his task at hand. "Sure, have fun."

From the next spot over, he heard Dolly go over the basic gun safety rules and procedures. He knew far more than the club's madam but wouldn't step on her toes. It never ended up well when anyone did.

He watched from the corner of his eye, imagining himself behind Jupiter, showing her precisely how to hold her arms and spread her legs. The sensation of her ass against his cock, the cool steel from the gun in her fingers before she pulled the trigger. *Dammit, get yourself together.*

Shaking his head, he trudged through the snow to

the next set of targets. He pushed his earplugs in, hoping they'd keep Jupiter's voice out of his head. Two guns started firing and he glanced over to see Dolly and Jupiter aiming at the large hay bales. Dolly's shots hit the outer rim of the bullseye, but Jupiter's bullets were more precise. Her stance was perfect, as if she'd done this many times before that afternoon.

His feet started moving toward them without warning. The closer he got, the more he was impressed. She was killing it. Finally, she stopped and turned toward them, a wide grin on her face. "How'd I do?"

Dolly's mouth gaped and her blue eyes sparkled with mischief. "Girl, you're gonna give Kevlar some competition, and he's the best shot in the club."

The three walked to the targets and he scratched his forehead, his black beanie sliding up. Jupiter pierced the bullseye ten out of eighteen times, the last eight straying to the inner circle.

"Holy shit." He met her gaze and she shrugged sheepishly. "Where'd you learn to shoot like that?"

"My brother mostly." She grabbed another magazine and slid it into place, the act so fluid, Rubble could've sworn she'd been doing it her whole life. "It's been quite a while since I shot." A lonely smile crossed her cheeks. "I guess some things kinda stay with you."

Rubble nodded. He knew full well that was true. But, what exactly did Jupiter mean by it? The wind whipped at their faces, and he pulled his beanie a little lower over his forehead. While Dolly raved over Jupiter's success, Rubble was content with watching the interaction.

Some things did stay with a person, and he had a feeling Jupiter was one he didn't want to miss out on. Suddenly, hurrying back to the garage didn't seem so important. He had a better way to spend his afternoon.

CHAPTER 11
JUPITER

Bubbles jumbled in Jupiter's stomach the entire next day. She'd met Yasmina only minutes ago and already loved her. Now it was time to open the front doors. She wasn't sure what to expect. No one loitered outside, which was not uncommon in the chilly Colorado temperatures.

Unlocking the door first, she carefully flicked on the Open sign, then hurried back to the register. Yasmina was baking up a storm in the kitchen behind her. The display case held savory treats and sweet confections made in the early morning. Jupiter ran her green-eyed gaze along the delicately formed and iced works of edible art. They were truly as heavenly as the name of their shop indicated.

The bell above the door clanged and she straightened to greet their first visitor. The jitters in her belly only doubled at the sight of Rubble. He wore his typical black beanie with an MC patch, jeans, and leather jacket. Her focus shot to his cap. She'd seen the plethora of tattoos on his skull, each one depicting a story. If she weren't so chicken, she'd ask about them, but going off the way he easily diverted the conversation to something else when personal questions came up, Jupiter opted against it. If the man wanted to share, he would.

"Good morning." She tried to make it sound cheery, but her voice cracked.

Rubble gave her a slight nod. "Mornin'." He inhaled and glanced around. "Something smells scrumptious."

"Oh, that's the raspberry tartlets. Yasmina took them out of the oven a few minutes ago." She adjusted the small sign that said *freshly made daily* on the counter, not knowing what to do with her hands. Opening day was important for a new business and she didn't want to let Queenie down.

"Just relax. People will come." He moved past her, hanging up his jacket on the coat rack. "Are there security cameras?"

Jupiter almost laughed at the swift change from encouraging to professional. "One facing the register." She pointed to the small camera in the corner.

Walking over, Rubble examined the camera, then

pulled out his phone. "I'll sync it to my cell so I get the live feed when I'm not here." He glanced around. "Is there a break room or office where I can set up? Don't want to linger." He cleared his throat. "I may scare away potential customers."

Frowning, Jupiter noticed the tinge of embarrassment flicker on his face. It was gone the next second. "Because of your height?"

His mismatched eyes met hers. "Mostly the tattoos." He pulled off the cap and chuckled. "They're not for everyone."

"That's dumb. You should be proud."

He lifted his left brow and slowly reviewed her form. "Oh yeah?"

"Mhm."

"And what about you? Aren't you proud of your new shop? Maybe you should post all about it on social media so your friends and family can see."

He was baiting her, and she wouldn't succumb to it. "Not a big fan of social media." She lifted her chin. "Mostly people bragging or bitching. Not my thing."

Rubble nodded and crossed the room. "Break room?"

She jerked a thumb over her shoulder. "There's an office in the back and to the right. The surveillance is already pulled up on the monitor."

"Thanks." He grabbed a muffin from the pink basket on the counter. "I'll check in on ya in a bit."

Hearing his boots echo down the hall, Jupiter let out her breath. She didn't have time to recover before the bell clattered again, this time with a handful of customers ready to try something sweet.

"WE SOLD OUT OF THE CHERRY TARTLETS!" YASMINA exclaimed, stunned when she saw the display case. "I can't believe it. Not even noon and we've sold out of something." She gave Jupiter a knowing look. "Guess we can bank on making more of those tomorrow."

Jupiter switched out the empty tray of tartlets for sugar cookies in the shape of snowflakes. "They were amazing, honestly. I've never had a better one."

Yasmina rolled her brown eyes. "You're saying that because we'll be together for the next few weeks."

Her thick accent forced Jupiter to smile. After hearing the story about how Nikita saved Yasmina and a semitruck full of women and children on their way to be auctioned as sex workers, she had to admit Macha had some stellar women associated with them. It gave her hope to know women could come out of a poor situation and flourish.

"Maybe a little, but they are fantastic. If I didn't

know better, I'd think you've been working in a bakery your whole life."

Yasmina's eyes dimmed. "I did back home. My parents were great bakers. I fear they're no longer living. The last letter I sent was returned weeks later." She sighed. "Once the business does well, I'll fly over to check on them. If they're gone, I'll say goodbye, but if they're alive, I'll bring them back to the States with me. They deserve the same happiness I've found in Colorado. It is home now."

Jupiter swallowed at hearing the sadness in Yasmina's voice. Her own family didn't know what had happened to her over the last ten years. She should've told them but couldn't bring herself to admit defeat. Not when they couldn't help. Only she could fix her mistakes. With a little help, that is.

"I think they'd like Snowshoe. Plenty of places to open a rival bakery."

Yasmina laughed, the sound as sweet as the donuts cooling on racks. "They'd like you. You're funny and have secrets. Just like me."

Before Jupiter could ask more, a customer walked in with three children in tow. It was time to bring in that cash so Yasmina could bring her family to Snowshoe.

Jupiter didn't have a moment to sit, let alone take a break, until the day was half over. She pushed back the strands of hair that had fallen loose over the morning and watched Yasmina rearrange the remaining goodies in the glass display.

"It looks like those raspberry tarts are a big seller," she said, taking an empty tray from Yasmina.

Yasmina nodded, a proud smile on her face. "An old family recipe. I used to make them as a child. I'm glad Colorado likes them as much as I do."

A pair of teenagers walked through the front door, the girls whispering about a new boy in town. Jupiter envied their carefree nature. They didn't have a damn thing to worry about except if the boy talked to them. She sighed, recalling her own teenage years spent doing the same thing. Her older brother used to scare away any boy that tried to ask her out. It was one of his more endearing yet annoying qualities. Tears suddenly welled in her eyes at the thought of Levi. She desperately wanted to reconnect with him but couldn't. She brushed away the tears before they could fall. *Not yet at least.* She had to be strong. Lyle couldn't hound her forever.

After helping the girls to a box of cream puffs, Jupiter looked to see Yasmina carefully watching her. Before she could ask Yasmina more about her family, the other woman spoke up.

"Queenie says we have much in common."

Jupiter dropped the coins into the register drawer and closed it with her hip. "Like what?"

"Men hurting us." Yasmina pushed back her dark hair and lowered her voice. "You don't have to be scared. No one in Macha will tell, especially me."

She wanted to believe her. Jupiter wiped down the counter instead of responding. Yasmina stayed put instead of retreating to the kitchen like she expected.

"If you'd rather not say, I understand. It's difficult to talk of for me too." Yasmina leaned against the back counter. "Nikita helped me a lot when I first arrived in Snowshoe. She even made sure I had someone to talk to about the abuse."

Jupiter paused the cloth in her hand and met Yasmina's eyes. The brown depths were filled with understanding, no trace of judgment present. Asking her about what happened didn't seem appropriate. Yasmina's treatment was no doubt a thousand times worse than her own.

Yasmina placed a soft hand on Jupiter's arm. "Don't do that."

Jupiter shifted on her feet. "Do what?"

Yasmina offered her a sad smile. "Think your situation wasn't horrific." She reached for Jupiter and placed a comforting hand on her arm. "You got out alive. That's all that matters."

Jupiter didn't even realize she'd been on the verge of tears until one slid down her cheek. Wiping it away quickly, she cleared her throat. "I should've left sooner. End of story."

Yasmina pulled Jupiter into a tight hug. "Don't blame yourself. He is the one to blame. He is the evil, not you."

Wrapping her arms around the smaller woman, Jupiter cringed at how thin she was. She couldn't imagine the atrocities Yasmina faced, but she understood in her own way. "We're both better off."

Yasmina broke their hug and smiled. "Yes, we are."

The bell above the door clanged and Yasmina rushed to help the customer. Watching her, Jupiter felt the urge to open up to Yasmina. At least a little. It'd help her heal and she needed that more than anything. Only someone who'd been in a similar situation could truly understand.

After the man left with a dozen chocolate cupcakes, Yasmina turned to her. "You don't have to tell me. It's hard, I know."

Jupiter shifted her weight. "It is, but I think it'll help if I talk it out." She took a breath, summoning her courage. "A week after I left, my ex found me holed up in a crappy hotel in Florida. He'd bribed the front desk lady. When I got back from working at a restaurant as a dish washer, he was sitting on my bed.

Reading the paper like he should've always been there."

Her stomach knotted at the memory. "I was terrified. I couldn't move from the doorway. He used that to his advantage and dragged me in by my hair. I should've braced myself before he backhanded me."

Yasmina squeezed her hand, silently encouraging her to continue.

"When I came to, he was gone. I was bruised, bloody, and missing my underwear. He'd taken all my cash and the few possessions in my room." She rubbed a hand over her stomach self-consciously. "He wanted me to be stranded and I was. Thankfully, the same person he bribed came to my rescue. She gave me all the cash she had including what Lyle paid her." She smiled sadly. "From that day forward, I never stayed in one place for very long. I got fake IDs and learned how to defend myself."

"Thank you for telling me." Yasmina hugged her again. "You're safe, Jupiter. Macha won't let him do that again."

More tears threatened to fall, but she held them at bay. Another customer came through the door and Jupiter hurried to find a tissue. When she passed the back room, she noticed Rubble returning to his chair. Her stomach pitched. If he'd heard, she had a new reason to steer clear of Rubble.

CHAPTER 12
RUBBLE

Watching Jupiter for eight hours was the worst form of agony. Her lithe movements and easy smile were only the beginning of his constant need for a cold shower. The pink-and-blue apron molded over her perky breasts perfectly, her jeans accentuating a round ass that his palm ached to swat. He was an ass man through and through, and Jupiter had an ass straight from his dreams.

He checked his cell. A message from Kevlar about having drinks later popped up and he replied affirmatively. Brewer sent a group chat about the Xtreme Winter Games opening ceremony on Sunday. Evidently, the MC wanted as many members present as possible to show support for the community. He'd tag along but would stick to the shadows. Working behind the scenes to see the job to completion was what he knew best. He'd done it in the Marines, and it was what he continued to do for Macha. Getting his hands dirty wasn't an issue. In fact, it was one of his more preferred methods of combat.

But the worst part of his day was overhearing the story Jupiter told Yasmina. That cut open his heart and nearly sent him on the hunt for the no-good prick. She deserved better than that from a man. Not confronting her about it was equally difficult. He wanted nothing more than to hear every detail so he could somehow save her from the pain.

"Hey, I made a fresh batch of ham and Swiss croissants. Do you want any?"

Jupiter's sweet smile made his automatic reply fade away. He wanted some all right. Some of her. *Dammit, man, stop.*

"Sure, thanks." He took the proffered croissants that were still warm from the oven and bit into one. The creamy Swiss cheese paired perfectly with the salty ham and buttery pastry. "Damn good."

She caught her bottom lip between her teeth, a smile just below the surface. "Thanks."

"How's business been?"

"Steady, but you know that."

He took another bite. "Yeah, I do, but hearing it from you is different than watching on the screen."

She shifted nervously as if his constant scrutiny

somehow bothered her. It shouldn't. He was there in case things went awry. Everybody knew it wouldn't, but Queenie still insisted on a Macha member at the bakery. After knowing Yasmina's past and recently hearing Jupiter's story, he now understood why.

"I like the brown."

"What?"

"Your hair." He finished the croissant and wiped his hands on his jeans. "It looks good brown."

Jupiter tucked the short hair behind her ears. "No, it doesn't, but it's nice of you to say."

"Why'd you dye it?" That question burned in his mind since he'd seen Jupiter switch from honey blonde to mousy brown. He also wasn't sure about the drastic lopping that had happened either. He liked a little something to hang onto when he was with a woman. *Fucking, stop.* He tamped down the lust running through his veins.

"Needed a change, I guess." Her green eyes darted to his mouth, and he fought the urge to pull her against him.

"Who're you hiding from?"

He'd asked her before, but she'd skirted answering. If she would only tell him, he could help. Rubble watched her closely and she gave her tell. Rubbing her thumb against each finger repetitively.

"I can't tell you."

He shifted to face her. It was more than he expected. "Why not?"

"Because I'm handling it. Queenie knows and that's enough." She turned to leave, but he caught her wrist. Immediately, she shrank back, fear scribbled on her beautiful face.

"Shit, Jupiter, I'm not gonna hurt you." He released her and stood. Cursing himself for not seeing the signs before, he held up his hands. "I swear to God. I'd never hurt any woman, let alone you."

Doubt filled her eyes. "What do you mean 'let alone me'?"

Aw, shit. He couldn't very well tell her how attracted he was to her or that he'd overheard her and Yasmina. She was already scared enough. "I meant someone under Macha protection." She seemed to buy that, and he swore silently.

"All this is new to me." She tightened the apron strings.

"Being protected?"

"Trusting that a man won't hurt me."

The urge to wrap his arms around her shoulders and comfort her overwhelmed him, but he wouldn't do it. Not when the last man abused that precious opportunity.

"You won't believe me, but that's okay. I can show you that Macha doesn't treat women like property."

A small smile crossed her kissable lips. "I've noticed that here and there at the clubhouse. Mostly with Queenie, Nikita, and Isa. Their men really seem to love and respect them." She met his gaze then moved toward the door. "I should go back to work."

"Jupiter?"

She turned. "Yeah?"

"Don't let one bad guy ruin love for you. We're not all like him."

"No, you're not." A soft smile played on her lips and wrecked him in a way he couldn't believe. He wanted more than her body. He wanted every inch of her soul.

He needed to punch something. Hard. Rubble snatched the athletic tape from the dusty chair and hastily wrapped his wrists. The more he focused on the tape, the less visions of Jupiter played across his eyes. It worked, but only for a few minutes.

Growling at his wandering mind, he climbed the stairs and entered the gym. Without a sparring partner, he had to walk past the boxing ring, the thick ropes tempting him with memories of past fights. His muscles itched to pound into flesh and incur ruthless damage.

Rubble found his favorite punching bag on the far left side of the gym. It was where he and his fellow Macha bikers went to let off steam, and it worked like a charm. *Most days.* Planting his feet, he tossed the first jab. The heavy punch thudded loudly in the vaulted space.

Somebody actually hit her. Laid hands on that sweet face. He swung with his left, adrenaline pumping through his blood. He'd observed Jupiter and Yasmina all day. The cute way Jupiter fixed her ponytail, still not used to the shorter length, was just the start. Already, he felt the walls shaking around his heart.

Rubble bounced on the balls of his feet. Club business was all he'd planned on doing today. Watch the bakery, make sure nobody tried to jack the register, and check up on the garage. That was it.

He clenched his teeth, face jerking at the memory of Jupiter curling back because she was expecting to be backhanded. After that, he couldn't keep his eyes off her. The desire to protect her every second of every day for the rest of her life haunted him.

Rubble kicked the bag and then rapidly punched it, spending the fury on it instead of the motherfucker who hurt Jupiter. He'd searched the Internet the rest of the day for Jupiter Quinn and discovered she went by her maiden name. *It's smart.* He wiped a stream of sweat from his brow. *She's damn smart.* He managed to backtrack her movements to Texas where he found the mother lode. That was the funny thing about engagement announcements. They tended to give more information than people thought.

He threw a left then two right punches before hopping backwards, his mind wandering further. Lyle Jones was an upstanding citizen who took over the family ranch ten years ago. From the outside, the guy looked squeaky clean. Not even a speeding ticket on his record, and Rubble checked. He pulled in every favor he could with the local police and was waiting to hear back from Kevlar's old lady and her FBI contacts for an in-depth search. Nothing seemed indiscreet about Mr. Bigshot which was why Rubble's stomach pitched. *Nobody's* that *good.*

Sweat trickled down his shirtless torso as he hammered the punching bag in rapid alternating combinations. If Jupiter was in Snowshoe, it meant there was a reason. *A goddamn good one.* The hint of bruises healing on her throat and face were enough for him. Hell, she could've said the bastard only yelled at her and he'd still be ready to rip the man apart with his bare hands. No woman deserved to be treated with anger. And Jupiter never would be again. Not if he could help it. *And I will.*

The punching bag suddenly stabilized, and Rubble whipped his eyes up. Brewer stood behind the large bag, holding it steady. "You looked like you could use some resistance." He smirked. "Don't want you busting this one."

Wiping sweat from the tip of his nose, Rubble grunted and nodded once. For the next twenty minutes, Brewer stayed silent while Rubble took his frustrations out on the heavy bag. By the end, every inch of him was covered in a sheen of sweat. He picked up one of the clean towels and ran it over his face. It wasn't like him to get overly involved with a woman, but here he was, on the edge. He knew what would happen if he took the next step. Knew what he was risking if he stuck his neck out there for a woman who clearly didn't want to be found. His stomach dropped at the thought of Jupiter leaving without a trace. He couldn't protect her if she ran away again.

"Drink?" Brewer held out a red sports drink.

"Thanks." He unscrewed the top and guzzled half.

"It's Jupiter, isn't it?"

Rubble started unwrapping his wrists. "Why do you say that?"

Sitting down on a bench press, Brewer shrugged. "I saw the way you looked at her."

"I look at all girls the same." He tossed the

wadded-up tape into a large trash can. "They're trouble."

"Yeah, yeah, you talk big, but I've seen you with her. You've never looked at a woman like the way you look at Jupiter." Brewer chuckled when Rubble glared. "No judgment here, brother. She's quite the lady." He stood and lowered his voice to say, "But I saw the bruises."

Turning around, Rubble stalked over to him and grabbed the front of his shirt. "And you didn't say anything to me? What the actual fuck is wrong with you? Somebody did that to her."

Brewer's usually cheerful blue eyes shadowed. "It wasn't my information to tell."

Rubble growled low then dropped his hold. The man wasn't wrong. It killed him to admit it, though. His role in the MC was to ensure the club's protection. Jupiter fell under Macha's outstretched wings. He wouldn't let her down even if it killed him.

"Dolly made enchiladas for dinner." Brewer took a step toward the door. "That was the main reason I popped in."

"What was the other?"

"To tell you Nikita's looking for you."

This got Rubble's full attention. "She must've found something."

Brewer shrugged and disappeared through the

door. The clubhouse wasn't too far away. He'd walk over after taking a quick shower. The blue and red ring mocked him as he passed it. It had sat unused for too long. Rubble aimed to fix that as soon as possible. He needed to spill some blood even if it was his own.

CHAPTER 13
JUPITER

Lyle: I miss you, pet. Send me a photo of that beautiful ass so I can show my friends.

Jupiter swallowed the bile in her throat, her mind spinning over how to reply. She glanced at the time. It was only nine at night, which meant he wasn't fully drunk yet. She walked further down the hallway toward the door to the back staircase. Other than nymphs coming and going from their downstairs lair, she was alone.

Her fingers hovered over the small keys of her phone. She chewed her bottom lip. No response was coming to her. She shouldn't reply, but a little part of her worried about what would happen if she didn't. When they were together, he demanded an instantaneous reply to any call or message. If she didn't comply…. Jupiter shivered at what Lyle used to do to her. *But that was then. This is now.*

"Everything all right?"

Squeaking, she jumped backwards and nearly bumped into a nymph with a tray full of beer. Jupiter placed a hand on her chest and lifted her gaze to the intruder. "Rubble."

She instantly cursed how out of breath she must sound. It happened every time she looked into his mismatched gaze. One blue, one green, his eyes were spellbinding, and she was instantly lost in them.

Rubble's brows knit together. "Sorry. Didn't mean to scare you."

"You didn't." Jupiter shoved the phone into her back pocket. "I mean, you did but I don't mind. Not when it's you." She slapped a hand over her mouth. "Shit, I didn't mean to…." She couldn't finish the thought.

A flicker of lust crossed Rubble's face and Jupiter's breath caught in her throat. She couldn't remember a time when a good man had looked at her like that. But Rubble wasn't good. He wasn't bad either. He was an MC biker. They practically had warning signs tattooed on their foreheads. He was bad news, but she couldn't resist. Not after years of being discarded at any given moment.

A whoop of laughter cut the tension and Jupiter

looked away. Staying here was reckless, especially with the way her stomach filled with butterflies whenever Rubble was near.

"Don't do that."

Jupiter met his eyes. "Do what?"

"Act all shy right after saying something that any man in here would love to hear from that pretty mouth of yours."

She parted her lips and his eyes focused on them. His boots shuffled closer and instead of moving away, Jupiter stayed where she was. The warm scent of freshly baked gingersnaps drifted down the halls. Somehow it mingled perfectly with the hint of motor oil and leather coming from Rubble's large form. Next to him, she was almost small. With the wall behind her, she had nowhere to run but found she didn't want to leave.

Rubble slowly lifted his hand and gently slid his thumb along her lower lip. She couldn't breathe, her body on fire for what he'd do next. He carefully tugged on the lip with his thumb, and she stifled a moan.

Tension sizzled between them. She was unable to look anywhere but his handsome face. The long, full beard summoned her curiosity and she timidly reached up, running her fingers over it. The coarse yet soft hair came as a surprise. She'd never felt one before. Not one as big as his.

Rubble pushed the hair away from her neck, focusing on her pulse there. His eyes met hers, concern evident. "If you tell me to stop, I will. I swear, Jupiter. I'll never hurt you."

He'd barely even touched her, but she already didn't want him to stop. He wouldn't hurt her. She knew it in her soul. It was evident in the way he controlled his muscular body to merely graze the skin on her collarbone. A man like Rubble could snap her like a toothpick, but he wouldn't. Rubble couldn't. She recognized that truth in his gorgeous eyes.

"Don't stop," she pleaded, tugging gently on his beard.

He moved closer. Jupiter sighed at the feeling of his warm, sweet breath on her neck. She closed her eyes the moment his lips touched her skin. For a split second, Jupiter forgot where she was. She wrapped her arms around his waist, pulling him closer still.

"Fuck, you taste as good as you smell," he said against her neck. His tongue darted out, circling before he kissed the spot. "Brown sugar and cinnamon."

When he switched to the other side of her neck, Jupiter's grip weakened. Every inch of her body flooded with heat, and she marveled at that small feat. No man had ever turned her on so quickly and with so little effort. He was the ignition to her flame.

A clatter from the kitchen snapped Jupiter back to

earth. Rubble must've felt her tense for he stepped back and watched her silently. His chest heaved more than before, and she couldn't help but dip her eyes to the sizable bulge beneath his jeans. She barely touched him and had this effect on him. It scared her to think of what could happen next. She returned her gaze to his. *What* will *happen next?*

"It takes every muscle in my body to not toss you over my shoulder and throw you on my bed."

She smiled, a warm flush taking over her face. "You haven't even kissed me. How do you know I want that?"

"I just do." Not giving her a moment to reply, Rubble leaned over and pressed his lips to hers. Jupiter gasped at the demanding yet enticing kiss. Lacing her arms around his neck, she slipped her tongue into his mouth, and he growled. The sound skidded along her spine, settling low between her legs. His tongue sought hers out, tangling with it so intimately and turning her knees to rubber. Seeing her plight, Rubble picked her up and she automatically wrapped her legs around his waist. He pushed her back against the wall, his kiss inhibiting her ability to think clearly. All she saw was Rubble. All she tasted was him. All she wanted was his body close to hers.

And just as quickly as he'd begun touching her,

Rubble paused. She whimpered at the loss, eyes opening to see concern etched in his features.

"Shit. I got carried away. I'm sorry." He carefully set her feet back on the ground, though Jupiter doubted she could walk on her own quite yet. He straightened his cut, the sergeant at arms patch proudly displayed on his breast.

"I'm not." She meshed her fingers with his, the dark tattoos foreign compared to her light skin. "But I need to tell you something."

"And what's that?"

"I'm—" A slew of Spanish words coming from the pool tables interrupted her and Rubble shot a stare down the hall.

He turned back toward her. "You're what?"

"Married." She let out a breath. "Technically. I filed for divorce but my hus—he won't sign the papers."

Rubble scratched his jaw and nodded. "Anything else?"

"Doesn't that matter to you?" She couldn't get a read on him. His face was like stone. It was eerie how easily he went from passionate lover to MC soldier in seconds.

His gaze softened. "No, baby girl, it doesn't. I assumed it was something like that." He gently traced the bruises on her neck and jaw. "Did he give you these?"

"In a way, yes."

A fierce expression crossed his features. He looked ready to punch someone. Instead, he let out a breath and tipped up her chin.

"If you decide tomorrow you want to leave Snow-shoe, I'll help hide you until your ex is taken care of." Rubble's low voice rumbled against her chest, eyes searching out hers. "But if you stay, Jupiter, I'll protect you. I'll make sure you're safe. And if nothing ever happens other than that kiss we shared, I'll be okay with it."

"But I—"

He placed a finger over her mouth, the look in his eyes telling her he'd much rather put his lips there. "I'm not a good guy either. I'm not him, but I've done some bad shit. You deserve more. You deserve better than a rough-and-tumble biker."

Jupiter slowly digested his words. He wasn't wrong. She hardly knew him. Hell, she'd arrived only a week ago. She wasn't thinking clearly. Kissing Rubble was a mistake. She inwardly shook her head. *No, I wanted to do that when I saw him.* There was something about him that made her trust he wouldn't hurt her.

Straightening her shoulders, she grabbed the back of his neck and pulled his mouth to hers. She didn't have to wait for him to react. He was there in an instant, lips devouring her. Lust floored her once more, the desire too powerful to be diminished.

"Don't make me throw this beer on you," a voice teased from down the hall.

Jupiter gasped, but Rubble didn't seem put off in the least. He kept a strong arm around her waist and lazily glanced over to the intruder. Dolly stood with a shit-eating grin on her face, a plate of cookies in one hand and a beer in the other.

"Hot from the oven. Better grab a few before I give them to the vultures." Dolly smirked, her bright blue eyes sparkling with mischief.

Rubble glanced down at Jupiter and offered her a small smile. "Come on. Might as well see what club life is like after being cooped up in your room."

Legs still shaky from their kisses, she held tight to Rubble as they made their way to the large living space where the rest of the club members, their old ladies, and nymphs were teasing and laughing. It didn't take Jupiter long to see why the club was a lot like a family. What she liked the best was the way Rubble kept her close by. Not always touching, but he was always within reaching distance. It brought a warm flutter to her heart and a worrying ache to her belly.

LATER THAT NIGHT, JUPITER LAY IN BED, A CONTENTED grin on her face. She'd joshed with nearly every member of Macha into the early morning hours. Hawk flirted more than the rest, but Brewer was right behind him. They stopped shortly after Rubble sat next to her on the couch. It was some sort of silent warning. At least that's what she assumed, since the two men were less flirty toward her from that moment forward.

She rolled over and tucked the excess blanket between her legs. Ignoring the kisses she and Rubble shared was the hardest part of the night. Never would she have guessed the tall, burly man with a wild beard and piercing eyes would be a gentleman.

Sighing, she thought back to their exchange. His lips caused enough mayhem that she imagined them caressing her again. If she invited him in at the end of the night when he walked her to the room, he might've said yes. *Maybe.* Rubble was a mystery. One she wanted to learn more about. *And since he's with us tomorrow at the bakery, I'll ask.*

She flipped to her back as a buzzing sound came from the side table. The new text from Lyle made her cringe. He was drunk and horny. It was always the same. This one was a brag about how much fun he was having. *I know what that means.* He wasn't alone. It should've hurt, but it didn't. Not after all the shit he'd done over the years.

Jupiter powered down the phone and turned her thoughts back to Rubble. *I wonder what his real name is.* The club names were as sacred as their patron, Macha, herself. Bikers earned their names. She was pleased to discover that hearing the origin stories were her favorite conversations to have. Even if she didn't stay in Snowshoe, she'd take a piece of it with her. Stories were everything. Macha was evidence of that.

A small part of her worried about what would happen if Lyle found her early. If his men tracked her down and they managed to drag her back to hell. A gust of wind shook the window, and a tremble ran through her body.

Maybe telling Rubble more about the situation is a good idea. She'd ask Queenie in the morning. For the time being, sleep was quickly closing in, bringing with it the revolving dream about Rubble and the other incredulous things his tongue could do to her body. She snuggled closer into the bedding, a nighttime smile on her lips for the first time in years.

CHAPTER 14
RUBBLE

"And you're sure this information is accurate?"

Cradling his cell phone against his shoulder, Rubble pulled out a cigarette and lit it. The leisurely afternoon snow settled on his black beanie and dusted his leather jacket.

"Yep, the Cutthroats are voting on a new Prez this week."

He took a long drag and watched the steady traffic drive into Snowshoe. The games began the next morning, and crowds were already gathering for the opening ceremony. It was the ideal time for their rivaling club to make a shit show.

"All right, thanks, buddy. Next time you're in town, I'll buy the first round."

The man on the other end of the call snorted. "You know I don't leave the beach unless I have to."

Nodding, Rubble knew it to be true. His old friend from foster home days had done well for himself, albeit illegally. He disconnected and shoved his free hand in his pocket. The duties of sergeant at arms weren't always fun, but he enjoyed the consistency of bad people being, well, bad. The Greenback Cutthroats in the next town over had finished licking their wounds after the ass whooping Macha gave them a few months prior, thanks to the FBI's help. The Cutthroats wouldn't ever disappear. Not completely. It was one of the constants. Typically, if a club was beaten, they either healed up or joined with another until they were great once more.

"You shouldn't smoke."

Rubble glanced to his left and noticed Isa walking toward him, all bundled up in a bright blue bubble coat and matching thermal leggings. She waddled more and more with every passing day. It'd been some time since he cared about one of the old ladies in the club. After years in the foster system with shitty moms, most rubbed him the wrong way. Isa, on the other hand, could light up a room by walking into it.

"And you shouldn't be out in the cold." He nodded to her belly. "Where you off to so early?"

Isa pushed her long braid behind her back. "The boutique of course. It'll be busy today with so many visitors to Snowshoe." A peculiar expression covered her face, and her hand grazed the swell of her stomach. "Ach, I swear this baby is kickboxing in there." She grinned at him. "Speaking of, when's the club hosting another MMA fight?"

Rubble blew smoke away from Isa. "Dunno. Hasn't come up at church."

"I'll bet Jupiter would enjoy watching you kick some arse."

He chuckled. Her lithe Irish accent was almost worth the bullets she caused last summer. "I doubt that very much. Jupiter and violence don't mix." He licked his lips, almost tasting the woman he couldn't get out of his head. "Which means Jupiter and Macha don't mix."

Laying a hand on his arm, Isa shook her head. "I thought that once too, Rubble. Then I met Doc, and everything changed." Her eyes took on a faraway gleam. "I love this club but not nearly as much as I love the man who showed me I was meant to be alongside him in it."

"No offense, Isa, but Jupiter isn't an MC princess." He met her eyes and recognized the fire there. "Has she told you about her ex—er—soon to be ex?"

"No, but I can guess." Isa's face shadowed and she huddled closer to him to block the wind. "I saw the bruises and how she reacts to some of the members."

"Then you know she needs to be as far away from

us as possible. Macha is my life, but it doesn't need to be hers."

Doc's truck pulled up to the clubhouse and Isa waved at him. "You Macha men think you know what's best for women to keep us safe. It's aggravating." She rolled her eyes. "But also sweet." She hugged him lightly. "Just once, let us make our own decisions. Jupiter will make the one best for her. I know I did."

Rubble helped Isa to the truck and opened the door. He nodded at Doc, who was recently back from running errands to the mayor's office. Once the truck left the parking lot, Rubble tossed the cigarette butt in the snow and checked the time. He had fifteen minutes before meeting with Nikita and the local sheriff. Keeping the town and Macha safe was his club priority. He'd check in on Jupiter and the bakery afterwards.

He hurried through the snow to the garage. All the motorcycles sat lonely in the back room. Fingers itching to use one, he kept walking. The snow wouldn't last forever, and he'd be on the open road once more. He grabbed a set of keys from his office. For now, he'd settle for the jacked-up Chevy he recently finished for a client in Denver. He'd freighter it next week, but one of the perks of working in the garage was test driving the vehicles. Jupiter would stay on the back burner for the next few hours. There'd be time to sort out the kisses they shared the night before. He'd make sure of it.

———

THE CROWD AT BOOZE & TATTOOS WASN'T OVERLY rambunctious, but Rubble kept his eyes peeled for trouble. He couldn't help it. Sitting in the corner of the bar, back to the wall, he scanned the tourists mingling with Snowshoers. Security was second nature to him after years in the military, not to mention his MMA and foster care days.

A burst of cold air touched him, and he swung his gaze to the tattoo parlor attached. Hawk greeted a customer covered in ink that was no doubt done by the artist himself. Turning back around, Rubble noticed the music shifted from country to rock. A group of ladies circled the small dance floor, their faces all smiles as they laughed.

A little part of his stomach jumped at the sight. They were so carefree. Not a worry in the world while they danced to a late '90s song. There'd never been such a time for Rubble. For as long as he could remember, he was on the defense. Getting drunk and having a night out wasn't in his memory bank.

"Need a refill, Rubble?"

His attention shifted to the nymph wearing tight

jeans and a shirt that showed off her flat stomach and solid C-cup breasts. The fact that his dick didn't jump at the sight of her worried him. Shaking his head curtly, he held his breath until the nymph left his purview. He needed to sink his dick in a wet pussy ASAP, but the club girl did nothing for him.

Surveying the nymphs at the bar, he grew increasingly aggravated when none of them even made his dick twitch. He stood and started his quarter-hourly stroll around the bar. Sure, they had a bouncer—one of the prospects—but protection was too embedded in Rubble's nature to leave it to someone else.

Doc and Snoop entered from the side door. Doc jutted his chin in Rubble's direction before heading toward the club's usual booth. Rubble would circle back to them shortly.

"Hey, big guy. You look like you could handle two girls," a woman called, grabbing his arm. Her equally intoxicated friend pressed against him, repeating the threesome offer.

"Not tonight, ladies," he said, brushing off their wandering hands. He pushed through the crowd, grateful neither one followed. He just wasn't feeling a drunken hookup tonight.

When his eyes latched onto the woman who had recently stepped foot inside, the other women in the bar disappeared. Sandwiched between Nikita and

Dolly stood Jupiter Quinn. Black jeans hugged her long legs. His mind immediately went to how they'd feel wrapped around his waist. She turned and he held his breath at the perfect way the pants gripped her ass. His dick was at full attention, and he hadn't even looked at the rest of her outfit yet. The people around him swayed to the music, but Rubble's feet were rooted to the spot. A deep crimson long-sleeved shirt and knee-high boots had him ready to toss her over his shoulder and swat her very spankable ass.

"You might wanna pick your jaw off the floor before she gets over here," Brewer teased, an empty tray under his arm.

Torn from Jupiter's inadvertent spell, Rubble looked at the redheaded man. "Yeah, um, good idea."

Brewer laughed his way back behind the bar. Rubble hated how a woman could have such a powerful effect on him. He shook his head. *Nah, I like it. That's the problem.*

"Hey, Rubble, how's it going?"

Closing the distance between him and the group of Macha women, he offered Dolly and Nikita nods. "Good."

He focused his attention on Jupiter. Her keen green eyes took in the bar's ambiance until her attention landed on him. "You look really nice."

Dolly chortled and linked her arm through Nikita's.

"Okay, we can take a hint. Jupiter, when you're done with this brute, come find us."

Jupiter's face turned a dark pink, but she didn't shy beneath his gaze. "Thanks. We stopped by the boutique and Isa hooked me up with some new clothes. She has amazing taste. I might have to buy an entire wardrobe from her."

He had to physically hold himself back from touching her. Every inch of him wanted to caress her soft skin and brush back the short hair from her face. Patience was what she needed, not him mauling her. "Yeah, Isa's got a good eye for detail."

She shifted on her feet, and he inwardly smacked himself for acting the dumbstruck fool. "You want a drink?"

"Sure. Vodka cranberry, please."

If he could've snapped the cocktail into existence, he would've. But he couldn't. He could barely make the mixed drink the proper way. "I'll grab it for you." He pointed to an open booth. "Be back in two shakes."

Jupiter lifted her brows, and suddenly Rubble wanted to dig a hole and crawl into it and die. "Shit, that was lame."

She placed a hand on his forearm, a cheerful grin on her face. "It was cute." She bit her bottom lip. "You're cute."

Rubble didn't know what to respond, so he didn't.

He hurried to the bar and wiped his forehead with his arm.

"Somebody hitting it off with a lady?" Brewer snagged a clean glass and filled it with beer, handing it off to a nymph.

"More like making an idiot out of myself." He gripped the edge of the counter and groaned. This wasn't normal for him. Even when he had been a horny kid, he didn't say stupid shit.

"So not suave?"

He gave Brewer a pointed look. "Not even close."

Brewer didn't try to hide his cocky grin. "What'll it be?"

After retrieving the drinks, Rubble made his way to the booth where Jupiter sat. Unfortunately for him, it was directly next to Macha's, and Nikita was leaning over the booth chatting with her.

Jupiter showered him with a grateful smile and took a sip of the drink. He wasn't much of a vodka fan, so he sat nursing his ice water while she and Nikita talked. It shouldn't have perturbed him that Nikita had her attention. Jupiter wasn't his. She wasn't anyone's. Despite that, Rubble wanted her all to himself. He craved her uninterrupted attention both clothed and otherwise.

He gritted his teeth, willing those thoughts to disappear. He had to go slow with her. She'd been through shit thanks to a man, and he wasn't about to repeat that. He'd get through the night. He'd watch her supple hips sway to music and not drink a damn drop of liquor. He'd listen to her light laugh, memorize the lithe way her legs moved. He'd make polite conversation. Then he'd grab the first nymph and fuck her until Jupiter's innocently seductive lips were a mere memory.

Only, he couldn't do any of that. Not when one touch from her silenced those thoughts.

Jupiter smiled at him from across the table. He took a large gulp of water. It was going to be the worst night of his life. But it was worth it to be near her.

CHAPTER 15
JUPITER

The scent of butter and freshly popped corn greeted Jupiter the moment she and Dolly walked into the arcade. No children's laughter greeted them. The arcade closed off after eight in the evening for adults only, or so said the sign on the front door.

"Come on, the guys are over there." Dolly grabbed her hand, pulling her toward the pinball machines. A group of bikers and their accompanying partners filled the space.

Jupiter glanced around the large arcade. Macha cuts were visible in every direction. Playful laughs filled the air, and she noticed the club girls milling about, going from game to game. They mostly stayed in groups of two or three, each woman dressed for optimal attention. There was no mistaking what they were there for.

"What guy wouldn't wanna win air hockey, then

fuck a girl in the arcade bathroom?" She rolled her eyes, staying to the edge of the biker group.

"Well, me for starters."

Jupiter whirled around and spun right into Rubble. Lifting her gaze, she met his steely eyes. "W—what?"

His gaze softened. "I'm not a big fan of bathroom sex." He shrugged. "Just doesn't do it for me."

"But the rest sounds good?"

Rubble leaned closer until his mouth hovered above hers. "When you beat a game, there's this high that surges in your veins. You feel invincible even if it's in a dumbass arcade." His eyes dropped to her lips, and she held her breath. He lifted his thumb to her bottom lip, grazing it. "With all that adrenaline pumping, yeah, sex sounds really good right about then."

Wetting her lips, Jupiter inhaled sharply at the hue in his mismatched eyes. A shot of desire pulsed between her legs, heart racing at the thought of what he'd do next. She couldn't just close the space and kiss him. *Could I?* She studied his lips, imagining them gliding across hers. He'd been distant the last few days and she hated it. This flirty behavior was precisely what her body craved.

"Wanna find out?" He eased back and held up two cards. "Fueled up and ready to go."

Not bothering to tamp down her giddy response,

she snatched one of the cards. "Let's do it." He smirked and Jupiter cringed. "Oh, God, not *it*."

"Patience, woman. We'll get there." Chuckling, he shook his head. "I'm a Skee-Ball legend 'round these parts."

Finding two open machines, Jupiter breathed a sigh of relief at his subject change and swiped her card. "Prove it."

Rubble mirrored the act, sending the balls rolling toward him. "Oh, I intend to."

Before Jupiter could read into any of his words, the timer started and they both tossed balls up the alley to the targets. When she sunk a ball in the highest point circle, she whooped and glanced at Rubble. Despite being a big, bad biker at all other times, he suddenly looked like an average guy as he tossed the heavy balls, hitting their mark every time. Jupiter's mouth dropped open.

"Better get going, Quinn, or I'm gonna kick your ass," Rubble teased lightly.

Snapping back into action, she rushed against the clock. She couldn't remember the last time she'd been to an arcade. The competitive kid in her was quickly coming to the surface. It felt good to be so carefree.

When the buzzer went off, they stepped back and watched the machine calculate the scores. Rubble nudged her arm with his elbow.

"Don't worry, I won't hold you to the bet."

"What bet?"

He wiggled his brows at her, and she rolled her eyes, recalling his earlier statement about sex. "Keep dreaming."

"Oh, I do."

The final score flashed on the screen and Jupiter scrunched her nose. Rubble had beat her by three hundred points.

"All right, smartass, I guess you are good at this game." She slid the game card in her back pocket, surveying the rest of the arcade. "But what about that one?"

Rubble followed her pointed finger. "The racing ones?"

She started walking backwards toward them. "Yup."

"The motorcycle racing games?"

Suddenly seeing her mistake, she laughed. "All right, probably not a good choice."

"What about some basketball?" Rubble looked her over. "You've probably got some hoops in ya."

"Oh, yeah. Point guard in junior high." They reached the hoops. She adored how easily they got along. His tough charade disappeared around her. "I was the best if I do say so myself."

Rubble rolled his shoulders back and forth, feigning

preparation for a big match. "All right, but this one's for a bet."

"Fine, what's the bet?"

He swiped his card and four basketballs rolled toward him. "Loser owes the winner a kiss."

She waited for the hoop to reset. "Seems kind of steep. More like an overall winner kind of bet."

"Not like we haven't kissed before." Rubble twirled a basketball on his middle finger, spinning Jupiter's axis right alongside it. "But I can work with that."

"Show off."

He leaned over and lowered his voice. "You have no idea."

Jupiter's nipples hardened at the insinuation. She met his playful gaze and he winked at her. If she didn't already find him attractive, this bantering side of him would reel her in.

"You're going down."

"Not yet, but soon enough if you play your cards right."

Her mouth gaped and he laughed as the timer started. "Are you always this crass?"

Rubble sunk the first shot. "Usually, yeah."

For the next two hours, Jupiter hauled ass, trying to beat Rubble at every game the arcade had to offer. She bested him in some, but he was the overall winner of the evening. With Rubble, their interactions weren't forced or even awkward. He was a playful flirt, and she was truly herself. That truth made her realize all the years she'd lost because a man kept her down instead of encouraging her to thrive.

"You okay?"

Jupiter finished the last sip of her cola and tossed the can in the recycling bin. "Sorry, I spaced out." She met Rubble's curious gaze. "I'm okay." The sounds of the arcade swarmed her. "Where'd everyone else go?"

Rubble glanced around the emptying arcade. "You really wanna know?"

She shook her head, suddenly realizing where everyone went. "No, I guess not."

"Guess we should cash out before they close."

Jupiter handed him the empty game card. "Actually, you can have my points. I doubt I have enough to get anything other than candy."

"Normally, I'd refuse that, but I've got my eye on that emoji alarm clock."

Following his gaze to the wall of prizes, Jupiter let out a loud laugh. "You aren't what I expected."

Rubble zipped up his club jacket. "What did you expect?"

He waved at the young kid who was behind the register turning off the games. They made it to the parking lot before she answered.

"The stereotypical biker, I guess." She shrugged, a

cold breeze taunting her light coat. "An asshole who chain smokes, only cares about sex, gets drunk, does drugs, and gets in tons of fights."

Rubble moved closer, blocking some of the chill with his large stature. "I'm not a big drinker and I never do drugs." He tugged the hood of her coat onto her head as the snow fell gently. "The rest I'm guilty of at times."

"So, you're an asshole who smokes, gets in fights, and is obsessed with sex?" Jupiter searched his eyes, their unique color holding her in place. The shivers down her spine weren't from the cold anymore. They were from the desire written in Rubble's eyes and her body's reaction to it.

He laced his arms around her shoulders and dipped his head lower. "I think I won the bet, and that means you owe me a kiss."

"Don't change the subject."

"I'm not." Rubble nuzzled her nose with his, the moment singeing the air between them. Jupiter's stomach flip-flopped at the connection. She shouldn't want to kiss him. They barely knew each other.

"Which one are you the most, Rubble? The sex addict or fighting god?" She meant it as a joke, but her tone didn't convey that.

Licking his lips, he stepped away and brushed a

hand over his face. "Let's get you back to the clubhouse."

Defeat washed through her veins. "Rubble, I didn't mean to upset you."

He stopped in front of his truck and unlocked it. Turning, he managed a crooked smile. "You didn't, baby girl."

But I did. She pushed down her anxiety the best she could. He wasn't Lyle. He wasn't a typical biker either. *He's one of a kind.*

Reaching for him, she grabbed both sides of his bearded face, pulling him to her waiting lips. His hands went to her hips, and he yanked her to him. Jupiter gasped at the primitive reaction. Tongue meeting his, she melted in his embrace. The frigid temperatures vanished the longer he overwhelmed her body and soul.

His hands drifted along her body, cupping her ass one moment and caressing her breasts the next. She moaned into his mouth, adoring the sensual electricity he amplified so easily until all she wanted was to lay him down in the parking lot.

Jupiter reached for his fly, but he put his large hand over hers to still their action.

"We can't." He pulled away, chest heaving and eyes glassy.

He was right of course. They couldn't make love in

a parking lot out in the open for anyone to see. Thrusting a thumb backwards, she already knew the answer but had to ask. It'd been a year since a man touched her. He was the one she wanted. The throbbing in her clit wouldn't relent until he did.

"Your windows are pretty dark."

He chuckled and snaked his arm around her waist, kissing her firmly. "With any other girl, I'd agree." He cupped her cheek. "But I want you all to myself, Jupiter. I want to feel you come alive beneath me." His eyes searched hers. "I want to hear your moans all night, not just in the backseat of my truck for a few minutes."

She started to pout until he added, "But after that first time, you can bet your ass I'm gonna fuck you wherever we are." He kissed her soundly once more. "We've got an early morning tomorrow."

Shivering now because of the cold, she reluctantly agreed. She wanted all that he said too. *All that plus some.*

CHAPTER 16
RUBBLE

The neon sign outside the bar and tattoo parlor blinked statically. The bulbs needed to be replaced. Rubble sent a text message to Brewer, reminding him it needed to be done as soon as possible. With all the new business thanks to the winter games, the club couldn't afford to lose any due to faulty bulbs. He'd checked in on every one of the club's businesses since leaving Jupiter at the clubhouse. *All except one.*

Turning on his toes, he headed to the garage. Since he spent the whole day watching over Yasmina and Jupiter, his duties at the shop went unattended. Flipping on a light, he made his way to the office and the mess of paperwork on the desk. It all made sense to him, which was the only reason no one dared touch it.

Rubble sank into the chair and tapped the wireless mouse until the computer screen lit up begrudgingly.

He didn't mind playing security guard for the bakery. In fact, he rather enjoyed seeing how Jupiter interacted with the customers and how determined her face got when she baked.

There was something special about her that went beyond the physical. Sure, she was drop-dead gorgeous even with newly cut and dyed hair that didn't do her justice in his opinion. But there was another quality about the stunning woman that made his stomach somersault every time she glanced his direction. He glared at the growing erection in his jeans, willing it to subside. *Not now.*

He started clicking along the keyboard, ensuring orders were filled for the next day's jobs. During the day, Kevlar ran the shop. The two kept in constant contact about the inner workings, new repairs, and the prospects working on the vehicles. So far, they had a decent group. Dealing with prospects was all part of club life. Most ended up patching, but he'd cut a few loose over the years.

Shaking his head, Rubble focused on the job at hand. Once he got caught up, he could go back to the clubhouse where Jupiter was hanging out with Dolly and the rest of the gang. Seeing her again shouldn't make his palms sweaty. But it did. *Every damn time.* These sensations were all new to him. He didn't get attached to women. *They're nothing but trouble.* He ran a hand over his beard. Except now, he didn't care about the possible trouble. Not when Jupiter was involved.

"Rubble, you in here?"

Rubble glanced toward the dark shop, recognizing Kevlar's voice. "In the office."

Heavy boots clomped through the garage until Kevlar and Nikita stood in the doorway. "You missed dinner again."

He shrugged. "Gotta catch up on shit." He went back to typing, fully aware of Kevlar's head shake.

"Loosen up, brother. Everything's taken care of here." Kevlar leaned against the door. "We both know you're looking for ways to stay away from a certain cute baker."

Rubble flipped through the stack of orders, keying in their codes on the computer. "No, I'm making sure Macha's taken care of, Kevlar."

"Mhm, sure." Nikita said, plopping into the chair across the table. "I heard back from my analyst about that certain cute baker and her past."

This got Rubble's full attention. He saved the last order and leaned back. "Well? What'd you find out?"

Nikita's eyes sparkled with mischief. She was one hell of an FBI agent even if it took him a bit of time to fully appreciate the kind of trouble she brought to the MC.

"Lyle's one evil motherfucker," Nikita started,

fishing out her phone and reading from it. "Looks like there's a history of domestic abuse all over the board. He's never been charged, though. All his indiscretions were wiped away by one of the judges in Texas. From our research, it looks like the judge is an old family friend."

That didn't surprise him. From what he'd gleaned from Jupiter, her ex's family wasn't one to trifle with. "What else?"

"Lots of sketchy overseas transactions." Nikita turned her phone around to show him the open FBI and CIA files on the man soon to be out of Jupiter's life. "He's sneaky. Plenty of offshore accountants to shuffle the money around, but multiple agencies have been working on nailing this guy for years. They're close too."

"How can we make sure that happens?" Sweat lined Rubble's brow. He needed this guy gone for Jupiter's sake, but there was a selfish factor as well. With Lyle put away, Jupiter was free. He swallowed hard at the possibility that Jupiter may just decide to leave Snowshoe behind and his broken heart with it.

Nikita stood and linked her arm around Kevlar's waist. "We gotta wait."

"That's bullshit."

She shrugged. "That's all we can do, Rubble. If the FBI or CIA gets too close, Lyle will scrub all open deviances and we'll be shit outta luck." She offered him a sad smile. "It's not what you wanna hear but give us some time. We'll get this bastard."

Kevlar nodded. "Don't worry, brother, Jupiter will be safe."

"Thanks." Rubble pushed back from the desk, resigning himself to the fact that they'd all have to be patient. "What's going on over there?" he asked, hoping to get his mind off the temporary dead-end.

Nikita grinned. "Hawk's teaching Jupiter how to play billiards."

The thought of Hawk touching Jupiter in any way gnawed at Rubble's gut. "What was for dinner?" He wasn't hungry in the slightest, but if he were about to watch another man be close to Jupiter, he'd need something to shove in his mouth to keep quiet.

"Cavatelli, garlic knots, and salad."

"Perfect." Standing, he turned off the monitor. "I'll catch up tomorrow."

Kevlar patted him on the back. "Sure, you will."

Rubble didn't like the tone in Kevlar's voice, but he let it slide. He wasn't in a joking mood. Right now, he needed to watch over Jupiter in case one of his dumbass brothers got a little too handsy.

She was a natural. At least that's what it looked like from his viewpoint on the other side of the room. Rubble finished the last bit of pasta and took his plate to the kitchen. He handed it to a nymph doing the dishes, giving her a swat on her ass before leaving her to her duties.

Jupiter's laughter caught his ear, guiding him back to the pool tables. She and Dolly were playing against Hawk and Cueball. From the looks of it, the ladies were losing. Both sides were slinging back beers, the steady tempo of the country song in the background drowning out the clinking of balls.

Rubble sat on the leather couch next to Kevlar. The other man nursed a whiskey in one hand and texted his old lady in the other. Despite everyone else drinking, Rubble didn't feel the need or desire. Jupiter muddled his mind more than alcohol.

"And that's another loss for you two," Hawk said with a cocky smirk. "Want to try again?"

Dolly placed her hands on her hips, face showing she was ready for a fight, but then Jupiter walked over and whispered something in her ear. The club madam went from fiery to mysterious in an instant.

Rubble sat up a little straighter, straining to hear their conversation better.

"All right, boys, rack 'em up." Dolly fished out a

wad of cash from her bra and placed it on the table. "But this time, we're playing for money, not glory."

Cueball and Hawk exchanged a skeptical glance. "Why don't we play for both?" Cueball suggested, fronting the money for the bet.

"Yo, Rubble, you want a piece of this action?" Hawk asked, walking over, and offering a cue stick.

Rubble eyed his brothers then the two women who looked much too intrigued. "All right, but we'll have to break it up to two tables."

Cueball nodded. "Only seems fair. Me versus Jupiter."

"And me versus Rubble," Dolly said with a sly grin.

"What about me?" Hawk pouted, left out of the game.

Kevlar finished his whiskey in one drink. "I'll play ya next game, brother. I have a feeling we should sit this one out."

Hawk reluctantly handed over his stick and sat next to Kevlar. "Fine, then I'm taking bets on the winners."

A group of bikers and nymphs slowly gathered side by side around the pool tables. Dolly didn't hide her confidence, flaunting it for all to see. Rubble noticed Yasmina join the group, her eyes never shifting from the club madam.

"Hundred bucks buy in. Winner of each game faces

each other for the big payout," Snoop said, taking the cash and stashing it in his pocket for safe keeping.

The balls were racked up on both tables, and Dolly and Jupiter were given the breaks. From that moment forward, Rubble noticed the group of bikers closing in to form a tightknit circle. There was no backing down now.

Dolly hit two balls in before missing the third. When Rubble glanced over to see how Jupiter faired, Dolly clucked her tongue.

"Oh, no you don't. Focus on me, big guy." She smirked. "If you're lucky, you'll get her the next round."

Tightening his hold on the stick, Rubble hated to admit she was right. He couldn't advance if he kept looking at Jupiter. Sinking four balls in, he grinned at the cheers from his fellow brothers.

The games ended at the same time, he and Jupiter the victors. From the looks of it, Jupiter's game was closer than his and Dolly's, but he wouldn't get ahead of himself. He'd rather have a tight game than it be a blowout.

"Looks like we've got our winners ready for a showdown," Snoopy said, grinning from ear to ear. "The game is nine-ball. Best of luck."

"Place your bets," Hawk chimed in, grabbing the outstretched money from prospects and patches alike.

Jupiter grabbed the chalk and rubbed it on the end of her cue stick. Her hair was pulled up in a messy bun. Tendrils of hair had fallen loose, resting comfortably on the back of her neck. Only she could make faded blue jeans and a T-shirt sexy.

Rubble eyed the other men. They'd all noticed the roundness of her ass and the outline of her braless nipples against the gray shirt. He gripped the stick until he had to remind himself not to break it. They could ogle all they wanted, but she wasn't going home with any of them. He'd make sure.

"You want to break?" she asked, slicing into his thoughts.

He met her gaze, the green depths curious with a hint of playfulness. "Ladies first."

Jupiter didn't need to be told twice. She lined up the shot and took it. Balls scattered across the table, two going in right away. "Looks like I'm one through seven."

"Nice shot." He stood back and watched her slide the pole between her hands. Her movements were lithe and fluid as if she'd done this her whole life and not just the last two hours.

She hit two more in then turned the table to him. "All yours."

Rubble walked by and the scent of brown sugar and cinnamon almost made him forget which balls he needed to put away. He cued up and easily hit two in but scratched on the next.

"Why don't we make this more interesting," Dolly said above the roar after each of them hit two more balls into the pockets.

"Such as?" Hawk called.

Dolly and Jupiter exchanged a secretive grin. "Loser is the winner's drink bitch until after the winter games." She held up her hand at the laughter. "And yes, the honor can be transferred if the winner sees fit."

Rubble chuckled, already knowing he wouldn't make Jupiter bring him drinks.

"Done," Jupiter called, raising her glass of beer.

The bikers cheered in response, clinking their glasses and bottles together. Suddenly, the idea of winning didn't seem so guaranteed.

Moving closer to Jupiter, Rubble leaned down. "Should I be worried you're a pool shark?"

She laughed and shook her head. "I don't know, should you?" Her green eyes twinkled, and it took every ounce of willpower to not capture her ruby lips then and there.

He lowered his voice and placed a hand on her waist. The merriment in her eyes quickly morphed into something more intense. "If you're hustling me, baby girl, I'll tie you to my bed and make you come until you beg me to stop."

Jupiter's breath hitched and her eyes darkened with lust. "I guess we'll find out soon, won't we?" She reached over and grabbed his cue stick. "To make it fair, I'll play with yours if you play with mine." Her face reddened at the statement, and she quickly hurried to take her shot.

Rubble's mouth dropped open at the sensual intonation. It wasn't what she meant, but he sure as hell knew she didn't regret it. He stood back and kept his gaze locked on her movements.

Jupiter lined up the stick and sunk the first ball. She redirected the next hit to get two more in the side pockets. A hush fell over the room as she reared back to take on the nine ball.

Her eyes drifted to his momentarily and Rubble clenched his jaw. She winked once then let the cue stick fly. The crowd watched in silence as the ball rolled toward the left pocket. It teetered on the edge before slipping in the hole. The group went wild in that moment. Beer sloshed on the floor, howls of joy and disappointment filling the air.

Jupiter stood and walked over to him. She placed a hand on his chest, eyes never leaving his. "Huh, I guess you *did* get hustled."

She could've stopped there, but she didn't. "You know, I'm feeling kind of thirsty after all that winning." Her brows wiggled and she fanned her face.

"Care to get me another beer, drink bitch?"

The bikers roared in laughter. Some slapped Jupiter on the back, others heckled him at the clear hustle. They all respected this woman. Rubble nodded. *And rightly so.*

Rubble was ready to bend her over the pool table and fuck her, but he wouldn't. Not yet at least. Jupiter loved the attention her recent win earned her. Men and women alike surrounded her, offering compliments, and slathering her with praise.

All he could do was watch. She'd won, albeit by cheating, but she deserved this positivity in her life. After all she'd been through, Jupiter deserved the best.

"Guess she fooled you."

He looked down and saw Dolly grinning from ear to ear. "You little shit. You knew the whole time."

Dolly playfully punched his side. "Aw, come on, Rubble. It wasn't all my idea. Give the girl a little credit."

And he did. He'd give her credit for being a crafty billiards player. Jupiter was a woman who knew what she wanted, and she didn't stop until she got it. She was quickly becoming his favorite person of all time. That worried him. He was falling for this wily woman and he couldn't help himself.

CHAPTER 17

JUPITER

"We should talk."

Jupiter looked over her shoulder at Rubble who stood to the left of the register. She finished bagging up the dozen sugar cookies and nodded. "Sure. Yasmina, can you man the front?"

The other woman came to the front and smudged flour on her cheek. "Break time?"

"No, Rubble needs to ask me about…." She looked to him expectantly.

"The Xtreme Winter Games."

"Right." She motioned to the flour on Yasmina's face, then followed Rubble to the small office in the back. He shut the door behind him. "I think we'll be able to meet the current orders for the games. Yasmina hasn't stopped baking in days."

"That's not what I wanted to discuss."

Jupiter smoothed her apron. "Yeah, I figured." She lifted her eyes to him. "Then what?"

"Your soon-to-be ex."

She wrinkled her nose and gripped the side of her apron. "Why do you want to talk about him? I'm handling it."

Rubble took the seat not filled with bakery boxes. "No, you're not. You think you are, but you're avoiding it."

"I really don't want to talk about this, Rubble."

He clenched his jaw then relaxed it. "Baby girl, you gotta talk to me. I can help."

"Yeah, because you love talking about your past."

He winced. "Fair enough. What do you want to know?"

She chewed on her bottom lip. He was offering insight into his youth and some part of her wasn't sure if she wanted to hear it. "You don't trust women except a select few that I've noticed. I overheard a prospect joke about how you think we're all trouble. Why is that?"

Rubble smoothed a hand over his burly beard and leaned forward. "My mom died when I was little. I can't blame her for anything except not being alive for me. I was almost immediately put into foster care. The women didn't care that I was an orphan. They only wanted the paycheck from the state. Some were verbally abusive, some physically. Being in Macha, we protect women, but sometimes that goes sideways. I shouldn't blame anyone, but I do." He paused and studied his boots. "Trusting anyone is tough, but women especially. I've never been in love, Jupiter. I never let myself be vulnerable like that."

Jupiter placed a hand on his shoulder. "I understand more than you know."

He nodded. "But I'm trying, baby girl. I'm trying my damnedest to break down the walls around my heart. I can only do that if you're honest with me." He met her gaze. "Please."

Jupiter worried her lips together. She wasn't sure how to react. Rubble had given her a glimpse into his childhood and all she wanted to do was wrap him in a hug and never let go. She had to share everything. It was only fair to them both.

"My lawyer has been arguing with his lawyer for eleven months, Rubble. Once they're done squabbling, I can get back to living."

He narrowed his gaze slightly. "You make it sound so easy."

"It is."

"Then why are you here, Jupiter?" He carefully took one of her hands between his two. She shifted her attention to him instead of the purchase orders on the desk. "You think he'll hurt you."

"Yes." She bit back tears. "Once he finds out where I am, he sends hired goons to bring me back."

Rubble's face darkened. "How many times have they caught you?"

"More than I care to admit." She cleared her throat, trying not to remember the last time. "I barely made it away a few weeks ago. They took me halfway to the ranch before I ran off at a rest stop." She pointed to the light bruises. "Lyle doesn't give up."

"He won't find you."

She half laughed, half cried. "He will."

Rubble gently pulled her onto his lap and gathered her against him. "If he does, he'll wish he hadn't." He kissed the top of her head. "You're safe, baby girl. You're safe with me."

Jupiter snuggled deeper into his embrace. She desperately wanted to believe him. The pessimist in her wouldn't completely allow it. *Okay, maybe for a few minutes.*

"The FBI is aware of your—Lyle's abuse. If he steps foot in Snowshoe, they'll be on his ass."

She sat up and stared at him. "What? How?"

He smirked. "Nikita is an FBI agent."

"I thought she just worked in an FBI office or something."

He squeezed her closer to his chest. "We got you."

For the first time, Jupiter believed him.

Lyle: So, you don't want any of my money? I'm surprised. We're loaded, pet. Don't you want a measly one percent at the very least? All I want is to see you and you'll get it.

Jupiter gripped the phone tighter, dots on the other end of the phone indicating that more words were on their way.

Lyle: Where are you hiding, my precious pet? I bought a present from Paris for you. It's one to die for.

Her stomach dropped low, and she took a step away from the bakery's front door. She'd been on her way to lock it for the night when the texts started pouring in from Lyle. At first, they were general messages. She could easily ignore those. But they quickly went downhill.

Lyle: Don't forget, if I go down for anything, I'm taking you with me. Those money transfers were under your name, Jupiter, not mine.

Looking out the window, she watched people walk

by toward the town center. The opening ceremony would begin shortly. Yasmina slipped out the front door an hour ago, promising to save her a spot in the bakery booth in hopes of increasing sales. Judging from the text she received from Yasmina five minutes ago, they were right to do so.

But those weren't the messages circulating Jupiter's mind. The onslaught of texts from Texas were the culprit.

Lyle: Fine, be a mute. You'll be lucky to walk away with your life, you bitch!

The more she read, the darker they got. Flipping off the lights, Jupiter stuffed the phone in her back pocket. *I'll show them to Rubble. He'll know what to do.* She finished the task at hand and loaded the last of the pastries into her Civic before making her way to the already full parking lot.

Spotting people walking away from a side street, she followed suit and found an empty spot big enough for her tiny car. Just as she climbed out, a voice made her gasp.

"Need any help?"

She turned and grinned at Doc approaching. "That'd be great, thanks. I have a few boxes to bring to the booth." She popped open the trunk and he smirked.

"A few boxes?"

The trunk was jammed full. She buttoned her coat and tucked the scarf around her neck. "Maybe more than a few. Think we can get it all?"

Doc held out his arms. "Oh, yeah. Pile it on me."

After managing ten bakery boxes on his long arms, Jupiter grabbed the remaining ten and closed the trunk with her foot. "I don't think I would've made it on my own."

"Not without help."

She followed him toward the center of Snowshoe. Blue streamers lined the streetlights, guiding them toward the main attraction. The streets were recently plowed, and Jupiter was wearing her boots, so she easily kept up with Doc's long strides. Everything about the town looked homey. On this street, mature buildings lined the way, each one having its own appeal. Snowshoe wasn't old, per se, but it also wasn't new. The residents enjoyed a happy medium and it seemed to attract visitors each winter for the Xtreme Winter Games.

"Have you ever been skiing or snowboarding?" Doc asked as they wove through the crowd.

"Actually, no." She chuckled. "My senior trip in high school was to Colorado but I never went."

"Too cold?"

"More like afraid I'd break my leg again."

Doc paused and offered her a cocked brow. "Say what now?"

"When I was eight years old, I broke my leg sledding." She shuddered at the memory. "Since then, I haven't had much luck in the snow."

"Can't blame ya there." He nodded toward the booth decorated with Macha's emblem. "Here we are. You and Yasmina are set up right next to the club in case you need a hand."

They reached the small tentlike structure with Heaven's Treats scrawled on the banner. Yasmina had a long line waiting, her pretty face a combination of flustered and enthused.

"Good thing you came when you did." Doc set his boxes on the table and helped Jupiter with hers. "I'll pitch in until you guys slow down."

"Oh, thank God." Yasmina nodded enthusiastically and the trio got down to work. They had a nice little system down by the time the line dwindled. Doc handled payments while Jupiter and Yasmina bagged the pastries.

When an announcement about the opening ceremony start time was made over the loudspeaker, the crowd shifted and gave them a short reprieve.

Yasmina fanned herself despite the overcast sky

and cold breeze. "Thank you for bringing more donut holes. Those are the best seller so far."

"Glad I made it in time, or you would've had an angry mob on your hands." Jupiter glanced at the boxes they'd gone through as well as the ones left over. They were a little more than halfway through the extra she brought.

"Are you staying for the ceremony?" she asked once Doc left to join the other booth.

Yasmina shook her head. "Nikita will be along shortly to take my place. I need to get some sleep before waking up early to start baking again."

"I can help if you want. If I have a recipe, I can make just about anything."

Offering her a kind smile, Yasmina rearranged the cookies on display. "Two of the nymphs offered already but thank you. We'll get you up at four one of these mornings."

A small part of Jupiter was disappointed. She wanted to be part of the hubbub of baking, not just the selling portion. Her phone buzzed in her pocket. *Plus, it'd keep my mind off that.*

They helped a handful more customers before Nikita arrived and Yasmina left. The mayor droned in the background; the crowd was clearly more interested in the popular athletes who would hop onstage next.

During a break, Jupiter surveyed the crowd. The

town square was alight thanks to twinkle lights and streetlights, along with plenty of spotlights that had been brought in. Uniformed officers moved through the crowd, alert and ready to pounce should the need arise. It gave her a moment of peace to know they were nearby. *But where's Rubble?*

She peeked over at Macha's main tent and didn't spy the tall man. Panic filled her stomach.

"He's up there." Nikita's voice broke into her worry.

"What?" She turned toward where Nikita pointed her finger.

"The watchtower. Rubble's up there."

Heat flooded her face, and she wrapped a banana nut muffin for a customer. "Why would I—"

"Because you like him." Nikita winked. "Don't worry, I won't tell. But you should know everybody already knows."

"They do?" More panic, this time localized to her heart. "How?"

Nikita gave a customer their change and crossed her arms over her chest. With her dark hair, piercing eyes, and skintight leather, she looked the biker chick part. The only give away was the FBI badge inside her jacket.

"Rubble."

"What'd he do or say?"

She shrugged. "Nothing. That's the thing." Jupiter gave her a confused glance, so Nikita explained. "Rubble isn't shy about speaking his mind. He did so when both Isa and I came to town. His life is the club. Has been since Reaper all but adopted him. The fact that he hasn't said a word about you to anybody is suspicious." She grinned. "But good suspicious."

"I don't know how to take that." Jupiter truly didn't. For all she knew, Rubble was the brute his name reflected… but only when he was with the club. When it was just the two of them, he was a giant teddy bear.

"It's a good thing. Rubble wouldn't ask around if the person didn't mean anything to him."

"He mentioned he spoke to the FBI about…." She didn't want to finish that line of thought.

"Your ex. Yeah, he did and I'm glad." Nikita held up her cell phone. "As it turns out, my buddy in Dallas got a tip about Lyle Jones a year ago. He's been on the Feds' radar, but we never had anything on him. Still don't." Her face bunched up in disgust. "But since Lyle has known about the divorce, he's lit up the bad guy beacon. Guess he's pretty intent on finding you."

The cinnamon roll in Jupiter's hand shook slightly. She bit the inside of her cheek and willed herself to stop reacting. It was easier thought than done.

"He won't, Jupiter." Nikita took the roll from her and bagged it. Her eyes softened and she offered a small smile. "Macha won't let your ex find you, and if he does, you can bet the ranch that Rubble won't let the man anywhere near you."

"I hope you're right."

"Sweetie, I'm never wrong." She winked again. "It's one of the perks of being me. Just ask Kevlar."

"Ask Kevlar what?" the man in question asked, walking up to the booth.

Nikita leaned over and kissed him. "That I'm never wrong."

He chuckled and gripped her chin before kissing her again. "Nope, she's never wrong."

Giving them a moment of privacy, Jupiter stepped foot outside the booth's warmth and watched the torch being lit on stage. The crowd roared with applause and a splattering of fireworks lit up the sky. She smiled at them. The start of a new adventure for all those present. She rather liked the idea.

CHAPTER 18
RUBBLE

For the first time in five years, no snow fell during the opening ceremony of the Xtreme Winter Games. Rubble watched the crowd from his perch above the makeshift stage in the town center. Thousands of winter sports enthusiasts were bundled up, faces aglow for the main event to begin the following morning. A group of teens snickered when the mayor started talking about the community's efforts and maintaining the games for future generations. The kids wouldn't be any trouble for the club. He wasn't keeping an eye out for dumbass teenagers. He was looking for a genuine threat.

The sheriff's deputy waved at him from the ground level. Working hand in hand with local law enforcement was key to Snowshoe's survival. The town appreciated Macha's security, and the club appreciated the town supporting their businesses. So long as no lines were crossed, Macha never had a quarrel with the politicians.

From his spot, Rubble could see the entire town square along with the array of booths and tents set up. Most had long lines, including Heaven's Treats. He'd noticed Doc and Jupiter arrive with supplies. It'd been hard not to notice Jupiter and even harder to remain at his post instead of whisking her away for a kiss under the cloudless stars.

Once, he caught her staring his direction. The watchtower was lit up for that very reason. They could see out, but the public couldn't see in. It was his idea and seemingly a good one until he couldn't catch Jupiter's green eyes from below.

The torch was lit on stage and was followed by fireworks. They weren't his favorite part of the event. The bright sparks and echoing booms reminded him too much of his time overseas. War had a funny way of unearthing regrets and lost friends when he least suspected.

Breathing in through his nose and out of his mouth like the VA doctor taught him, Rubble closed his eyes for a millisecond until his heart stopped pounding in his ears. When he opened them, he saw Jupiter standing outside the bakery booth, smiling up at the fireworks. His heart clenched again, this time in a new and frightening way. Suddenly, he needed to see her, talk to her, tell her how bad he felt when she wasn't near.

"All clear, Rubble." The deputy said, climbing the stairs. "We'll lock down the square for the night." He smiled. "Go enjoy yourself. I'll see you tomorrow."

Nodding, Rubble didn't need to be told twice. He hurried down the steps and through the crowd. Groups of people were already celebrating the event as the band on the stage pumped out lively music.

Rubble made quick work of the sidewalk, steering clear of the beer tent at the other side of the square. He didn't need alcohol to do anything in life, let alone tell Jupiter how important she was to him.

Reaching the bakery's booth, he nodded at Nikita and noticed her odd smile. If he weren't intent on speaking with Jupiter, he'd ask what Nikita was up to. Instead, Nikita hopped over to the Macha tent. He was never more grateful for the privacy.

Jupiter finished with the customers, and he stepped inside the small booth. The scent of brown sugar laced with cinnamon drifted to him and he inhaled her essence.

"I was wondering if you'd stop by." The shy smile on Jupiter's face was too adorable.

"My shift was over, and I thought I'd see how things were going." He sought out her gaze, but she kept her eyes focused on the streusel bites. Not discouraged, he took a step closer and tilted up her chin. Gorgeous light green eyes stared back at him. Just like that, his favorite color changed from black to the hue of her eyes. "How're things going, baby girl? Anybody giving you a hard time?"

"No." She bit her bottom lip, her tell showing.

"Jupiter, tell me."

"I, um, started receiving more text messages today."

He searched her eyes. They weren't spam texts. They were harassing ones. "Show me." It wasn't a command, but he'd fish the phone out of her back pocket if she didn't obey.

Jupiter handed it over, a customer stealing her attention while he reviewed the slew of messages.

Lyle: You better never stop running. I'll find you and you don't want that to happen, pet. You'll beg for mercy by the end. The doctors won't even know how to fix you. I'll take my belt and—

That's when he stopped reading. If he kept going, he'd surely crush the phone in his fist. He flipped the phone off and resisted the urge to drive down to Texas and deal with the asshole himself. *Holy fuck. The guy is a lunatic.* Rubble shifted his weight and watched

Jupiter's exchange with the customers. She was sweet as chocolate pie. *What kind of man could hurt her?* He already knew the answer.

"I put it away when I got here." She moved for the phone, but he kept it out of reach.

"You don't want to read the new ones." He tucked the phone in the interior pocket of his jacket.

Her eyes shadowed. "That bad, huh?"

Tugging her to his chest, Rubble pressed a kiss to the top of her head. Her body shook slightly, and he hoped it was from the cold. He could fix that here and now. He couldn't force her to feel safe. She had to do that on her own.

"This is club business. Okay, baby girl?" he whispered. "Nobody threatens Macha."

She eased back enough to meet his gaze. "I'm not Macha."

"The fuck you aren't." He kissed the tip of her nose. "You're living under Macha's roof and working under our name. You don't have to be patched to be Macha."

Jupiter nodded. He knew in his gut she'd never been cherished by a man before. He'd right that wrong for as long as she'd let him.

Rubble cradled her jaw and kissed her top lip. Her eyes closed automatically so he repeated the act on her bottom lip. "Jupiter, I'm trying to be patient, but you make it so damned hard."

"Then don't be patient." She lightly kissed his mouth, and he swallowed the urge to consume her on that very spot.

"Don't say that if you don't mean it."

A family of tourists walked to the booth and started ordering, summoning her away from him. Before she went to help, she pressed her lips to his cheek. "I mean it, Rubble. I want to feel protected by you."

She walked away, taking his heart with her. Resisting Jupiter wasn't going to happen anymore. Not when she wanted him, and he wanted her. He let out a steadying breath, the hard-on in his jeans begging to be freed. *Later.* He'd show Jupiter precisely how he planned on protecting her.

CHAPTER 19
JUPITER

Stray firecrackers echoed in the distance, red splashing across the sky through the bakery's window. Jupiter and Rubble volunteered to take the remaining pastries and cash to the store for safekeeping until the next day. With only the back light on, the late hour combined with the looming truth that her past was catching up with her set Jupiter on edge.

She finished putting away the boxes of treats and walked to the front where Rubble stood watching out the window. Macha's emblem on his broad back stood out amid the feminine colors in the shop. He looked like the ideal brooding male with his shoulders slightly hunched, eyes narrowing on every movement outside, and arms ready for action should the need arise. She set the pouch of cash in the safe then silently watched him. *It'd be so easy to fall into this world. To fall into him.*

As if sensing her gaze, Rubble looked at her. "Ready to go?"

Leaning her forearms on the counter, she nodded. "Whenever you are."

"All right, I'll warm up the truck." He moved to do exactly that, but suddenly she couldn't let him. The need to feel something other than fear overtook her better sense. *Just because I have to leave eventually doesn't mean I can't see how a man should treat me.*

"Wait."

He paused at the door and turned. "For what?"

Her stomach dropped at the look in his mismatched eyes. She'd never be able to choose a favorite. One green and one blue were each too unique to decide between.

"I don't want to go to the clubhouse yet." She tugged off her coat. "I want to spend time with you without being interrupted by one of your brothers." She smiled faintly. "Not that they're not great, because they are. I just want some time alone with you."

Rubble shifted on his feet, uncertainty lining his handsome face. "Are you sure?"

"Very."

He turned the lock on the door and slowly walked toward her. "I don't think I can control myself if we're alone." His eyes dipped to her lips. "You know the effect you have on me, baby girl."

Jupiter came out from behind the counter and closed the distance between them. She gripped the lapels of his leather jacket and searched his eyes. Maybe it was the mountain air summoning her courage or the intense reaction she had to him that spurred her on. All she knew was that she desperately wanted him.

"I don't want you to control yourself. Go wild, Rubble. I want to feel everything you've got."

In one smooth move, Rubble was there, arms around her waist, lifting her off the floor. She wrapped her legs around him, lips fused to his as sparks ignited. The scream of the fireworks outside was nothing compared to the heat flooding her veins.

She gasped when he rested her on the cool countertop. He pulled back slightly, sliding her loose shirt down her arm to place feathery kisses on the naked flesh. Her heart thudded loudly in her ears, and he repeated the act on her left side. Shirt now barely covering her breasts, Rubble gently tugged the material off and hissed out a reverent curse.

He watched the rise and fall of her chest and Jupiter held as still as possible. Her B-sized breasts weren't what he was focused on. It was the scars on her chest that held his rapt attention. Not wanting to answer those unasked questions, she unclasped her bra and let it fall to the floor. His warm hands were there in an instant, enclosing her breasts, making her fear evaporate.

"I'm usually an ass man, but you have one perfect set of tits," he said before closing his lips around her right nipple. Jupiter gasped and arched her back. His teeth grazed the tender flesh, sucking on it hard until stars danced in her eyes. She caught her breath just before he moved to her left breast, his free hand holding her tighter to him.

Jupiter tugged at his jacket, needing to feel his body's warmth without the confines of clothing. He eagerly obliged, shedding his jacket and long-sleeved T-shirt, but keeping his jeans properly buckled. Standing in the muted darkness, she took her time reviewing his tattoos. They were as beautiful as she anticipated. Tracing them, she recognized the coiled serpent and Marines emblem on his ribs. Similar military tattoos wound across his form. Without a doubt, more lay etched on his back. She swallowed hard, her gaze traveling along the powerful lines of his muscles and finally to the bulge in his jeans.

"Don't be scared." Rubble tipped up her chin. "Please. I never want you scared of me."

His tone was so soft, sweet even, that she couldn't be fearful if she wanted to be. Not when this massive man was in front of her, his voice so unlike the rest of his ruggedness.

"I'm not." She cracked a small smile. "I'm more worried you'll be disappointed."

He shook his head. "Not possible, baby girl." He cupped the left side of her face. "If all we do is this right here, I'll go to sleep happy."

She smirked and hopped off the counter. "But not satisfied." Reaching for his belt, she unbuckled it, pulling the zipper down next. "And I want you satisfied because I know you'll do the same for me."

Rubble's large hands squeezed her ass. "Fuck yes I will."

Kicking off her boots, Jupiter shimmied out of her jeans. When she looked up, Rubble had done the same. They both kept their underwear on, but he couldn't disguise what lay beneath his. The thick erection couldn't be hidden, and a shiver of concern crippled her mind.

"When was the last time you were touched?"

She lifted her gaze from his groin. "A year."

He shook his head, fingers sneaking beneath the blue panties hugging her hips. "You deserve better." His lips tickled her neck, the touch spurring her desire. "If you were mine, I'd fuck you twice every day at the very least, until you know how a man should treat you."

Jupiter closed her eyes as his lips trailed down her chest, stopping to encompass her nipples, but not staying there long. "I'd wake you up every morning kissing you right here." He kneeled, his breath stopped at her panties, slowly pulling them down until she was fully exposed to him.

He held her steady as she kicked them away, her breathing staggered from his words and actions. Jupiter clung to the edge of the counter behind her, her knees wobbling. Rubble kissed her thighs, stopping at her knees then back up to her hips. His light touch turned possessive when his nose disappeared into her thatch of springy curls. Jupiter gripped his smooth head, eyes wide at the act she'd only experienced a handful of times.

"Spread your legs, Jupiter. I want to taste you."

She did as he instructed, not regretting it once his tongue dove into her sex. She leaned against the counter and held him tighter against her, his mouth exploring every facet of her pussy.

"You're so sweet. I knew you would be." He looked up from his kneeling position on the floor, beard glistening with her arousal. It turned her on more and she grinned, pushing him back in place. Rubble didn't waste any time; his tongue flicked her clit and she inched closer to release. When he slipped a finger inside of her pussy, she bucked automatically. He moved it so fluidly, slowly summoning her orgasm. He groaned against her and she caught her bottom lip between her teeth. It'd been too long since a man touched her. Everything he did was heaven.

He added another finger, and she started to sway her hips in time with his movements. Closing her eyes, Jupiter felt a familiar yet foreign sensation building low in her belly. She couldn't remember when she felt it last. She clenched her thighs around Rubble's head, lightning firing through her body as she came undone. Her mouth dropped open and the sound of her moans echoed through the empty bakery. Her hips shook uncontrollably, legs weakening the longer the orgasm clenched her. Rubble was there, lapping up every drop and keeping her steady as she rode out the rest of the wave while she cried out Rubble's name.

At last, her body relaxed, mind still humming from the delectable sensations. Rubble hopped to his feet, arms there to catch her wobbling body.

"Holy…." She met his eyes, a playful smile on his face. "I don't even know what to say."

"Oh, you said plenty. Or should I say, moaned plenty?" He smoothed his beard. "It's the hottest thing I've ever seen or heard."

He kissed her deeply, the taste of her orgasm on his tongue. It turned her on even more than she was before. Reaching down, she palmed his cock. It was hot to the touch even through the boxer briefs. "I want to see you."

Rubble nodded and his dark underwear was gone in a flash. He stood completely naked in front of her, cock alert and ready for action.

Jupiter traced the long and thick member. Pumping it in her hand, she kissed his chest covered with tattoos and a trail of small curls that led down his sternum to his groin. Her lips grazed several scars. She noted them for later and licked across the tattoos. Teasing his copper colored nipples with her teeth, she swirled her tongue across them and grinned at his sharp inhale. She kept moving further down his body to the heaven she longed to sample.

Kneeling, she licked the length of his cock. It bobbed hungrily in response, so she did it on the other side. She massaged his balls with her free hand, dipping her tongue to them briefly. Rubble let out more shaky breaths the longer she teased him. She gripped his thick cock and lifted her eyes to his. They were glassy with lust, desperate for her to complete the transaction. The power she held over him right then was euphoric on its own. A man at her mercy was a whole new experience.

Holding his gaze, she slipped the tip of his cock into her mouth, sucking hard. His hips jerked forward, longing for her to accept more of him. She twirled her tongue over his tip, keeping her eyes focused on his. The strain in his face was more than she could bear.

She needed to taste all of him. The desire pooling in her sex demanded it.

Putting him out of his misery, Jupiter opened her mouth and swallowed his cock until it hit the back of her throat. He wound his fingers in her hair and she bobbed down on his length, sucking until her cheeks caved.

"Fuck, Jupiter, if you keep that up, you're gonna make me come."

His cock hit the back of her throat again and he gripped her hair tighter, pushing her toward him. Gagging slightly, she rolled his balls between her fingers, adoring the manly groans it earned her.

Before she could suck him dry, Rubble stepped away, stealing his cock from her mouth. He grabbed beneath her arms and hauled her off her knees. Pushing back her hair, his unique eyes searched hers. Fireworks from outside shone through the large window, casting him in perfect light. He was the most beautiful man she'd ever seen.

"You're a damn good surprise, baby girl. Never imagined you'd enjoy making a man beg for more."

She lifted her neck up and bit his bottom lip. "I never did until you."

Leaning down, he caught her mouth and wrapped his arms around her, settling them on her ass. "I'm going to fuck you now. Are you ready?"

Jupiter nodded, craving more of what this man had to offer. Her body needed to experience all of him.

"I can't promise I'll be gentle." He grabbed a fistful of her hair, carefully wrenching her head back so he could kiss the length of her neck.

Shivers raced across her body. She adored his possessive yet loyal touch. "I don't want gentle, Rubble. I just want you."

He dropped his hold and lifted her to the counter. The cool glass against her naked form made her shiver. Just as she remembered where they were, Rubble sheathed his cock with a condom and entered her. Jupiter's mouth dropped open and her toes curled.

"Oh, God." Goose bumps scattered across her skin, her nipples pebbling as she adjusted to his girth.

Rubble stilled, brows knit in hesitation. "If it's too much—"

"It's not, I swear." She gripped his muscular fore-arms and kissed him roughly. "Please don't stop."

He pulled out and slammed back into her. A soft moan escaped her mouth, warmth spreading like wild-fire. Rubble kept his pace, thrusting in and out of her pussy. When he tugged her body further up the counter, cock hitting her deeper, she dug her nails into his back, gasping at the new sensations.

"Like that, huh?"

She managed a nod, words lost to her.

Rubble grinned deviously and propped her legs on his shoulders, plunging even deeper. That was when Jupiter lost control, climaxing once more. She coated his cock, hips convulsing with the strength of her ecstasy.

Before she could come down from the bliss, he pulled her off the counter and twirled her around, pressing her body against the cold glass. He entered her once more and she sighed at the now familiar sense of fullness. His hips moved wildly, his breathing staggered. Jupiter gripped the counter, desperately trying to steady her body for his powerful thrusts.

Rubble pulled her upright, his large hands holding onto her breasts. His balls slapped her ass, their rhythm one she'd never forget. When he moved one hand down to her clit, she gasped. He rubbed his index and middle fingers between her folds, the friction building toward another orgasm. She tried to move, but he'd completely immobilized her. His fingers sped up and her breathing hitched as she drew closer to the cusp.

In the reflection of the display case, she caught sight of his strained face and pumping muscles. It was just too much. She cried out his name, her pussy quivering around his cock. Rubble let out a loud cry and joined her. His lips moved deftly across her back as they drifted down from their high.

Tenderly spinning her around, he rested his forehead against hers. Their breaths mingling together almost as intimately as their bodies had moments before. Jupiter kept her eyes wide. She wanted to see it all. If they only had a limited time together, she needed these memories to keep her going for years to come.

"Rubble."

"Yeah?"

"Can we do that again?"

A cocky smile crossed his face. "Oh, yeah, baby girl, we're doing that again." He playfully swatted her ass. "Right this very minute."

Jupiter barely had a moment to register what he meant when he entered her again, slower this time. She clung to his shoulders. *Forget leaving. I'll stay here with Rubble.*

CHAPTER 20
RUBBLE

Jupiter was a little nympho. Rubble paused the cup of coffee before it met his lips. *My nympho.* How he wanted that to be true. He wanted Jupiter as his and only his. The sounds she made…. Rubble shifted in his seat. His dick was eager for more of her. He wanted to be the only man to hear those beautiful cries.

He sipped his coffee then grabbed another cup for the naked woman in his bed. They'd gone three rounds at the bakery, using the space in a way that'd never leave his mind. They then headed back to the club-house for an entire night of lust-fueled sex that left them both pleasantly exhausted.

"Where've you been?" Hawk asked, walking inside from his smoke break. He eyed the second cup of coffee. "Somebody have a little crème brûlée at the bakery?"

"Ooh, Jupiter, huh?" Cueball stepped in behind him, a similar teasing smile on his face. "Was she bonerrific?"

He tried to flip them the bird but couldn't with his hands full. "Fuck the both of you."

Hawk chuckled. "Nah, I'm good, brother. I'll catch a nymph soon enough. But you should hurry up to your old lady before she misses you too much."

Rubble narrowed his gaze and Hawk wiggled his brows. This was new. Being on the receiving end of shit about women wasn't the norm for him.

"Don't forget church is in two hours," Cueball yelled after him.

Ignoring them, Rubble took the stairs two at a time, careful not to spill the coffee or upset the blueberry muffins stuffed in his jacket. Hawk and Cueball hollered more sexual innuendos after him, but he let them have their fun. He'd get them back later anyhow. The two were notorious with the club girls.

He reached his room and frowned at the shut door. Setting down one of the cups, he opened the door and grabbed the coffee before closing it with his foot.

"Wakey, wakey, sleeping beauty." He placed the cups on the nightside table and smoothed back Jupiter's unruly hair. Mascara stained the skin around her eyes, but he didn't give a damn. She was gorgeous no matter what. *Plus, that's kind of my fault.* His mind turned to their shower romp sometime around three in the morning. It was well worth the effort to hear her breathy moans in the acoustic setting.

"What's in there?"

He glanced down and saw her eyes glued to his jacket. "Blueberry muffins."

She giggled and sat up, taking the first one he offered. "That's stupidly cute, by the way. You sneaking muffins in your very tough biker jacket." She took a small bite, a speck of sugar clinging to her bottom lip.

"You think so?"

She took another bite and nodded. More sugar clung to her lips this time. If he didn't know better, he'd guess she did it on purpose. The sheet fell from her chest, revealing her perfect tits. *Fuck, woman, you're killing me.*

He couldn't resist. Leaning over, he licked her lip clean and nibbled at the seam of her mouth. She opened insatiably to him, her tongue mingling with his. Even without the sugar-dotted muffin, she tasted like heaven's treat.

Easing back, he pulled on her bottom lip with his thumb. The lustful gleam in her green eyes told him not to stop. His cock jumped inside his jeans. That bastard always wanted some pussy and Jupiter's was his new addiction. But Rubble didn't want to overexert her. They were running on limited fluids and even less sleep.

"Aren't you hungry?"

Jupiter grabbed the back of his neck and pulled him on top of her. "Famished."

He couldn't argue with that. Quickly shedding his clothes, he pulled on a condom and was in her warmth seconds later. She was always so fucking drenched, which made her pussy impossible to resist.

"Hold tight, baby girl. I'm gonna fuck you good and hard."

Jupiter parted her lips to speak, but he captured them instead. They didn't need words. *We need this.* He pushed into her deeper and her eyes rolled back. *Lots and lots of this.*

***

"WILL YOU TELL ME ABOUT THE SCARS?"

Rubble propped up his head on his fist. They'd finished another round, the scent of sex lingering in the small room. He'd never leave if he had his way. Taking in the freshly tousled strands of her short hair, his eyes fixed on her own set.

"Whenever you ask." He cautiously traced one of her scars. "Will you tell me about yours?"

Jupiter swallowed, her gaze dropping to the bed.

He wouldn't push but couldn't let the subject drop entirely.

"Yes, but not today." She covered his hand and squeezed. "I'd rather focus on happy things."

"Well, talking about my scars won't set a happy mood." He chuckled, fighting the horny side of him when Jupiter kissed the back of his tattooed hand.

"All right, then how about your tattoos? Surely, they have friendlier stories?"

He glanced at the artwork proudly displayed on his skin. "Some do. Some don't." Cuddling closer, he took her hand and placed it on his chest. "Point to the one you want to know about, otherwise we'll be here all day."

She grinned and quickly scanned his torso. "This one."

Eyeing one of his first tattoos, he nodded. "I got that when I was living in my last foster home. The people were decent, but I didn't like rules. Still don't, honestly." He reviewed the faded tattoo in black handwriting. "I was deep in MMA fighting. I had a coach and trainer and plenty of fights lined up."

"Of course I'd be attracted to a man who pommels people for a living."

"Used to, baby girl." He kissed her forehead. "Now, it's just a good workout."

"Born in ash. Die in rubble." Her finger traced the

saying he thought so wise as a seventeen-year-old. "Your MC name was your fighter name."

"Yep. When Reaper found me, I was in some trouble and he offered to help."

"What kind of trouble?"

He stared at the wall, memories flooding him. "Illegal fights meant illegal money, and as it happened, my coach and trainer weren't the best dudes to hang out with. My name was linked to some shady shit, and they were going to let me take the fall. Thankfully, the Feds took mercy on me as did Reaper. Can't say I regret anything." Tucking back her hair, he kissed the top of her head. "Any different choice would've meant a different outcome. And I like where I'm at. Right here, right now."

Jupiter kissed the tattoo. "So do I."

"All right, none of that," he said when she started kissing lower. "You gotta tell me something. It's only fair."

She pouted, the look too adorable on her face.

"Yo, sex addict, church is starting," Kevlar said, pounding on the door.

"Fuck off, Kev."

"Payback's a bitch, brother. At least I'm not out here cranking one out to the two of you. Hawk on the other hand…."

Rubble frowned but couldn't be mad. He climbed

off the bed and yanked the door open. Only Kevlar stood in the hallway, the aforementioned brethren nowhere to be seen.

Kevlar's easy smile dropped. "Oh, good, you're up." He glanced down and whistled low. "Whoa, very up. Might wanna fix that before you come to church. Boulder may get jealous 'cuz his dick is the size of a tic—"

Slamming the door, Rubble held back a chuckle. His best friend of many years couldn't even be shaken after seeing him buck naked. It was why they got along so well. They were both deviants.

"You're going, then?"

He quickly dressed and pressed a kiss to her lips. "Yeah, I'd better, since I'm the one in charge of this thing. Get some rest before your shift at the booth starts." He walked to the door. "I'll be by later to check in. And to sneak you away to fuck the cold right out of you," he confirmed when a knowing smile crossed her lips.

Desire flushed her face, and he resisted the temptation that lay between those long-ass legs he loved having wrapped around his waist. He had club business. His dick could wait.

CHAPTER 21
JUPITER

Lyle: My men are closing in, pet. Enjoy your freedom while you can.

Gliding the brush through her short hair, Jupiter stared at her reflection in the large mirror. The bruises from Lyle's goons were gone. Only the memory of them remained. Adjusting the towel around her chest, her eyes roamed over the small scars. Most were burns from Lyle putting his cigars out on her flesh. She closed her eyes, the smell of burning skin drifting into her memory.

The text from Lyle early that morning came to her mind. She'd snuck a glance at the phone while Rubble was asleep. It couldn't be helped. She had to know how close he was getting and when she should leave.

Macha had too many good people in it to get tangled up in her web of horrors. *Even if Rubble keeps insisting.*

She set the brush aside and swept the locks into a messy bun on top of her head. It wasn't as cute as when her hair was longer, but it'd work for a full day of manning the booth during the games.

"Hey, Jupiter, how was your night?"

Looking over her shoulder, Jupiter caught sight of Nikita walking into the community bathroom. "Hey. It was… fun."

Nikita smirked, turning on the shower. "Just fun?"

"Um, yeah, what else would it be?"

Crossing her arms over her chest, the other woman cocked her head to the right and lifted her brows expectantly. "Oh, I don't know. Maybe thrilling, surprising, and orgasmic?"

Heat rushed to Jupiter's face and she stammered for a complete sentence. "I, uh, um, we were—"

Nikita chuckled and shook her head. "I'm giving you shit."

Jupiter relaxed and managed a smile.

"If anybody deserves a happy ending, it's Rubble."

"Why's that?"

Stripping off her tank top and pajama pants, Nikita walked to the shower and checked the water temperature before stepping inside and closing the curtain. "He and Kevlar go way back. They were in the military together. Even had a few close call OPs."

"Really? Rubble never mentioned."

"He wouldn't. Most guys don't like to relive the bad times overseas."

Jupiter toweled off her body and grabbed the bottle of lotion. "Can't blame them. Trauma tends to stick with you no matter how hard you try to escape."

"Sounds like personal experience." Nikita popped her head out of the shower, eyes curious. "Wanna explain?"

"Not really, no."

"All right. My door's always open." She closed the curtain again. "Plus, I know a little already thanks to Rubble. I won't snitch. I'm an FBI agent after all."

That made Jupiter smirk. The woman was the typical sassy biker chick, but Nikita's job title was unexpected. Normally, the Feds stayed away from MCs. *But this club is different.*

"Are you going to watch any of the events?"

Jupiter finished moisturizing her legs and moved to her arms. "I'm not sure. Yasmina mentioned wanting to see the snowboarders, so I'll man the booth while she does that."

"Snowboarders are cool, but the skiers are my favorite." Steam rose from the shower stall, filling the rest of the bathroom. "I'll try and convince Kevlar to take over so you can check it out."

Sensing a kinship already, Jupiter agreed and after promising to catch up later, hurried to her room to dress. She pressed her lips together as the night before flashed in her mind. Rubble was unlike any other man she'd slept with, not that the list was horribly long. Somehow, Rubble made her feel alive, protected, and adored all at once. She shimmied her jeans over her hips and buttoned them. It was a sensation she'd gladly repeat as often as possible.

A new message popped up on the burner cell. Grabbing it, she reviewed the text from her lawyer in Dallas.

Neffenger: Everything's going as planned. Will contact you soon with more news.

Jupiter gripped the phone a little tighter. Their plan was a bit ballsy, but she didn't have any other choice. Lyle set up corporations under her name to avoid tax repercussions on the family business. Her lawyer was working on skirting the potential criminal issues Lyle liked to hold over her head. It gave her little peace, but it was better than the alternative.

Letting out a shaky breath, she replied and stuffed the phone in her back pocket. The safest option would be to tell Rubble about her plan, but she didn't want to risk his involvement. *As if he isn't already involved.* She pulled on her fur-lined boots and donned a stocking cap. Her reflection in the small mirror made her chuckle. Everything she wore had Macha stamped on it. *Including my heart.*

"You can't be serious."

Rubble's left eyebrow quirked up, a wickedly cute grin on his bearded face. "But I am. You said you didn't know how to ski." He nodded to the large mountain behind them. "We're in the perfect place for you to learn."

"This is a horrible idea," she muttered, but allowed him to help her click ski boots into the long skis, nevertheless.

"We won't start on the double black diamonds, don't worry." He kissed her forehead before adjusting her pink hat. "Green's the way to go… for today."

Jupiter's eyes widened and her mouth dropped open. "You're gonna kill me."

He shook his head, only a select few tattoos peeking out on his neck. The rest of him was covered in winter gear just like hers, only it was black instead of pink. The bright color was Queenie's idea. The club's old lady was worried about not being able to see Jupiter if an avalanche occurred. *Yeah, that makes me want to ski.*

Rubble guided her to the chairlift nearing them. "All right, once the chair's close enough, hop on."

"You say that like it's super simple."

"It is." He nodded to the operator in the nearby station at the bottom of the mountain. "Denny over there won't let you face-plant."

Carefully stepping toward the chairlift, Jupiter rolled her eyes. "No, but you might," she mumbled under her breath. It wasn't true. Rubble would never let anything bad happen to her if he could help it.

"Okay, you ready?" Rubble scanned her face, worry reaching the corners of his eyes.

Before she could respond, the chair neared, and she squealed, carefully leaning backwards and into the seat. Rubble's hands hovered around her waist but never touched. The lift slowly rose, taking them higher.

"Holy shit, I did it!" She turned awestruck eyes to Rubble.

"No doubt in my mind." Adjusting the ski poles, he grinned. "Now, enjoy the view. It'll be a lot different on the way down."

Turning her gaze to the mountainside, Jupiter inhaled the crisp air and watched skiers below. Some zipped down the paths while others teetered before falling. The sun shone brightly overhead, no clouds in sight. She breathed a grateful sigh. *Learning how to ski during a storm would be five times worse.*

"I always liked riding these even if I wasn't skiing." Rubble swung his legs precariously, nothing below but blankets of snow to catch a fall. "During the games, I usually bounce between mountains, checking in with local authorities, and breaking up fights if needed."

"Why does Macha care so much?"

He turned questioning eyes toward her. "What do you mean?"

"Motorcycle clubs aren't known for being decent. They're terrifying, ruthless, uncaring assholes who do drugs, have tons of sex, and create havoc with anyone who spits in their direction." She noticed a teenager wipe out below on a snowboard, a wide smile on his face despite the fall. "But Macha isn't like that."

Rubble chuckled, the deep sound resonating in her own bones. He placed his left arm on the top of the seat behind her. His mismatched blue and green eyes were full of mischief, a common expression when they were together.

"Macha is all of the above, Jupiter. We're ruthless assholes when we need to be. Uncaring when someone threatens those we love. We'll fight anyone who disrupts our way of life. Yeah, drugs happen, but we regulate that shit for our club and the town." He tipped up her chin and searched her eyes. "And hell yeah, we have lots and lots of incredible sex, but Macha *is* different, baby girl. Surely, you've seen it. We're not a mainstream MC. We're better."

She swallowed hard, the intensity of his gaze making her belly turn somersaults. "How do I know if I should trust you?"

He pushed back her short braids. "Trust your gut. It hasn't been wrong yet."

Rubble read in between the lines of her question. It wasn't the first time the quiet mountain of a man had done that. He was an enigma in the MC world.

"We're getting close to the top. You ready to dismount?"

His words snapped her attention back to the present activity. Taking a breath, she faced forward and saw the small hut at the top of the slope. "Maybe I'll just ride this all the way back."

"Oh, no you don't." He linked his arm through hers. "Don't pull me down. I fall like a tree. It isn't pretty, believe me."

Laughing at the imagery, Jupiter gripped his arm tight, and they easily hopped off the chair and slid away while the lift continued happily around the circle.

"Over here, beautiful." Rubble waved his ski pole toward a path marked Green.

I can do this, she repeated to herself. The trail wasn't overly busy, just a few tourists here and there.

"What about that? Shouldn't I try the bunny slope first?" She pointed to the sectioned off area where children and first-time skiers practiced.

"Nah. You got this, come on."

Grumbling, she followed him to the trail and stuck the ski poles in the snow. "All right, teach me, sir."

His eyes darkened at her last word. She'd meant it as a joke, but the way he reacted made her mouth dry. He'd mentioned tying her to his bed during the billiards game. It wasn't a joke. Not in the least.

"I like the way you say that." Rubble delicately kissed her. "But for now, we'll focus on skiing and not sex."

A surge of desire shot through Jupiter's pussy at the underlying promise. Suddenly, she didn't want to ski. She'd rather explore his insinuation.

"How about some highlights?" He slipped on his sunglasses, the sun poking out from behind the clouds. "If you need to fall, do it on your side, not face-first or on your ass."

"I have a feeling I'll be doing that one a lot."

"Always watch out for other skiers, especially since some assholes like to zip down the easier trails to fuck with newbies," he said as an experienced skier did exactly that. "Keep your knees bent slightly and hands in front of you. Always keep your skis together unless you're stopping, then do a pizza move."

"A what?"

He started sliding down the slope, then turned his feet in toward each other, forming a pizza slice shape. "Pizza."

"And now I'm hungry."

He smirked and walked back uphill to her. "You try."

Jupiter positioned herself according to his instruction and slowly pulled her ski poles out of the snow and pushed forward. She moved slowly down the slope and turned her feet in like he instructed.

"Perfect. Now, if you ever need to stop another way, shift left or right. I don't think we'll have any trouble today." Rubble said from beside her. She hadn't even noticed him join her. "This trail isn't very steep, and you don't need to turn unless you want to get fancy. Think you're up for a little faster?"

"Better now than when it's busier." She slipped her ski goggles over her eyes, the buttered croissant from breakfast jumbling in her gut.

"That's the spirit." He pushed off and Jupiter watched for a good ten seconds before she did the same.

Gripping the poles tight, she tried to remember what Rubble taught her. The soft whir of snow beneath the skis combined with the gust of air hitting her puffy coat made her grin beneath the polka dot scarf. She quickly caught up to Rubble, keeping her body balanced in the middle of the skis.

"You're doing great!" he encouraged, keeping a safe distance from her.

Jupiter couldn't see the smile but heard it in his voice. For the next ten minutes, they skied down the mountainside, picking up speed little by little. The closer they came to the bottom, the more skiers they saw.

"Careful. People aren't the best at getting out of the way in time."

Rubble easily maneuvered around a slow skier. Looking to the end of the trail, Jupiter's pulse skyrocketed. A mother and daughter were up ahead in her line of travel. *Shit!* She cast frantic eyes to Rubble, but he was having his own trouble with a group of teens on snowboards. Suddenly everything he said was a jumbled mess.

The ski lodge loomed ahead, and she sent a quick prayer to the snow gods for a safe landing. She was going to crash. How hard was the only question.

The mother and daughter hadn't moved yet, and she was almost on them. Seeing a snowdrift to the left, she shifted her weight and moved her feet ever so slightly. Suddenly, the skis roughly jerked, and she barreled toward the embankment. The hard snow knocked out her breath, body tumbling to a stop at the pile of snow. Manly shouts and feminine screams cut through the ringing in her ears. The only one she heard was Rubble's.

CHAPTER 22

RUBBLE

Fuck! Rubble unlocked his boots and jumped onto the snow. Heart pounding in his ears, he hurried past the growing crowd to the snow heap Jupiter not so gracefully plowed into moments earlier.

"Move!" He shoved back a man, not giving a damn how sharp his tone was or if he'd done any damage. His girl was in trouble and he hadn't prevented it. Sourness engulfed his mouth and his blood chilled.

Finding Jupiter's bright pink outfit, he quickly assessed the situation. No limb was catawampus and the snow around her remained white. Her head, on the other hand, was out of sight.

"Get Doc from the lodge. Now!" he snapped at a prospect loafing around a group of snow bunnies. The prospect nodded and sprinted toward the large resort and Rubble kneeled in the snow. "Jupiter, can you hear me?"

A muffled sound from the snow responded, and he let out a relieved breath. She wasn't unconscious. Scooping the snow away from her face, he swallowed at the sight. Jupiter almost looked comfortable with the top half of her body wedged deep. The little mascara she wore earlier streaked around her eyes and down her cheeks. *Tears.* He gritted his teeth.

"Baby girl, what hurts?"

Jupiter burst out laughing, makeup smearing more. "Oh my God, am I stuck in a snowdrift?"

"Uh, kinda yeah."

She laughed more and winced when she attempted to dislodge herself from the packed snow.

"Don't try to move. Doc's on his way. He'll know how to get you out safely." Rubble couldn't see any damage, but then again, internal wounds were a different story.

"We should do that again." Jupiter rubbed her bright red lips together. Her entire face was flushed from the cold. "I really liked skiing until the end."

Heart still not recovered from seeing her wipeout, Rubble pushed up his black hat and shook his head. "Dammit, woman, how can you talk about skiing again after diving headfirst into a snowbank? Do you have any idea what could be wrong with you? You could have a broken neck for Christ's sake!"

Her bright grin drooped, and genuine tears welled her eyes.

"Shit, baby, I'm sorry. This isn't your fault. It's mine." He leaned closer and wiped away the hot tears rolling down her cheeks. "I shouldn't have rushed you. This is my fault."

"I was trying to avoid the lady and her daughter. You couldn't very well move them for me." That cute smile made its way back to her face and he cursed himself for the half-wit idea of skiing in the first place.

"Brother, what happened?"

Hearing Doc's voice made him focus on the situation. "Hang tight." As badly as he wanted to kiss her, he refrained.

Standing, he met Doc's concerned eyes. "She hit the drift pretty hard after tumbling. Didn't wanna move her in case her neck was injured."

Doc nodded and stooped to Jupiter's level. "How're you feeling?"

"Kind of cold, but otherwise okay."

"Can you feel your legs?"

"Yeah."

"Okay, good." Doc waved at the paramedics he'd brought with him. "We'll get you out and have you back on the slopes in no time."

Rubble bit his tongue. His idea of a lively afternoon nearly killed her. There was no way in hell he'd let her on skis again. The two paramedics brought over a snow stretcher and the trio got to work digging Jupiter out. Rubble tried to help twice, but his hands shook so severely, he had to step away. He'd seen his fair share of gore and disfigured bodies thanks to years in the military and in MMA, but this was different. This was someone he cared about more.

Five minutes later, Jupiter was safely onboard the rescue sled and headed toward the lodge. The crowd cheered then dispersed as quickly as it formed. Rubble could barely move. His legs were heavy, chest laboring with each step he took in the snow.

"She'll be all right."

Rubble glanced at Doc, who was walking in step with him. "I did this."

"No, some tourists did." He shrugged. "You can't keep Jupiter in a bubble. Shit will happen to her whether you're around or not."

Rubble clenched his hands to fists. "That's what I'm afraid of."

Doc playfully backhanded Rubble's arm. "Come on. I convinced the paramedics to take her to the lodge instead of the hospital. Her neck is fine and I'm pretty sure the rest of her too, but they'll check her just in case."

They reached the lodge, the paramedics carefully shuttling the stretcher through the doors. Rubble couldn't cross the threshold. Even if she was perfectly healthy, his reaction to her accident wasn't.

"Is this what it feels like?"

Doc paused at the doors. "What?"

"Loving someone."

The former paramedic smiled faintly. "Yeah."

"Damn." Rubble leaned his back against the lodge. "She laughed."

"What?"

"Jupiter was laughing when I found her." He crossed his arms over his broad chest. "Fucking laughing. Not worried if she was hurt but wondering how crazy she looked in the damn snowdrift."

Doc chuckled. "Well, she did look pretty nuts. Like one of those cartoons where they stick straight out. Gotta admit, it was funny. Should've gotten a picture for Isa."

Rubble glared at him and Doc held up his hands. "All right, all right. I'll go check on your lady. Try not to hunt down the poor tourist who caused the accident, all right?"

"Can't make any promises."

Doc snorted then walked into the lodge, a gust of warmth reaching Rubble for a split second. His muscles burned from the recent events, but he wouldn't leave the lodge until he was certain Jupiter was unharmed.

Finding a bench, he swept off the snow and sat. He felt a vibration from his pocket and fished out Jupiter's phone. Multiple missed calls and texts greeted him. They were all from her soon-to-be ex. He read a few messages, jaw tightening the longer he skimmed them. The last one solidified the ache in his gut.

Lyle: I found you, my precious pet. Hiding in Colorado. Such a stupid idea. Be there soon.

His fingers itched to send a reply that'd send the man straight to a safe house, but he wouldn't. Crushing the man under his boot also sounded like a good idea, but he couldn't afford it if he lost. In such a short time, Jupiter became his everything, and he'd die before letting that asshole of a man touch her again.

Damn, I need to bring this to Prez. She wasn't an old lady, but neither was Nikita when they helped her. Jupiter needed the club's support, and he was damned sure she'd get it.

He stuffed the phone back in his coat and pulled out his own Android. Dialing, he didn't have to wait long for the call to connect. "We have a situation."

"With…?"

"Jupiter."

Rubble held his breath, waiting for Reaper's response. If Queenie were nearby, there'd be no questioning the answer. Jupiter meant more to him than any person he'd known. If he had to fight her ex on his own, he'd do it.

"Church at eight tonight. I'll send the text."

"Thanks, Prez."

"Don't thank me yet, Rubble."

He hung up and seven seconds later, the MC members group chat had a new message. It eased his anxiety but only minutely. *Well now I know how Kevlar felt when he asked the club for help.* Macha hadn't flinched at the scenario. *But this is different.* Jupiter wasn't a club princess or an FBI agent taking down a rival MC. Jupiter was a battered woman on the run. Surely, his club wouldn't let him down. *I never have.*

CHAPTER 23

JUPITER

"Any pain here?"

Jupiter winced. "A little, yeah."

Doc carefully rested her left arm in a sling. "The good news is nothing's broken."

"And the bad news?"

"You're gonna have a shit ton of visitors." He stood and grinned. "But the main one you'll like, I think."

Glancing at the door, Jupiter wished Rubble would stroll through it. Since arriving at the lodge, he hadn't stepped foot in the room, and she didn't understand why.

"He'll be along eventually."

She looked up at the club's doctor. With his slightly longer hair than the rest of his brothers and a swoon worthy smile, Isa was lucky to snag such a guy.

"Thanks for everything you did." She sat up and

tried to adjust the pillow behind her back but having her arm in a sling made it quite the endeavor until Doc helped.

He walked to the door and paused. "Rubble knows a good soul when he meets one."

"You think so?

"I know so." Doc grinned. "Try to take it easy for a few days."

Jupiter offered him a weak smile. "Thanks, I will."

Doc closed the door quietly behind him, leaving her alone in the room that had been decorated as if torn from a wilderness cabin. Macha's entire lodge seemed to have a recurring theme. The giant fireplace visible upon opening the front doors and the woodsy rooms only reinforced her impression.

Glancing at the bear-shaped clock, she sighed. She was late to help Yasmina with the bakery. Their little skiing adventure wasn't supposed to end this way. Wriggling into the blanket, she pulled it over her head. "Maybe I'm bad luck. Shit keeps happening when I'm around."

"Or maybe you're good luck."

Rubble's voice sent shivers down her body. She slowly pushed off the soft coverings and met his eyes. He stood in the doorway, overtaking it with his tall frame and wide shoulders. The black beanie cap sat in its usual place, but the Macha stamp on the front was crooked. The blue plaid shirt beneath his open winter coat brought out the color in his right eye. His long, wiry beard was disheveled, whether from the elements or him running his fingers through, she wasn't certain. All in all, Rubble commanded the room from the moment his shadow graced it.

Jupiter sat up and his gaze went to the sling on her arm, his expression making it clear that his tough guy façade was just that. The regret in his perfectly mismatched eyes spoke the volumes she'd always want to read. She'd heard the worry in his voice, but actually seeing him looking so rugged yet docile spun her world off its axis.

"Doc said—"

"He told me." Rubble took a giant step toward the bed, the room shrinking more the longer he stayed there.

"Just a sprained arm and some bruises. I'll be back to normal in a day or so." She scooted to the edge of the bed and frowned when she saw her boots and coat on the other side of the room. "See, nothing to worry about. I'm right as rain."

Rubble closed the distance and knelt on the floor next to the bed. He grabbed her hand and kissed the top. "I'm sorry. I should've been more careful."

"I'm fine, seriously." She tried to escape, but he held her in place. "Rubble, honestly, I'm—"

He cut off her reply by putting his lips over hers. The coolness of his mouth sent a new form of goose bumps along her skin. Grabbing the back of his head, she pulled him closer, opening her mouth to taste him. His tongue interlaced with hers as bursts of craving filled her stomach.

Rubble eased back, eyes warring with hers. "When you fell, so did I." He brushed the hair out of her face. "I fell so fucking hard, baby girl."

Jupiter looked him over for damage. "You fell too? Are you hurt?"

He laughed, shaking his head. "Fuck, this is why I love you. Never worrying about yourself, only others."

The air in her lungs escaped in a loud whoosh. "You… you love me?"

"Yeah, I do." He kissed the tip of her nose.

Jupiter's heart throbbed in her ears, the realization of his words hitting her hard. She pulled away, hands shaking and beads of sweat lining her brow. "I can't, Rubble. I'm not somebody you can love."

He frowned and rocked back on his heels. "What do you mean?"

She stood and paced the shining hardwood floors. "I'm married for starters."

"You're midway through a divorce."

She tossed him an unbelieving glance. "Secondly, I'm a hot mess and probably leaving Snowshoe soon.

No doubt my ex found out where I am, and I have to keep moving."

"Aren't you sick of running, Jupiter?" He sat on the bed and reached for her. "Macha can give you a life here. I can give you a life. Please let me."

Jupiter worried her bottom lip between her teeth. His face was so earnest. He believed every damned word he said. "I can't have children," she blurted before she could stop herself. "At least I don't think I can. Lyle blames me because I couldn't give him the one thing he thinks a woman is good for." Tears pricked her eyelids. She held them at bay despite the tremble in her voice. "I probably can't give any to you either."

She stopped pacing to watch the news sink in. Every man wanted kids. An heir to carry on the family line. Rubble would be no exception. "Well, say something. Now's not the time to be a mute brute."

Finally, he stood and walked over to her. Tilting up her chin with his fingers, he softly kissed her lips and she braced herself for the impending dismissal.

"Baby girl, you couldn't be more perfect for me if you tried."

"What?"

His fingers unraveled her braids. "I'm pretty sure I can't have kids either. I had an accident during my time overseas in the Marines. The doctor said I was lucky to be alive, but I'd probably never have kids myself. I don't need any to be happy, Jupiter." He kissed her forehead. "I just need you. I don't want to ever wake up without you in my life."

His quiet words crumbled the dam she'd made. Tears rushed down her cheeks. She buried her face in his chest, the scent of leather overwhelming her. Never in her life did she think a man would not only accept this but love her because of it.

"Our flaws make us perfect, baby girl." Rubble cradled her face in his callused hands. "I'm damned sure you were made just for me, Jupiter Quinn."

His soft words made her emotions surge over the edge. This man was her everything. Not able to wait another second, she fused her mouth to his, moaning when he cupped her ass and picked her up off the floor. Her back hit the wall roughly, but she didn't feel anything except the hard lines of his body against hers.

"Wait, wait." She pried her lips away, panting at the loss.

"What's wrong? Am I hurting you?"

"No, nothing like that, I just...." She searched his unique pair of eyes. "I don't know your name. Your real one, I mean."

Rubble smirked. "Is it that important?"

"I want to know who I'm kissing." She traced his jaw. "The man I can't live without."

"When you put it like that, how can I resist?" He set her feet on the hardwood. "Kassian Hardy."

The name fit like a glove. Common yet unusual, not unlike his characteristics. "I like it."

"Well, don't let my brothers know. They'll never let me hear the end of it."

"Doesn't Kevlar know?"

He fixed the hem of her shirt. "Yeah, he and Reaper are the only ones. And now you, I guess."

"Thank you." She wrapped her free arm around his waist and hugged him tight. A sense of comfort washed over her.

"Anything for you, baby girl."

And she believed him. He wouldn't lie to her.

CHAPTER 24

RUBBLE

Church started like every other time. Boulder recapped the last meeting then moved on to the club's financial matters. None of it felt the same. This time, Rubble's ass was in the hot seat. His happiness was on the line.

He shifted his weight in the comfortable leather chair, left leg bouncing beneath the solid wood table. Doc sat across from him, a knowing grin on his face. Doc had walked in on them in bed an hour ago, hoping to check on Jupiter before church. Since her accident, Rubble hadn't allowed himself to be intimate with her, so his brother hadn't seen much. She argued for the opposite treatment, but she was recovering and needed some time. He wouldn't put her at risk.

Jupiter was halfway out the door when he left for church. She and Yasmina had to make a run to the grocery store, their supplies dwindling thanks to the busy time for the town. He wouldn't see her until that night unless he snuck away from his rounds early.

The conversation moved on to the Xtreme Winter Games. Thus far, the club had raked in quite the amount of dough thanks to their numerous businesses. The lodge was profitable, of course, and the tourists seemed to enjoy all the club's covert dealings.

"Sergeant, you got something to bring before the club?" Reaper's voice snapped Rubble from his thoughts. He glanced around the room. Not a single seat was empty.

"Many of you have met Jupiter Quinn." They answered with a round of nods, so he continued. "I recently found out the reason she came to Snowshoe." His leg wouldn't stop jiggling so he stood and placed his fists on the tabletop. "About a year ago, she left an abusive relationship. Been on the run ever since. She reached out to Queenie for help and I'm damned glad she did." He watched the club's reactions. A few members remained passive, but the majority were pissed. And for good reason. They wouldn't be in Macha if they treated women like shit.

"Her ex found out where she is and instead of running, I—she wants to stay." Rubble paused and waited for someone to speak up.

Kevlar didn't disappoint. "When's he gonna get here?"

"Not sure. According to a recent text, he knows where she is, so he could be here within the week. He also could've sent that to spook her into taking off again. He's hired men to follow and capture her. I guess they finally caught up." He met Kevlar's eyes and saw the wheels turning in his mind.

"You think he'll kill her?"

Rubble grabbed the folder from under his seat and tossed it on the table. "Here's the shit I have on him. After talking with Jupiter and seeing photos of what he did to her in the past, yeah, it's very possible he'll kill her and not think twice."

Brewer stole the folder and opened it. Kevlar and Cueball moved in for a closer look as he flipped through the information. "How'd you find all this?"

When Rubble paused, Kevlar chuckled. "Kita, right?"

Rubble nodded. "She offered, and I had to protect the club." He looked to their president, who sat back with fingers meshed on the table. "Prez, the call is yours. I'd like to keep Jupiter under Macha protection until her ex is handled."

"Handled?" Reaper's brows rose. "How so?"

Rubble's cheek twitched. Despite all the ways he wanted to deal with the slimeball who dared raise an angry hand toward Jupiter, he wouldn't go off the deep end. "The Macha way."

Hawk snorted. "We all know that means skirting the lines of legality."

He whipped his gaze to Hawk. "You got an issue with the way Macha handles dickheads?"

Hawk flipped to a page in the folder. "No, but if you've got a personal stake in this, the club deserves to know."

This got Reaper's attention. He sat up in his chair and motioned for the folder before putting on his glasses and reviewing the documents the FBI gathered. Not one club member uttered a word while he read for a solid five minutes. Sweat lined Rubble's brow. He'd never been on this side of the table before. Never asked the club for help. He was the sergeant at arms for God's sake! He didn't ask for help. He gave it.

Finally, Reaper shut the folder. "He's a jackarse, that's for damn certain, but Hawk's right. Do you have selfish intentions with bringing justice to this man?"

Gripping the edge of the table, Rubble looked him square in the eye. "Hell yes."

"Then let's vote." Reaper grabbed his small gavel. "Macha, you've heard the plea before our table. What say you?"

"Aye." Kevlar said, standing. He nodded to Rubble.

"No man loves this club more than Rubble. If he's asking, it's serious."

The rest of the room joined in, and the *ayes* echoed in Rubble's ears. He looked to the president at the head of the table. Reaper offered him a small nod and slammed down the gavel.

"It appears Jupiter Quinn is officially under Macha protection. What's the plan?"

Relief coursed through Rubble but so did adrenaline. They had a job to do. He leaned over the table and laid out his simple yet foolproof strategy. He'd keep Jupiter safe. Macha would do the rest.

"You sure you're ready for this?"

Rubble took in the splendor of Hard Hitter jammed packed with tourists and Snowshoe residents. The familiar thrill of fight night filtered through him. It'd been way too long since he'd smelled the scent of sweat and blood blended together inside of a tight fighting ring.

He met Brewer's blue eyes. They were bright with excitement. "Yeah, I'm ready." He looked the other man over from head to toe. "What about you? You have the first fight."

Brewer bounced on his toes, blue shorts and sneakers his only apparel other than boxing gloves. "I'm gonna smear this guy."

Slapping his back, Rubble hoped his old friend was

right. He led Brewer to the ring and held up the ropes so he could enter. While Brewer hopped around with a local MMA enthusiast on the other side, Rubble stayed on the outskirts.

A voice over the loudspeaker announced the first competitors and the rules. He didn't need to listen. His mind was elsewhere anyhow. The knowledge that Jupiter would eventually show up made him sweat for a whole new reason. The last-minute club vote on hosting the fight tournament made her cute little nose wrinkle with uncertainty when she found out.

The bell rang and he stopped searching the noisy crowd for Jupiter. *She may not even come.* He shrugged aside that possibility and focused on the fight. Brewer was holding his own in the ring. A few of his jabs and kicks had the other man on the defensive.

Noticing the fighter favor his left leg after Brewer's last kick, Rubble gripped one of the rings and yelled, "Lean port!"

Brewer didn't acknowledge him but jabbed his fist in the man's face, laying him out flat. They'd developed shorthand queues over the years fighting together. Rubble slowly paced the small space between the ring and crowd. His muscles itched to jump in and pummel until the other man tapped out.

Using an elbow strike, Brewer managed to get the other man off-balance before going in for the knockout.

He kicked the man's left thigh, and the sickening sound made Rubble shiver. It'd been way too long. Brewer kept up his jabs even as the man struggled from the floor. Finally, Brewer tucked him into a choke and wrapped his legs around the man's waist until he submitted.

The onlookers cheered and jeered, but Brewer didn't seem to mind the hecklers. He stood and pounded his gloves on his chest, yelling his first-round victory. The referee called the first win and the fighters retreated to their corners for a small break.

"You're doing great," Rubble praised, offering Brewer a bottle of water.

Sitting on the folding chair in the corner, Brewer took out his mouthguard and squirted water in his mouth and on his face. "Thanks for the tip."

Rubble hopped up and assessed his brother's wounds. The bruises couldn't be treated, but he could help with the few cuts. Making quick work of the flowing blood, Rubble smeared petroleum jelly on the rest of Brewer's exposed skin. That simple trick had helped him more than once over the years.

"All right, you're good to go." The bell clanged for the next round and Rubble slid under the ropes to the safety outside.

For the next two rounds, Rubble offered encouragement and advice. He didn't have time to wonder about

Jupiter. Instead, he maintained his trainer role and hooted with pride when Brewer was announced the overall winner of the match.

He hooked an arm around Brewer's neck. "You were kickass."

"Thanks, brother." Brewer chuckled and wiped his face with a towel. Women and men alike slapped Brewer's ass as they made their way through the crowd.

Once they reached the locker room, Rubble left Brewer to shower and recoup. The next fight had already started and plenty of people milled about the gym. It was a superb turnout even compared to previous tournaments.

Getting the event put together wasn't as hard as he thought it would be. With the winter games going on, plenty of tourists and MMA supporters were ready to join in on the fun instead of merely watching. *Also helped that the mayor's a big fan of MMA.* He smirked, recalling the hour turnaround on the permit.

The club hastily rented folding chairs for the tournament since the bleachers had been requisitioned for the Games. Curls of smoke filled the air and Rubble's mouth watered. He needed to release his pent-up anxiety, and since his fight wasn't for another hour, he escaped out a side door and lit up a cigarette.

Inhaling the nicotine, he watched cars enter the

parking lot. For many people, the fight was something new to do. He didn't mind one bit. The improvised concession inside boasting snacks and both alcoholic and virgin drinks would boost the club's finances along with the cover charge.

"Aren't the fights inside?"

Jupiter's sweet voice made him glance to his left. Sure enough, the tall woman who haunted his mind stood there wearing leggings with Macha's logo on them, her shirt hidden by a long gray coat.

"Yeah, but the amateurs are on now." He flicked his cigarette butt into the snow and glanced behind her. "You here by yourself?"

He knew he was being overprotective, but he had a damned good reason. She was under Macha protection, which meant one of the members should always be with her.

She rolled her green eyes, and she stuffed her hands in her coat pockets. "No. I came with Dolly and Nikita. I saw you over here and thought I'd say hi."

Rubble shifted his boots in the snow. It'd be so easy to wrap her in his arms and kiss her senseless. *Not like we haven't done it before.* He cleared his throat and tried not to think about each time he'd felt her body against his. He needed to stay clearheaded before a fight. Thinking about Jupiter only distracted him.

"You here to watch the crazies or just experience the bloodbath?"

"Honestly, I'm only here for one reason." She caught his gaze, and his pulse quickened.

"Oh, yeah?" He moved closer. He couldn't help it. She was the light at the end of his tunnel. "What's that?"

Jupiter slid her hands up his chest and he held his breath. She laced her fingers around the back of his neck, pulling his face down to meet hers. "To see you."

He searched her eyes, only seeing longing there. Gripping her hips, he pushed down thoughts of taking her then and there against the side of the gym. "You have no clue how badly I want to fuck you right now."

Instead of answering, she nipped his bottom lip. "I'll tell you what." She kissed his cheek. "After your fight, I'll make sure the locker room is all ours." She tugged on his beard. "And you can do whatever you'd like."

Rubble's dick jumped at the suggestion. He didn't need any more incentive, but knowing that she'd be in the crowd gave him new perspective on the fight. "Baby girl, I love that you're offering, but you've never seen a fight, have you?"

She shook her head, but the lusty gleam hadn't diminished from her face. Kissing her forehead, he thanked Macha for sending her to the club's door. "It's not pretty, believe me. The last thing you'll wanna do is me."

Frowning, Jupiter stepped back. "Well, then I'll be there for whatever you need. How does that sound?"

He cupped the back of her head and kissed her hard. "Sounds perfect to me."

"Rubble, you gotta get in here. This kid's walloping Hawk." Cueball called from the door.

Jupiter giggled and linked her arm with Rubble's. "Well, I guess it's time to see what you've been bragging about."

Rubble kissed the top of her head. "Ready or not, here we come."

ADRENALINE FLOWED THROUGH RUBBLE'S MUSCLES. THE humidity in the gym rose with each additional spectator. They were down to the final battle. Whoever won this match would walk away the victor.

Rubble glanced over at the kid from Waverley. He was ten years Rubble's junior and about five inches shorter. On any normal day, he wouldn't bother to let the kid go three rounds before tapping him out. But tonight was different. He wasn't the same fighter. Not when young guys had professional trainers while he merely had his brothers. He'd taken some hits but dished them out too.

Jupiter's cheer rose above the crowd. He couldn't help focusing on it. He heard her voice everywhere. Having her ringside was a mixed blessing. He loved the idea of her watching, but if he lost, they'd both be disappointed. *Me more than her.*

He met Brewer's eyes, the final bell echoing in Rubble's ears. The other fighter had managed to get a few decent jabs at him in the first round. Blood and sweat ran down his face, stinging the cut above his left eye.

They circled the ring, both of them ready for action. Rubble did his damnedest to tune out Jupiter's enthusiastic tone, but it crept in nevertheless. He wanted to show her how he could protect her. How he'd always protect her.

Swinging his left arm then his right, Rubble gritted his teeth when the other man blocked the blows and countered with a jab to his gut. He caught his breath before the fighter tried to drop him. Grabbing the shorter man, Rubble tossed them both to the floor, their sweat mingling in a mass of muscles and masculinity.

The elbow to his right ear made a sharp ringing sound and he loosened his grip. The fighter took the advantage, flipping them and jamming his gloves into Rubble's shoulder. Wincing at the pain, Rubble kicked off the mat and jumped to his feet. He wasn't about to let this shithead best him.

The referee stayed out of the way but was always nearby just in case. The roar from the crowd further deafened Rubble. He couldn't pick out Jupiter's voice anymore. Meeting the other man's gaze, he looked for injury. They both had gashes on their faces and bruises forming along their torsos.

You can do this. He moved on the balls of his feet, mirroring the other man. Just one good punch and Rubble would come out the victor. The swell of shouts and screams echoed in his ears. The recent blow to his strongest shoulder made the decision easy. He'd go with a roundhouse kick then smash the guy. *If he lets me.*

The younger fighter tried to take him down with a flying knee, but Rubble sideswiped him and landed a punch to his stomach. It knocked him backwards and Rubble used that to his benefit. His glove hit the man's face in an uppercut and before he could recover, Rubble tripped him, smashing him down on the mat. Using his weight against him, Rubble locked his legs, holding the fighter's arms above his head.

With the referee coming close to watch the final position, the crowd went wild as the younger fighter struggled. Rubble increased pressure with his arms, tightening every muscle until finally, the other man tapped Rubble on the foot, signaling his submission.

The ref shouted the end of the match and Rubble dropped his hold. His muscles ached but in the best possible way. He got to his feet and let the referee hold up his arm. The cheers sounded so familiar yet harrowing in a way. It brought back all the fights and lonely nights that followed.

Rubble nodded to the other fighter then ducked beneath the ropes. Jupiter was there in an instant, wrapping her arms around his neck and kissing him hard. More shouts sounded, adoration and catcalls alike.

"You won!" She beamed at him, looping his arm around her shoulders as they walked to the back. They stopped just shy of the locker room, surrounded by the milling crowd that seemed to have already forgotten the recent fight.

Rubble licked his bottom lip, the bitter taste of blood meeting his tongue. He reached over and gripped her chin. "You're here, so yeah, baby girl, I won."

She pressed her lips together and lowered her gaze. His girl was too damn cute. Leaning down, he placed a gentle kiss on her mouth. It was all he could manage now.

"Come on, Rubble, let's get you cleaned up and

back to the clubhouse." She pulled him toward the locker room. "I think there're a few places I can kiss without bruises. One in particular."

Her eyes lowered to his dick and his pulse jumped. *No one should be this happy.* But he was and he was damn glad too.

Rubble playfully swatted her ass. "Lead the way, baby girl."

CHAPTER 26
JUPITER

"Be back in twenty."

Jupiter waved at Yasmina before disappearing into the crowded town square. Stars dotted the skyline over the bright lights that shone in the near distance for the half-pipe competition. After she'd grabbed sugar cookies decorated to look like snowboards and skis to restock the booth, Jupiter would be back to watch the next round of competitors.

She hurried on foot through the streets. Tourists of all shapes and sizes lined the cobblestones. Some were drunk, and others were high, judging from the pungent scent of marijuana, but most were just genuinely happy to be at the Xtreme Games in Snowshoe. She smiled at the sight.

The bitter cold bit her fingers when she reached the bakery and pulled out the key to unlock it. A day had passed since Rubble told her about Macha's plan to keep her safe. Any messages from Lyle went through Rubble and the club. She didn't see any of them. It unnerved her at first, but finally being protected from the constant barrage of words freed her.

A loud cheer came from up the street. No doubt one of the more famous snowboarders was at the top of the course, ready to show off for the adoring fans. Hurrying to the back room, she spotted the trays of cookies already prepackaged. The bakery was killing it at the games, and she couldn't be prouder.

Balancing the trays on her arms, Jupiter walked toward the front of the store. The bell above the door jangled and she paused. All the lights were off, and the Closed sign was in the window. A familiar tingle skittered up her spine, palms sweating beneath the trays. Heavy footsteps echoed, the sound of rustling clothes evident in the darkness.

Eyes alert, Jupiter slowly backed up and set the cookies down before her trembling hands dropped them. Digging out her phone, she dialed Rubble's number as she peeked around the wall separating the ovens from the storefront. A slender silhouette stood in front of the counter, the black Stetson hat sending her stomach into a tailspin. *Lyle.*

Blood rushed in her ears, the hum of it overwhelming the steady click of Lyle's boots. She swallowed the bile rising in her throat and kept her eyes glued to his every movement. He looked the same. The hat hid his face, but she knew that smug look was in his eyes. *He found me just like he said.*

The phone against her ear finally registered. "Jupiter! Baby girl, what's going on?"

Lyle swiveled in her direction as if he'd heard Rubble's anxious voice, and she smothered a gasp. He continued to glance around the shop but didn't spy her. Jupiter sent a grateful prayer that the darkness hid her. She slowly moved backwards to the exit in the alleyway, cookies long forgotten. The handle to the back door jiggled against the small of her back. She couldn't answer Rubble. She could barely breathe, the air in the room stolen by the man who haunted her dreams.

Pushing open the door, she glanced up and down the alley before sprinting south toward the town square. Hair plastered to her face from sweat or tears, she couldn't decipher which, Jupiter rushed through the crowd. She scanned the tents, searching for Macha's. Loud music from the stage amplified the adrenaline coursing through her veins. Every tent looked the same beneath the starry sky.

Looking over her shoulder, Jupiter clenched her hands into fists. Lyle finally caught up to the edge of the crowd, his dark eyes scouring the tourists for her.

Seeing him should've caused her to melt into a useless puddle. Eleven months on the run from his horrors had brought her to Snowshoe. It was the one and only place that gave her a sense of safety and belonging. She needed to fight for that. She took a cleansing breath, attempting to wipe away the past. It didn't work, but it gave her a moment of clarity. *I have to get out of here.*

Acting quickly, she ducked behind a group of tall men heading toward the beer tent. Jupiter pulled the wool hat lower on her head, grateful she'd dyed her hair darker. She blended in better tonight, especially when everyone was bundled up in warm coverings.

Cheers from the half-pipe caught her attention and she moved toward it. The best place for her was in a large crowd. No one would grab her there. She could disappear and find someone from Macha among the onlookers.

Jupiter reached the seats overlooking the snow-boarders spinning and flipping on the faux snowbanks crafted for the event. She took the steps two at a time, her long legs eating up more distance between her and Lyle. Just before she reached the top, a rough hand grabbed her waist and yanked her backwards.

Struggling in the hold, she opened her mouth to scream when another hand clapped over her mouth.

"Jupiter, it's me. You're okay."

The sound of Rubble's voice muted her fear and she

relaxed against him. Turning, she met his gaze and her body started shaking, adrenaline waning. "I… he…." She couldn't get the words out. Her tongue wouldn't allow her to say the frightening words.

Rubble's eyes darkened. He nodded to someone behind her, and Jupiter saw Kevlar on the other side of the bleachers. She hadn't even noticed him there.

Rubble pulled her into the law enforcement booth, and she noted the radios lining the small space along with surveillance cameras. A man in deputy attire exchanged a glance with Rubble then ducked outside.

"He's here, isn't he?"

She managed a nod. "He came into the shop."

Rubble's jaw tightened. "He what?"

"I didn't lock the door behind me." She bit the inside of her cheek to keep from crying. "I should've. It's not safe. Shit happens here too. I don't know why I thought it didn't."

He rubbed her arms. "Baby, focus."

His voice snapped her out of her tailspin. "I went to the back to get the cookies then heard someone enter the shop."

"Did he see you?"

"I don't know. Maybe? He could've heard me."

"His PI must've told him where you work." He ran a hand over her head, smoothing her hair. It comforted her more than she could imagine. "Probably got him on camera at least. That'll help narrow down the search."

"How?"

Rubble motioned to the set up and focused his eyes on the screens. "A few FBI agents were assigned to the Xtreme Games. Looking for some scum or whatnot. Evidently, the Rockies are a great place to hide out." Rubble pulled out a chair and sat, pulling her onto his lap. "We added Lyle Jones's driver's license to the list of possible threats, so anytime he shows his mug, the cameras track his movements."

His fingers flew over the keyboard, the screens lighting up on faces as the camera scanned the crowd. Finally, the one face she loathed lit up bright green and several photos popped up as the cameras followed him through Snowshoe.

"There he is." She couldn't pry her gaze away. Lyle wasn't even trying to hide. Four men flanked him, each one helping him find her. None looked familiar, but that didn't surprise her. Lyle liked to switch up his hired help in case she started recognizing them.

"Jupiter."

She blinked, but Lyle was there even when she looked away.

"Jupiter, you're safe."

She cleared her throat, a tremble in her voice. "He's

in the same state, Rubble. The same damn town. No, I'm not safe."

In one swift move, Rubble cradled her face in his hands. She couldn't look at the monitors if she wanted. His tattooed hands obscured her vision of anything but him. "Don't you fucking dare."

"What?"

"Think about running." He pushed up her warm hat. "I can see it in your eyes."

Jupiter bit her bottom lip. She *had* been thinking exactly that. "It'd be easier. I'd just vanish. Nobody would get hurt."

"Nobody but me."

She averted her eyes. His were too full of emotion. She couldn't stand the love those blue and green eyes emitted. It tempted her too much. "Rubble—"

He gripped her chin and forced her gaze back to him. "No, don't tell me it's for the best or whatever bullshit you were coming up with. You're mine, Jupiter. Nothing is going to change that. Not some asshole ex or your fear of being loved." He traced her bottom lip with his thumb. "I want you to know what it's like to be truly loved by me. Let me love you, Jupiter. Please."

The pounding in Jupiter's ears was different now. The truth in his eyes spoke to her even more than the words that passed his lips. Rubble loved her. *More than*

I deserve. She couldn't abandon this kind of connection. Snowshoe was home. He was her home. But a small part of her worried for his safety. Lyle wouldn't stop until she was either his or dead. She couldn't put Rubble in the crosshairs. After the fight the other night, he wasn't at one hundred percent. *Lyle's guys will chew him up and spit him out.*

Jupiter reached up and smoothed his beard, kissing him gently. "I won't try to leave. I swear."

She meant every word. Even the ones she kept to herself.

JUPITER STOOD OUTSIDE THE DOOR WHERE MACHA'S MEN currently discussed her ex's sudden appearance in Snowshoe. She pressed her ear against the door but couldn't hear a damn word. They all spoke in low tones, the hum the only thing she could decipher. Only ten minutes passed before the door opened, spooking her away from her obvious spot outside.

She moved back and watched the club members file out of the room. None looked jovial as they had earlier in the day. Each had determination written on their faces. Her stomach dropped, already knowing what that meant. They were going to confront Lyle.

Rubble was the last to leave with Kevlar at his side.

He stopped just shy of her, his handsome face strained. "Baby girl, what're you doing out here?"

"I want to help."

"No." His automatic dismissal pissed her off.

"Why not? I know Lyle better than any of you." Rubble started walking and she hurried to keep up. Despite her long legs, his were longer. "Rubble, please, let me come with you."

Rubble came to a sudden halt and whirled around. His piercing eyes bore into her, his face a mixture of fear and stubbornness. "You're not going anywhere near that asshole if I can help it."

She lifted her chin. "What're you going to do, put me on house arrest?"

A hint of a smile graced his lips. "Tempting, very tempting."

Rubble started walking again and Jupiter groaned. "I can distract him so you can make a move."

They finally reached Rubble's room. "I'm not putting you any more at risk. Nobody knows his plan. He could be packing serious heat." He gently cradled the side of her face. "I won't lose you, Jupiter."

She leaned into his large hand and closed her eyes. He meant well, he truly did, but so did she. They could defeat Lyle together if only he'd let her help.

"And that's why Hawk's staying behind to protect you."

Jupiter's eyes flicked open, and she suddenly saw the shorter man behind Rubble. "I don't need—"

Rubble's mouth over hers silenced the rest of her reply. She melted into his embrace, the sturdiness of his arms wrapping her in a hug she never wanted to leave. When he finally let go, she noticed the sheen of moisture in his stunning eyes.

"If you're there, I won't be able to concentrate. Please, baby, don't fight this." He brushed his lips across her forehead. "Just stay."

Jupiter wanted to pound her fists against his massive chest and yell at him for his quiet yet swaying plea. "All right, I'll stay."

He kissed her cheek, his beard tickling her. "Good girl. I'll be back soon."

She watched him walk down the hallway. He didn't stop to look back. He trusted she'd be in his room when he returned. Jupiter glared at Hawk. She'd try. For Rubble she'd try to resist the urge to run.

CHAPTER 27

RUBBLE

He read her eyes so easily. Jupiter wasn't going to try and leave. She'd just up and do it.

Rubble reluctantly dropped his hold on the woman he desperately wanted to tie to his bed until this matter was settled. He wouldn't. *No matter how tempting.*

"We knew he'd come eventually," he said as his phone vibrated in his jeans. He fished it out and read a new text message from Doc. "The boys are following him. We'll get this settled once and for all, baby girl."

"I know you will."

He walked to the door, ignoring the blatant lie. No matter what he did, Jupiter was wary of the outcome. He gritted his teeth, anger growing in his gut. She didn't trust him, and it tore him up inside.

Seeing Hawk, he called him over. "Take her back to the clubhouse and do not leave her side."

"Yeah, got it, Sarge."

Rubble grabbed a fistful of Hawk's leather jacket and brought the other man closer. "If any goddamn thing happens to her, it's your ass."

A flicker of fear flashed in Hawk's eyes. "I'll keep her safe until you get back."

"Text me when you're there." Rubble dropped his hold and glanced back to see Jupiter watching them. *Good, the woman better realize she's driving me insane.* "Hawk's taking you to the clubhouse."

"Wait, why?" She pinched her brows together, her frown cuter than he deserved. "You said you'd keep me safe, and now you're passing me off on some other biker?"

He tucked her hair beneath her hat. "That's exactly what I'm doing. I can't think straight when you're near me. You steal my focus, Jupiter." His cock jumped at the way her tongue darted out to wet her lips. It felt like months since he'd savored her. *But now's not the time.*

"Stay with Hawk, and for the love of the goddess, don't try to escape." He placed a demanding kiss on her lips and walked in the opposite direction. The applauding crowd drowned out any response Jupiter called his way. He couldn't afford to hear it anyhow. He had a job to do.

Meeting up with Doc and Kevlar, he pulled up the

surveillance on his phone. "Lyle was last seen near the Grand Old Hotel on the main drag. If we catch him tonight, it's all over."

Kevlar swiped through the footage. "Kita's on standby if we need her."

"Let's get this bastard," Doc finished, tossing Rubble the keys to a truck parked nearby.

Rubble never let up on the gas pedal, and they made it to the hotel in under five minutes. Their arrival would've been more dramatic on Harleys, but the winter weather dissuaded that approach.

The crunch of the snow beneath Rubble's boots the same sound he wanted to inflict on the man they were there to confront. He caught sight of Boulder and four prospects at the door. His club was already ahead of him, but they'd let him make the entrance.

"You all remember the plan?" A chorus of silent yeses greeted him. "We're not here to bash heads. It'll be civil."

"There's nothing civil about you scaring the devil into him," Kevlar added with a nod.

Rubble rolled back his shoulders. He'd do more if nobody stopped him. For now, scaring would suffice.

Two prospects held open the doors for the rest of the bikers to file into the hotel's lobby. It was one of the nicer places in the city. The floors were waxed daily and there was a shiny chandelier above their heads.

"Room 210," Brewer said, catching up to the vanguard.

Rubble took the keycard. He didn't want to know how the redhead obtained the room number or key. They split up, half going up the stairs, half riding the elevator.

Once they made it to the second floor, three men in dark-colored suits greeted them. The flash of metal on their hips didn't daunt anyone. They all carried.

"Mr. Jones is expecting you," one of the men said, motioning to the room, door held open by another bodyguard.

Kevlar, Brewer, and Doc exchanged glances. They were all thinking the same thing. *It's a trap.* Since the other half of their posse hadn't arrived, Rubble assumed more of Jones's men were keeping them at bay. It was the four of them versus God knew how many in the room plus any hidden throughout the hotel.

Rubble shoved by the man who spoke, his shoulder colliding with him as he passed. It knocked the hired hand off balance and Rubble smirked. The gun in the small of his back itched to make an appearance, but he resisted. One wrong move and the whole place would erupt in bullets.

Crossing the threshold, Rubble swept his eyes around the room. Three more men were inside, surrounding their boss who was sitting on a comfortable looking couch with the TV on in front of him.

"Yes, yes, come in and have a seat." Lyle clicked to a new channel, a pay-per-view one with music as bad as the acting, before he turned to greet them. "You all must be the infamous motorcycle club, Macha."

Kevlar jutted up his chin. "And you're the asshole who beats women."

Lyle chuckled, crossing his left leg onto his right knee. "I see my lovely wife has been running her mouth."

"She's not your anything," Rubble growled, taking a step closer. Brewer shot out a hand to stop his approach and Rubble glared at him. The other man withdrew, but the apprehensive look on his face remained intact.

Sitting forward, Lyle grabbed a decanter of amber-colored liquor and poured it into a glass. He was too calm. Even the Texan accent sounded too serene. "Jupiter is my *everything*, and you're biker scum." He grinned, the expression more vile than friendly. "And you've found her. Thank you for that. The last eleven months without her were hell." He sipped the liquor. "But we'll be reunited soon enough, and I'll never take her for granted again."

One of his bodyguards moved forward with a black

briefcase, and Lyle said, "For your troubles, I've enclosed five hundred thousand dollars."

Brewer coughed into his hand. It was a lot of money.

Rubble was rethinking the concept of a civil outcome. He looked at Doc and Kevlar to find their gazes equally disturbed.

"What kind of man offers us half a million dollars to hand over his wife?" Rubble curled his hands to fists, ready should the need arise.

Lyle pushed up his Stetson, black like the rest of his apparel. His beady eyes shot ill-humored daggers at him. "You slept with her, didn't you? You lucky bastard."

Rubble couldn't stop his snarl. Lyle chuckled darkly before standing, finishing his drink, and sauntering over to Rubble.

"I won't hold it against you. She's one fine piece of ass." He shrugged, scanning Rubble's Macha vest. "Hell, she's probably slept with twenty men since leaving me." He brushed a speck from Rubble's shoulder, eyes meeting his. "Probably all good-for-nothing bikers like you."

Refusing to take the bait, Rubble narrowed his gaze. "She doesn't want to go with you."

"Of course she does." Lyle stepped away, palms up. "Women don't know what they want, so we as men have to tell them. She'll be happy once she's back at home. In my bed. With me." He stood behind a reclining chair, hands resting on the top. "But since it sounds like your chivalry is getting in the way…."

The second bodyguard placed another briefcase on the bed and popped it open.

"One million. Cold, hard cash." Lyle sighed. "Just think about what that could do for your little club. Or how easy it'd be to keep it for yourself. One mil split four ways is a lot of money, boys."

The four exchanged glances. They were on the same page. No amount of money would tempt them to hand Jupiter over to an abusive psychopath.

Rubble shook his head. "No deal."

The fabricated defeat on Lyle's face only pissed off Rubble more. He'd done enough research on the man to know he wasn't giving up. The Jones family allegedly stole the land they owned in Texas after a poker game gone awry. Rubble wouldn't put anything past this man.

"I saw you the other night, you know." Lyle leered at him. "At the fight. You did well too. Back in your prime, I'll bet you were a sight to see."

A horrified slither crept down Rubble's spine. The bastard was in town at the fight night. *That or one of his guys was.* Either was more than possible.

He took a step forward, and this time no one

stopped his approach. "Leave Snowshoe or there'll be hell to pay."

Snickering, Lyle closed the distance between them and shoved Rubble's chest. The audacity enraged Rubble and agitated the bruise from the fight. He winced, and Lyle preened.

"You're injured. You wouldn't last five minutes with my fighters." He snapped his fingers and the room flooded with more men. "Take the money and tell me where I can find my wife."

"Fuck off and I'll let you live."

"You give me no alternative." Lyle laughed, but the humor didn't reach his eyes. "If you won't take my money, you'll take my vengeance."

His thugs sprang into action, each one attacking Macha's bikers. Rubble ducked a punch from one man but got sideswiped by another fist. Rubble pushed through the brute, eyes trained on the man deserving of such a punishment. Blood trickled down Rubble's brow and into his eye, the blow to his side finally catching up to him. Rubble stepped to the left, kneeing the man in the gut, then smacking him to the floor. He glanced at his three brothers, each one busy with their own hired fighter. For one quick moment, he considered helping them, but the sight of Lyle scurrying off toward the door stopped him.

Jumping around the fallen bodyguard, Rubble

hustled to the front door. Just as he reached it, Lyle whirled around with a 9mm in his hand and Rubble slammed to a stop, holding his hands up.

"Back the hell away, biker, or I'll shoot you dead in the eye."

He couldn't make the shot, but Rubble wasn't going to chance it. "Be reasonable. Jupiter simply wants her own life. Can't you let her have it?"

Lyle threw back his head and laughed. "Fuck no. She's mine 'til death do us part' and I intend to make her death long and extremely drawn out."

Rubble took a step toward him, and Lyle shot off a round. The bullet whizzed past Rubble's side, catching a sliver of his leather jacket before hitting the wall. Before he could register what happened, he felt a jab to the right side of his head. He fell in slow motion to the unwelcoming floor, blood swimming in his eyes.

The last thing he heard was Kevlar yelling at him. Then it all went black. Jupiter's face was the only thing his mind could summon.

CHAPTER 28

JUPITER

Hawk hadn't budged from outside Rubble's door since Rubble left. He didn't answer any of her questions and barely let her leave to use the restroom. Jupiter was on room arrest. The longer she stayed confined to Rubble's sanctuary, the more she scolded herself for wanting to leave. He'd recognized her lies. He'd done it so many times over the last few weeks. He knew her better than any other man ever had. It scared the hell out of her, but it also gave her a sense of belonging. No one could affect her the way Rubble did with a single kiss.

"I'm hungry," she said, knocking on the door.

Hawk sighed. "I'll get you a sandwich if you promise to stay put. Rubble will kick my ass to Mexico if you sneak out."

"I won't leave." She meant it this time. She

wouldn't leave. Not until she knew Rubble was all right. A group of Macha bikers were on their way to confront Lyle. It sent her anxiety into overdrive. They didn't know what they were walking into. Lyle seemed liked a dumbass rancher, but he was much craftier than his guise. *If only Rubble had let me go.*

Jupiter chewed on her thumbnail. She sat on the bed, the frame squeaking softly. Eyeing the room, she noticed how tidy it was. His Marines background was showing. She smirked and lay back on the bed, the ceiling fan oscillating slowly. It had been turned on every time they slept together. She'd mentioned it to him in passing, but he'd remembered, and the damn thing was never turned off.

The door swung open and banged the wall beside it.

Rolling her eyes, Jupiter leaned up on her elbows. "Please tell me there was some of that leftover chicken Queenie made for my—"

Rubble stood in the doorway and her words dropped off. The light behind him blocked out his face. When he stepped inside and shut the door, he turned the lock as well. Blood stained his exposed skin and clothes. A cry caught in her throat at the damage done to his face.

Getting to her feet, she rushed to him. "Oh my God, are you all right?"

He winced and eased away from her touch. "I'm fine. Just a scuffle."

Jupiter frowned and pointed to the streak of blood on his cheek. "You call this fine? What the hell did you do?"

Rubble snapped his eyes to her. "Defended myself, that's what." He walked to the bed, tearing off clothes as he took lumbering steps.

It was then that she noticed him favoring his left side. Streaks of blood covered the tattoos on his bald head. His face pinched with pain as he slid off his jacket.

She covered her mouth with her hands. "He did this to you."

Pulling off his shirt, Rubble nodded once. "He had more bodyguards than we expected."

"You idiot! Of course he did!"

Rubble whirled around, his eyes fierce. "One million dollars, Jupiter. That's how badly he wants you back as his punching bag."

The blood drained from her face. "What?"

"He offered it to us. Cash." Rubble kicked off his boots and unbuckled his belt.

Fear suddenly crept into Jupiter's mind. If one of the club members wasn't as noble as Rubble, she might not make it out of Snowshoe alive. "No one wanted to accept it, did they?"

He pulled his belt through the loops quickly, the zing stinging the air between them. "How can you even ask me that? After all we've been through, you honestly believe Macha would sell a woman."

She didn't know how to respond. She didn't want to believe it, but her history with Lyle didn't leave her trusting many men.

Rubble groaned and shook his head. "Jesus, Jupiter. None of my men would ever betray a woman like that. That's not us. That's not Macha. I thought you knew that."

"So did I, but it's a lot of money, Rubble. What if one of the new guys makes a deal with Lyle?"

She went for the exit, but he made it there first, his long legs eating the distance. "Oh, no you don't, baby girl." He trapped her against the door, hands on either side of her head.

The metallic scent of blood clung in the air, and she closed her eyes. It wasn't all Rubble's, that much she could tell. *But some of it is.* She couldn't live with his blood on her conscious.

"I wouldn't blame you," she finally said, opening her eyes.

Rubble let out a weary sigh. "Goddammit, Jupiter, you drive me crazy."

She lifted her brows, but he silenced any question with his lips over hers. Whimpering, she laced her arms around his neck. His solid body slammed against her, pinning her to the door almost as roughly as his lips took hers. Lust poured through her veins, warmth blossoming in the pit of her stomach. She'd never known a man like this. He was the tinder she so desperately needed to stoke her inner fire, and he did it so easily. Rubble made every emotion come to the surface.

He tore away her shirt, the ripping of the thin fabric heating her cheeks and enticing her further. Her bra fell away, and he captured her nipple in his mouth, teeth grazing the taut bud. Jupiter arched into him, the sensations shooting like stars behind her eyes.

Rubble grabbed her by the waist and tossed her on the bed. Before she could recover, his muscular body was there, pulling her up to the headboard and peeling away her jeans and panties. She was completely bare against the soft bedding. She tried to kiss him, but he gripped her wrists in one hand and propped them above her head.

"I warned you, baby girl." He kissed the hollow of her neck, sending tremors along her spine.

A moment of panic settled through her at his intentions. Using his belt, he looped it through her wrists then around the steel headboard. She tugged at the restraint, testing the strength.

Rubble pulled away, leaving her alone in the middle of the bed. "Nah, it won't budge, believe me."

Jupiter's chest heaved. She couldn't escape but she didn't want to when it came to Rubble. "Are you going to leave me here?"

He chuckled and ran his hand over the front of his jeans. The bulge there told her no, but the look in his eyes swayed her otherwise. "Gotta clean myself up." He opened the door. "I might be awhile. Perfect opportunity for you to think about your behavior."

Her mouth dropped open and her eyes bugged in response to his words. She was tied to his bed. Naked. *Just like he promised.*

CHAPTER 29
RUBBLE

Washing the last bit of blood from his skin, Rubble watched the pink water circle the drain below him. His cock stood at full attention despite the frigid temperature of the water running down his body. The knowledge that Jupiter was not only naked in his bed but tied to it as well gave him the stiffest erection he could remember having.

He couldn't give her what she wanted yet. She needed to understand he was in this for life. He didn't want anyone else. *She needs to understand I'd never let anyone betray her.* He'd never lay a malicious finger on her body. It wasn't his style. But Jupiter had to learn she couldn't run away when shit got rough.

He shut off the water and draped a towel around his waist. The mirror's reflection hurt more than the injuries themselves. There'd be a scar or two, but he'd survive. The same could be said about his brothers. They all walked away with minor cuts and bruises. He leaned closer and poked the spot next to his left eye that was already a dark shade of purple.

Glancing down, he snorted at the tented towel. "All right, all right, dickhead, I'm going." Even when he wasn't hard as a rock, his body craved Jupiter's in a primal way. From the moment he walked out of the hotel, he had to get home to her. Had to feel her soft skin under his.

Rubble gargled a bit of mouthwash, getting the taste of blood out of his mouth. The only thing he wanted to taste was Jupiter. *And I will.*

He walked out of the bathroom and down the hall. He stood in front of his bedroom door for a good ten seconds before opening it. The lights were low, a lamp by the window casting the room in a warm glow.

Jupiter popped her head up, pressing her legs together but unable to hide her nakedness. "I wasn't sure when you were coming back."

Rubble's gaze slid over her pebbled skin, her nipples hard and longing for his tongue. "No matter what happens, I'll always come for you, Jupiter." He meant it with his entire soul. Even if he were shot twenty times, he'd crawl home if only to see her beautiful face one last time.

Walking to the bed, he ran his knuckles down her

chest to her hips. "Don't hide from me," he said, gently nudging her legs open. "You're too beautiful for that."

The vein in Jupiter's forehead eased, her body finally calming after he'd left for fifteen minutes. He massaged her heavy breasts one at a time with his left hand while tracing along her side with his right. She squirmed beneath him, body anxiously begging him to touch her in other, more intimate places.

Straightening his spine, Rubble walked over to the closet and grabbed two more belts. Turning around, he saw the hesitation vanish from her face. There was no worry, only acceptance and desire. She finally trusted him. *It's about damn time.* He slowly walked over and grabbed her right ankle then the left, tying each one to the bedpost. She was tall enough that the bedframe fit this position wonderfully. Any other girl wouldn't be able to reach, but his girl…. Yeah, his girl was just the right fit.

Legs properly restrained, he stood back and took in her majesty. The belts were loose enough she could move slightly but tight enough that he had full control over her body. He had to touch her. His dick demanded it.

"Please, Rubble, I can't stand having you so close and not being able to feel you." Her eyes pleaded along with her pouty lips.

"Fuck, woman." He dropped the towel, his erection

bobbing at the newfound freedom. Climbing on the bed, he positioned his cock level with her mouth. She didn't bat an eyelash. Opening her mouth, she took his cock deep in her throat. He clenched his jaw and gripped a hand on the bedframe. She bobbed her head, sucking him her only focus. Without a doubt she gave the best head. The soft velvetiness of her mouth made his balls tighten, but he wouldn't give in to her yet. He pulled his cock out of her reach, climbing back off the bed.

"Macha went to bargain for you tonight, Jupiter." He wiped the slobber from her bottom lip. "We bled for you, and you thought we'd be swayed by money." He paced around the bed while her eyes followed him at every turn. "I trust you more than any person in the world, but tonight, you wounded me."

Jupiter let out a weak breath, the belts stretching her limbs slightly. "I didn't mean to, Rubble."

"I know. You've lived in fear for so long." He leaned over and nuzzled her nose. "But now it's different. I need you to see that I'm different. Macha's different."

Her bottom lip quivered, and tears welled in her eyes. "I do. I'm sorry. I panicked and I shouldn't have. I know you'd never betray me."

Rubble gripped her chin, forcing her eyes to lock with his. He never wanted to see those olive-green eyes mournful. "No, I wouldn't, and neither would Macha."

She nodded. "I'm scared, Rubble. Scared that this isn't all real."

"It is, baby girl." He kissed the tip of her nose.

"I don't know how to be in love with someone good. I'm not used to it."

Seeing the truth in her eyes, he climbed on the bed and kissed a line from her belly to her lips. "I'm not a good man, but I want to be for you."

"You already are."

He couldn't resist anymore. She'd endured long enough. Hell, so had he. Under his watch, she'd never suffer again unless it was requested. He kissed her thoroughly, his tongue touching every part of hers. Kissing down her ribs, he settled at the apex of her legs. Already, her inebriating scent called to him. Slipping a finger between her curls, he closed his eyes at the wetness there.

"I think somebody likes being tied up."

"Only by you."

Rubble licked her slit and murmured, "That's my girl," before indulging in her tender clit. She bucked against him, her tiny nub of nerves swelling beneath his mouth's attentions. She tasted richer than any dessert he'd ever tasted. Feasting on her would always satisfy his hunger.

Jupiter lifted her hips and he slid two fingers into her pussy. Her core pulsed around them and he groaned. She was driving him crazy both sexually and emotionally. Pressing a thumb to her clit, Rubble increased the friction of his fingers, making his cock jealous.

His name rang out in the silence, Jupiter's come dripping from his fingers and to his waiting tongue. He lapped it up eagerly, never wasting a drop. Her quakes slowed, but the moans didn't. He'd have her coming again the moment he was inside her.

Sheathing himself in a condom, Rubble sunk into her slippery pussy, her walls gripping him tighter than before. He braced himself, allowing Jupiter to relax enough for him to plunge in and out of her. The belts held her wrists at bay, but she tugged, nonetheless.

Catching her lips, he tangled his tongue with hers, sharing the delicacy of her passion with her. "Don't fight them, baby girl. It'll hurt."

"Then take them off." She lifted her hips to greedily accept his thick cock and he nearly blew his load. The lusty whisper coupled with the way she gripped him was enough to make him clench the headboard until his knuckles were white.

He shook his head. "So bossy even when tied to a bed." He nipped the side of her neck and increased his tempo, needing to make sure that when she called his name, it could be heard all the way up on the roof. He didn't have to wait long. Jupiter cried out, the high-pitched moan better with his name repeatedly on her lips afterward.

Her legs wobbled beneath him, but he wouldn't relent. His girl needed more. The look in her green eyes demanded more and he'd give it to her one solid inch at a time.

Reaching down, he unbuckled the restraints and hoisted her ankles onto his shoulders. Jupiter bit her lip to keep from screaming, her white come coating his cock.

"Swear you'll never leave," he said, bottoming out against her G-spot.

"I swear."

"Swear you love me."

She panted as another orgasm crested. "You know I do."

Just as she clenched him hard, Rubble let himself go. He held her hips against his, her orgasm finishing him off. Her wild eyes met his, their connection too strong to break. Once spent, he reached over and freed her wrists. Jupiter wrapped her arms around his neck.

He nuzzled her cheek, the perfume of their bodies filling in his nostrils. "I love you, Jupiter, more than I should be allowed."

She kissed his forehead, the sweet act one he could get used to. "And I love you, Kassian."

Hearing his name on her lips broke something inside he'd kept built around his heart for so many years.

"I haven't heard someone call me that name in almost twenty years."

Jupiter leaned up until she was sitting on his lap, cock still fully embedded in her. "You should hear it more often. It's really a nice name." She lightly scratched the back of his neck. "Not that Rubble isn't completely accurate. You do have one hard dick." Her eyes lit up when he cocked his hips, ready for a second round.

Threading his fingers through her hair, he kissed her as she slowly rode his dick. This time wouldn't be fucking. This time would be even better.

CHAPTER 30
JUPITER

Rolling over, Jupiter's arm hit the empty spot beside her. It was warm. Rubble hadn't been gone long from the bed. She opened her eyes and glanced around the room, hoping to catch him sneaking out. His muscular form didn't meet her gaze and she grabbed the spare pillow. He'd mentioned leaving early for club business, but she didn't know what that meant. Some days he was blatantly clear about his jobs, but it wasn't one of those days.

She tried to fall back asleep but sounds from the hallway and downstairs interrupted her attempts. Sitting up, she stretched her arms above her head and yawned. Her muscles whined from the new positions they'd been exposed to under Rubble's care.

She swung her legs to the side and stared at the remnants of their lovemaking. Three belts lay precariously on the floor around the bed. The fourth she knew was wrapped around Rubble's muscular hips that very moment.

A jolt of lust spun low in her belly, the night before flashing in her mind. It wasn't merely sex or even fucking. They shared a deep connection every time their bodies came together as one. She shivered at the thought. Such a bond terrified her. She'd never felt it with anyone before Rubble. Somehow, the tough man delicately tore down her defenses until she unabashedly trusted him.

Light streamed in through the window beneath the half-drawn shades. Snowflakes fell leisurely outside, reminding her the day ahead would be another cold one. Walking to the dresser, she pulled out a drawer and found a fresh set of clothes. Most of hers were upstairs, but Doc's old lady had dropped off a few sets of clothes from the club shop the night before. She'd make do with the leather pants and shirt that had both been designed by Isa.

Holding up the red long-sleeved shirt with a small Macha emblem on the left breast, Jupiter smiled. It didn't look like much, but the fabric would be warm enough for a day outside in the elements. It was one of the benefits Isa's clothing line boasted, and one tourist bought into daily.

Jupiter pulled on a pair of Rubble's sweatpants and

a baggy sweatshirt before tiptoeing to the community bathroom down the hall. Forty minutes later, she stepped outside and grinned at Yasmina waiting by the blue truck in the parking lot. Two of the club prospects were already in the back, mandated protection after the prior evening's kerfuffle. She'd rather have Rubble or at least men she knew, but those club members had other tasks. They couldn't babysit two women baking all day.

"You're smiley this morning."

Jupiter opened the passenger door and climbed inside. "Why wouldn't I be? The snow is gorgeous, temperature in the double digits and—"

"You got some last night."

Her cheeks flared. "Well, yeah."

Starting the truck, Yasmina cranked the heat and let it idle. "I heard about what happened at the hotel."

Jupiter slipped on a pair of gloves, the harsh temperature of the new day greeting her. "Nobody got hurt, did they? Rubble only told me bits and pieces."

"To protect you, I'm sure." Yasmina offered her a small smile. "The club men actually did have a few injuries, but they're fine." She warmed her hands in front of one of the vents. "These men are good, you know. They rescued me and many other women and children for no reason other than we needed help."

"What kind of men do that?"

"Macha's men."

Nodding, Jupiter accepted the truth. Rubble's clan was much more than men who liked to drink and ride motorcycles. *They have a purpose.* It was the one thing missing in her life. She'd never truly had one other than being Lyle's trophy.

"Are you interested in any of the men?"

Yasmina shook her head. "Not my preference if you catch my drift."

"Oh, shit, sorry. I shouldn't have assumed."

She waved a hand. "But to answer your question, there is one woman I like very much. She is sweet, tough, and the rowdiest woman I've ever met."

Jupiter instantly knew who she meant. "Dolly."

A pink blush crept across Yasmina's cheeks. "Am I that obvious?"

"All Macha women are badasses, including you, so I did see a certain affinity but didn't realize it was more than that." Jupiter turned on the radio, Rock music softly filling the cab. "I guess I've been so involved with Rubble I haven't noticed."

"She's usually busy with the nymphs; we don't get a lot of time alone." Yasmina's pretty smile drooped. "I don't even know if she would like to be with me."

"Of course she would. You're amazing."

Yasmina shifted the truck into gear and they

rumbled down the busy streets. "Thank you, but I don't think I'm what she's used to."

Thinking back to when Jupiter saw a few of the Macha nymphs, she shifted in her seat. They were gorgeous, they had to be, but Yasmina was better than a sex doll. She had gumption and beauty that wouldn't fade over the years.

"If you like her, tell her."

"Yes, because that always works out." Yasmina turned into the alleyway behind the bakery. "It's easier to not say anything yet." She offered Jupiter a smile. "I've lived without love for this long, I can do it a little more."

The two prospects checked the alley before nodding. The women climbed out of the truck and unlocked the bakery door. "Don't wait for life to happen, Yasmina. Because it won't. You'll keep reliving the same day until you're old and bitter. Believe me, I know from personal experience." One prospect held open the door while the other one walked inside. He returned moments later with a slight nod saying that his search was clean. Jupiter and Yasmina walked inside.

"You say these things and they make sense." Yasmina flipped on the lights. "But I do not know if I have the courage."

After placing her purse in the small office, Jupiter

tied an apron around her waist. "You won't know until you try."

Yasmina preheated the ovens and pulled her hair into a tight bun on top of her head. "This is true. For now, we bake for the many hungry tourists."

The two grinned and started collecting the necessary ingredients for the recipes. Jupiter let the conversation drift away from Yasmina's feelings for the MC's madame. If it were meant to be, it'd happen one way or another.

She poured sugar into the mixing bowls, doing the mental calculations for the recipe. Listening to Yasmina's sweet, accented voice helped calm Jupiter's nerves. Rubble left out a few details from the skirmish and she needed to hear them. *Just like I need to find a way to get Lyle away from here, so he doesn't hurt anyone else.* There was only one way she was positive would work. *I have to go to him.*

CHAPTER 31
RUBBLE

Nursing a glass of cola, Rubble leaned back in the booth. Normally, he wouldn't come to Booze and Tattoos, but with the recent firefight, he needed to get a little distance. Jupiter was so entrenched in his mind that everything else seemed murky.

Two nymphs swayed their hips to the Led Zeppelin song playing on the jukebox. Before Jupiter, the two might've enticed him into a night filled with inconsequential sex. Now, though, he didn't want any woman's touch but Jupiter's.

"Sure you don't need a splash of Jack in there?" Brewer asked, settling across from him in the booth. Only a handful of patrons were scattered amid the tables, not unusual for the early afternoon.

"Nope. You know I don't drink much."

"Sure, I do, but you've barely had a drink since

Jupiter strolled into town. Care to explain?"

Sizing up the bartender, Rubble took a sip of the soda. Brewer didn't typically volunteer for the gun fights. Fists were more his style. A fact Rubble appreciated, since Brewer was the best spar partner in the club.

"I'm worried."

"About the club or her?"

Rubble rested his gaze on the door that led to the tattoo parlor. Legs and Snoopy were there, lips locked as per their usual stance. "Can't it be both?"

Brewer shrugged. "I guess, but you've never been this concerned about a woman before. Hell, you gave Kevlar and Doc plenty of shit when their old ladies needed help."

"But I still helped them."

The song changed and more customers filed into the bar. They were tourists, judging from the look of their wide eyes when the men saw the nymphs making out on the dance floor. Rubble'd never get sick of watching those reactions.

"Since Mr. Texas didn't play nice, what's the next plan?" Brewer knocked his knuckles on the table. "Plan B isn't that appealing, honestly. The less Feds around the better." He lowered his voice. "Doesn't bode well for business here."

Rubble glanced around the bar. Sure enough,

several men and women looked perfectly at home, but no doubt had a hit or two of drugs on them. The club didn't judge. They couldn't. All he cared about was ensuring Macha survived whatever it faced. Unfortunately, he couldn't predict the whirlwind Jupiter brought or the outcome now that her ex found her.

"Nikita is a last resort. I'm hoping that guy will leave Jupiter alone once the club has made a proper introduction."

"Without bodyguards, I presume."

"Exactly." Rubble finished his drink and sighed. He was tired. Tired of always having his defenses up. He never realized how sick of it he was until Jupiter. *Damn women ruin everything.* He smiled inwardly. He'd let Jupiter ruin every one of his days.

"You heading to the finals tonight?" Brewer asked, standing and waving at incoming Macha members. "The snowboarders look pretty good this year."

"Yeah. I was thinking of bringing Jupiter. She'd enjoy watching, I think. Would get her out of the club-house too."

Hawk and Kevlar reached them and squeezed into the booth.

"Double whiskey for me and a Guinness for Hawk," Kevlar called to the nymph behind the bar then turned toward Rubble. "I'm surprised to see you here. Figured you'd be handcuffed to your girl."

"I've got two prospects watching Yasmina and Jupiter," Rubble said, shifting in his seat.

Hawk lifted his brows. "Hold up. You, the sergeant at arms and protector of all things Macha, aren't watching your old lady when she's in potential danger. What the hell is wrong with you?"

Rubble narrowed his eyes. "Fuck off, Hawk."

"Yeah," Kevlar piped up. "Delegating is important in the club. Especially when it's something you don't care about or want to do."

Rubble eyed his brothers. Each one had a shit-eating grin on his face and a knowing gleam in his eyes. He deserved every bit of the grief they were giving him. "My shift starts in two hours."

Drinks arrived at the table, momentarily pausing the conversation. Once the nymph left, with a pinched ass courtesy of Hawk, Kevlar lifted his glass.

"To Rubble. Oh, how the mighty have fallen. Welcome to the pussy-whipped crew, brother."

The bikers clinked glasses while Rubble held up both middle fingers. They were right in teasing him and he could handle it. The only downside was that he truly did want to leave and find Jupiter. But he couldn't. He had to find a way out for her sake as well as Macha's. He failed miserably at focusing with her nearby, tempting him. No, he'd let the prospects earn their right to prove themselves while he figured out a better plan. *One hour and fifty-five minutes until I see Jupiter.*

Sitting back, he watched his brothers josh and curse with each other. The brotherhood was the biggest perk to MC life. He always had his family no matter what hell they suffered. Once Jupiter was free of her chains, she'd join the Macha family too. He'd make sure of it. Jupiter was his. The night before only cemented it for him. No other woman would warm his bed but her. She'd wiggled her way into his heart and now he never wanted to be rid of her.

An hour into their drinking, Doc came into the bar, Isa at his side. Rubble didn't think anything of it until he noticed Yasmina and the two prospects assigned to her and Jupiter's safety. Warning bells siphoned all humor from him.

He stood, teetering the table from his sudden move. "What the hell are you doing here?"

"Rubble, give 'em a break. They didn't know she'd do this," Doc said, his words only sending Rubble's pulse skyrocketing.

"Speak!" he boomed at the prospects cowering in front of him.

"Jupiter. She, uh, gave us the slip," the shorter of the two prospects said quickly.

"How?"

The other one opened his mouth but then thought

better of it and nudged his buddy. "She said she was going out for a bit of air. Eggy and I didn't think anybody would be dumb enough to take her in broad daylight."

"So, you let her go out by herself?" Rubble's hands curled into tight fists.

"Pretty much, yeah. We checked on her after a couple minutes, but she was gone."

"We searched for her, but came up empty," Eggy stuttered, fear filling his face. "Sorry, Rubble."

That was the last straw. Without thinking, Rubble decked the first prospect then the second. Both men teetered before dropping to the floor, out cold. Chest heaving, he whirled around and was grateful his brothers were already on their feet.

"When they wake, tell them if Jupiter is harmed at all, I'll be back for them," he snapped to the nymph kneeling beside the prospects.

Not bothering to check to see if his brothers followed, Rubble pushed through the bar and out into the elements. Darkness had fallen, and snow along with it. Beer and stale smoke greeted his first inhale, but he didn't care. He stomped toward his truck, irate at himself more than anyone. He'd left Jupiter alone and he'd never forgive himself if something happened to her. He couldn't live without her.

CHAPTER 32
JUPITER

This was a stupid idea. Jupiter swallowed the bile rising in her throat. The hotel doors loomed ahead, the warm glow from inside almost leering at her. Her ex would know the moment she stepped over the threshold. His bodyguards were always on top of that shit. *But I have to get him the hell out of Snowshoe.* The only surefire way to do that was to face her fears. Face her demons. *Face the devil himself.*

She could hear the roar of a crowd in the distance. The announcer's booming voice bounced off the mountains, a winner finally named in the half-pipe competition. She wiped her palms on the leather pants, sweat drenching them despite the frigid temperatures.

She told her feet to move, but her boots refused to take a step closer to the doom awaiting inside. Heart pounding against her ribcage, she clenched her jaw and forced herself through the glass doors. She tucked a loose strand behind her ears, the rest of her hair in braids Yasmina insisted on weaving while they waited for the cookies baking.

A short man stood behind the desk, eyeing her curiously. She didn't need to check in. Lyle would find her. Steering toward the large sitting room to the left of the entrance, Jupiter followed the crackling sounds of the fireplace. It was a cozy spot with several comfortable chairs facing the wood fireplace and books lining the built-in bookshelves along the wall.

A blue chair furthest from the hearth caught her attention and she unceremoniously plopped into the plush upholstery. The clock on the wall ticked loudly, announcing the new hour with chimes. It was eerily still. Thanks to the winter games, the hotel was all but empty.

She worried her bottom lip and closed her eyes. *I can do this.* The severe abuse she'd survived suddenly surfaced from the depths of her soul, the pain begging her to flee before it all happened again. *No more running.* She promised Rubble those very words, but now it didn't sound like such a good idea. Running was the only thing keeping her alive the last eleven months.

"There you are, pet."

The Texan twang to the words sent a frigid shiver

down Jupiter's entire body. Opening her eyes, she braced herself for the inevitable backlash. Instead, she found Lyle's haughty face filled with humor. Satisfaction filled his dark eyes. She was officially caught in the snare.

Standing, Jupiter stuffed her hands in the pockets of her jacket. Her fingers grazed the cool metal. It was her last resort. If Lyle couldn't see reason, she'd serve the justice he long deserved. A stocky man stood behind him, and she narrowed her eyes trying to read the patch on his cut. He didn't look like a Macha biker, but she could've sworn she recognized the familiar emblem.

She lifted her chin. "Don't call me that. I'm not your pet."

His easy smile drooped, and Jupiter felt her stomach drop. She couldn't let him see her scared. She was better than that. The last year proved she could face him without shriveling to his whims.

"Come, darling, I have a fine merlot in my room." He turned on his heels." No doubt you're dying to drink something other than the swill these people call wine in Colorado.

"No."

He swiveled to face her again and Jupiter held back her tears at the pure evil in his dark eyes. "Such a fiery tongue you have suddenly. It's almost as if you've forgotten your place, pet."

Jupiter steadied her breathing. She wouldn't let him slide that easily. "Ready to sign the divorce papers?"

Lyle chuckled, lifting a cigar to his lips, and inhaling the rich flavor. "Over my dead body."

"That can be arranged."

CHAPTER 33
RUBBLE

This damn woman will be the death of me. For the first time ever, Rubble didn't mind the sentiment. He'd lay down his life for Jupiter. He gripped the steering wheel tighter, wishing it were the handlebars of his Harley instead. The cigarette hanging out of his mouth tasted like shit, but he couldn't calm the hell down without it either.

"Brother, you need to let off on the gas pedal a bit." Kevlar grabbed the handle above the door as the truck took the turn faster than expected. "Seriously, Rubble, crashing will get us nowhere."

"She thinks she can be the sacrificial lamb for Macha." Rubble shook his head, inhaling the nicotine and flicking ash out the cracked window. "I swear to the goddess, I'm going to bend her over my knee and not let her go until both cheeks are red as cherries."

Kevlar chuckled but attempted to pass it off as a cough when Rubble glared his way. "She's a Macha woman through and through. I don't know why you expected her to roll over and submit. She's been running from this douche for almost a year. I'd want some justice served by my own hand too."

"Justice?" He stopped at a red light. "What do you mean?"

"Oh, shit. I should've told you earlier. Isa saw Jupiter cleaning a gun this morning." Kevlar straightened his cut. "Jupiter said it was hers. Isa didn't even tell me until an hour ago. I'm sorry, brother."

Rage fueled Rubble to press harder on the gas the moment the intersection was clear. His woman was in the grips of an abusive man and had managed to sneak in a sidearm. He couldn't be mad about that. In fact, it made him proud. He was angry at himself that he wasn't watching her every second until the matter was put to bed. He knew better. His damn emotions got in the way.

"Damn woman. I just hope it isn't used against her," he grumbled.

Snow blasted the windshield and he flipped on the wipers. Jupiter survived years under a cruel man's thumb, and he'd seen her shoot a weapon. His girl could protect herself.

"I know you're not used to this."

Rubble shot the other man a confused glance.

"Not being in control," Kevlar added. "Nobody suspected she'd waltz right into his hotel."

Jupiter's sweet face swam in front of Rubble's eyes. She was so innocent, yet a secondary nature simmered under the surface. "She's trying to protect us."

"Even more reason to love her."

"Loving her isn't the issue, brother." He pulled into the hotel parking lot. "I'm afraid of how much I love her. If something happens to her...." His voice dropped to a hoarse whisper. "I'll lose my very soul."

Kevlar clicked a magazine into his gun. "Then we better not lose either one of you."

Rubble nodded and climbed out of the truck. More Macha bikers were on their way to the hotel. He'd sent a text to his brothers the instant he left the bar. As appealing as rushing in and shredding the hotel room with bullets sounded, he couldn't be brash. One stray bullet and the love of his life would be gone forever.

Motioning to the incoming vehicles full of his brethren, Rubble waited until the crew was unloaded and ready for action. Reaper wasn't among them, opting instead to keep a few members behind in case of a double-cross. He'd have thought of that himself if his heart weren't involved in this rescue mission.

"Hawk tapped into the security system." Rubble glanced at the man who nodded. "This guy has guns on every floor. He moved to a bigger suite on the top floor. It's tucked in the corner, so Klink and Snoopy, you take the fire escape. Cueball and Doc will each take three prospects and clear the hallways. Kevlar and I will go up the service entry and sneak up the rear stairway once it's been cleared."

Rubble felt snow land on his cheeks. The cold didn't bother him. The worry lining his brothers' eyes did. "If you can't handle this, leave now."

The Macha men glanced between themselves, but no one moved.

"We're in this together," Doc said, clapping a hand on Rubble's back. "Let's go get your girl."

CHAPTER 34
JUPITER

Curls of cigar smoke mingled with the crisp air on the balcony overlooking Snowshoe. Every other puff hit Jupiter's face and her stomach lurched for more reason than forgetting to eat lunch. Lyle didn't bother to snuff out the cigar before tossing it to the snowbank below. He turned slightly and held out his hand. She wanted to smack it away and shove the small gun she had concealed to his ribcage. But she didn't. She couldn't.

"Pet, I've missed you." The malevolent glow inside of him lit up his dark eyes, no soul staring back at her. "Come give me the hug I've desperately been awaiting."

"Go fuck yourself."

If she thought her words would catch him off

guard, she was sorely disappointed. Lyle chuckled, the low sound snaking up her spine.

"I see being around the biker gang has loosened your usually tight tongue." He placed his hand on the small of her back and forced her into the room. One of his bodyguards locked the glass door and stood in front of it, cutting off that possible escape route.

"No, being around Macha has shown me exactly what I want in life."

Lyle narrowed his eyes. "And what is that? A poor biker who treats you like a piece of meat? A lifetime of constantly worrying about money?" He clucked his tongue and slowly grazed her neck with his fingers. "That doesn't sound like the woman I know."

Jupiter held in the inevitable shudder. He didn't deserve the satisfaction. "You don't know me anymore. I'm not the same woman you met all those years ago." She straightened, holding her chin a notch higher. "I know who I am and what I want." She pulled out the folded papers from her jacket. "And I want you to sign these and leave me and the club the hell alone."

Licking his bottom lip, Lyle slowly scrutinized her. From the glint in his eyes, she knew he was undressing her in his mind. The familiar darkness didn't scare her anymore. The fear that he'd beat her until she passed out wasn't gone, but it didn't agitate her either. Being around Rubble and Macha bolstered her courage. She wouldn't let this man destroy her life again.

"Perhaps I will." He loosened his tie, the act one she'd seen too many times before she passed out. A lump formed in her throat, his movements sickening her. "But not until after I have one final night with you."

The hired men didn't move and for a brief second, uncertainty wavered in her mind. The heaviness of the weapon in her other pocket calmed her and she rubbed it reassuringly. "No."

Lyle stopped his approach, hand on his belt. "Excuse me?"

"I said no."

"I'm your husband, Jupiter, whether you want to admit it or not." He stalked closer, eyes taking on a demonic hue. "I have needs. Needs you, my wife, can appease." He reached her and gripped her hair, yanking her face to his. "And you know I enjoy it when you struggle, so please"—he laced his free hand around her throat, choking her slightly—"*please* struggle."

Jupiter's heart raced, but her mind was clear. She slid the gun out of her pocket and jabbed it against his heart. "Sign the goddamn papers, Lyle, or I'll become a very rich widow."

Worry flickered in his putrid eyes and he snarled,

holding her tighter. "Some people can get away with murder, pet. You're not one of them." He bit her bottom lip, drawing blood. "But I am."

Cocking the gun, Jupiter readied her finger to squeeze the trigger. She'd done it many times before but always at a target. Shooting a man of flesh and blood was completely different. She hesitated and Lyle used it to his advantage. He grabbed her wrist and flung the gun out of her grip. A shot rang out, and one of his bodyguards let out an anguished cry and clutched his leg, hit by the wild shot.

A thud echoed in the hallway and the door splintered open. Ducking down, Jupiter moved toward the sofa's safety. More bullets riddled the room, manly shouts morphing into curses. Warmth sprayed the side of her face, blood dripping down her chin. She muted a cry, praying it wasn't Rubble's. *Where's my gun?*

Looking up, she spotted Lyle hunkered behind the reclining chair. Her eyes dipped to the floor and she winced. The gun sat between them by the fireplace, accessible to both. Lyle met her gaze and leered before pointing his gun at her. She dove just as he let off a round. The bullet hit the standing lamp, shattering the glass. Jupiter fell with a thud and tucked into a ball. She didn't have time to evaluate how painful it felt or the throbbing pulse in the arm previously injured from her skiing disaster.

"Come out, pet, and let's finish this," Lyle sang in a mocking voice.

She peeked around the sofa and saw several Macha bikers throwing punches at the hired goons. Only two men with patches lay on the floor, but she couldn't tell if they were injured or dead. She hadn't spotted Rubble yet and that fact soured her mind.

Crawling on her belly, she moved for the patio. If she could get outside and hop over the side, she'd land on a snowdrift. The fall wouldn't kill her. She'd been through worse broken bones. There was no way she'd make it across the room to get her gun. Finding one of Lyle's bodyguards on the floor, she grabbed his discarded weapon.

"Jupiter!"

Rubble's voice made her pause and bite back tears. The gravelly baritone was thick with emotion. His was the voice she loved. And the same one she couldn't afford to lose.

Carefully, she poked her nose around the side of the couch and saw him at the door. His burly frame filled it easily. *Oh, thank the goddess.*

His mismatched eyes scanned the room, his lips moving silently as he searched for her. When their eyes met, she saw his breath of relief. Carefully, she moved toward him, grateful his brothers were keeping Lyle's thugs occupied.

Rubble took a step closer, but the tenderness in his eyes waned in the next moment, one she couldn't prevent. Lyle stood and peppered bullets toward the doorway. One of them hit Rubble in the chest. Jupiter's ears rang from the incessant firing, and she screamed, the sound inaudible among the chaos. She turned and walked without hesitation toward Lyle, pulling the trigger.

Lyle jerked around in the onslaught of bullets. She didn't stop shooting until the gun was empty, her final bullet hitting him in the neck. He crumpled to the floor. The once white carpet was now drenched in blood.

Jupiter didn't stop her assault, her rage taking over after years of abuse. She kicked Lyle's immobile body, cursing what he'd done. Tears streamed down her cheeks, mingling with blood and creating a vortex of agony on her clothes.

Strong arms wrapped around her torso, yanking her away from the mess. Her hearing finally recovered in time to hear a gruff voice say, "You really think we don't wear bulletproof vests, baby girl?"

Jupiter wiggled free and whipped around. Rubble's easygoing smile greeted her, and she smacked his chest, the act only reinforcing his statement. "You aren't hurt?" Her gaze dropped to the blood in his beard and streaked on his face.

Rubble cupped her chin and shook his head. "The only thing that hurts is when you're not with me."

Fresh tears surfaced, and she closed the distance to his lips. The sweet yet masculine taste of his mouth elicited a sigh she knew damn well she'd never forget. Rubble wrapped his arms around her, pulling her off the floor and tucking her legs around his waist. She couldn't kiss him enough. She'd never leave this man. He was the other half of her soul.

"Hey, love birds, let's go. Sheriff will be here soon."

Kevlar's voice seemed to snap Rubble out of the trance her lips cast on him and he reluctantly set her back down on unsteady legs. "We need to get you cleaned up."

It was then that she glanced at herself. Blood soaked through her clothes and her hands were blotched with red. She took in the room. Bodies lay at every exit. Macha hadn't just burst through one door, but every door they could find. For a brief moment, Jupiter couldn't breathe. The magnitude of what not only Rubble but Macha had done for her was too heavy.

"What will the sheriff say?" She clung to Rubble's leather jacket. "Will they arrest me? What about you? I can't live with you paying for my sins. I'm the one who started all this. I brought them to Snowshoe."

Tucking a strand of hair behind her ear, Rubble

offered a small smile. "I'm not going anywhere, baby, don't worry. It was self-defense" He jutted his chin toward the bodies then back to her. "These men weren't upstanding citizens. They all have records and are wanted for one thing or another." He gently pulled on her earlobe. "They would've killed you if we hadn't intercepted."

She looked toward the door as a man in a sheriff uniform arrived. "They'll believe your side of the story?"

"We don't get our hands dirty for the fun of it. Macha protects our own." He kissed the tip of her nose. "And you, baby girl… you're as Macha as they come."

A flutter of excitement mixed with relief coursed through her veins. She sighed, the weight of Lyle's abuse and betrayal leaving her. Looping her arm through Rubble's, she nodded and followed him out of the room, not looking back. The past was officially behind her and would never return.

CHAPTER 35
RUBBLE

The shower he was sharing with Jupiter following the shoot-out would never leave his memory. It could've been a simple wash and dry, but that wasn't what his girl wanted. It wasn't what his girl *needed*. He lowered his gaze and watched his cock disappear into Jupiter's mouth. Water sprayed against his head, the heat nothing compared to how hot her mouth was as she swirled her tongue around him. He placed a hand against the side of the shower, willing himself to hold out until he properly satisfied her.

Jupiter lifted her gaze, her gorgeous green eyes compelling him to come then and there. He wouldn't even if his balls begged for it. Water dripped from her eyelashes, her breasts rubbing against his legs with every bob of her head. She applied more pressure with her mouth, sucking until her cheeks hollowed.

Giving in slightly, he rocked his hips until he was fucking her mouth with his dick. She harmonized with his motions by reaching down to cup his balls, massaging them at each thrust. He'd never enjoyed sex like this before. With nymphs it was a deed. With Jupiter it was so much more. He wanted to see the light burn in her eyes. He wanted to feel the way her nipples tightened beneath his mouth.

She pulled him out, sliding her tongue along the underside of his length. Reaching his balls, she sucked one into her mouth and he felt light-headed. His toes curled when she repeated the act with the other one then returned to his cock. He couldn't wait anymore.

Tugging her off the floor, Rubble kissed her hard. He dipped his fingers between her legs and he groaned at how wet she was for him. "I want to fuck you now."

Jupiter pulled back and shook her head. "I want you to come on my face and mark me as yours." She brushed her fingers through his beard, pulling lightly. "Then, I want you to fuck me in your room." She leaned closer, her hot breath tickling his ear. "Fuck me until I scream your name."

If Rubble thought he was hard before, his dick disagreed. He didn't even have a chance to reply before she knelt back down in front of him and swallowed him whole.

"Anything my girl wants, she'll get." He started

thrusting into her mouth again, hitting the back of her throat and making her gag. She didn't fight it, choosing instead to moan every time he slipped through her lips.

After another minute, he couldn't resist. Rubble pulled his cock out of her mouth and aimed. Jets of hot cum shot along Jupiter's face, dripping on her nose and mouth. She met his gaze and swirled her tongue on the tip of his dick before licking her lips. That alone made his balls clench, and he was ready once more for her.

"You're going to kill me with sex."

She grinned and wiggled her eyebrows. "What a way to go."

CHAPTER 36

JUPITER

When she saw the purple bruise above Rubble's heart, Jupiter realized the magnitude of what happened a mere hour earlier. The webbing shot in every direction, bringing tears to her eyes. After they returned to the clubhouse, he'd left her to Queenie's care while he checked on the rest of his men. It was his duty to look out for Macha, and he did his job damned well. Her injuries had been minimal. Scrapes and bruises but nothing more.

She stood alone in the shower until Rubble joined her five minutes later. The adrenaline high from the shooting couldn't be helped. All she wanted was his skin against hers in the most intimate manner. After satisfying his need and a fantasy she never knew she had until that night, she stood nearby and watched Rubble apply bandages to his open wounds. She offered to help, but her man was stubborn.

Now, Jupiter's fingers traced the mark that, without a bulletproof vest, would've been fatal. The low lighting in his room cast shadows across the rest of his muscular form. Cuts, both fresh and already scarred, stared back at her. She hadn't caused them, but she felt responsible, nevertheless.

"Don't you dare blame yourself."

Looking up, she met Rubble's unique gaze. He traced her bottom lip with his thumb.

"How is it you know me so well?"

He ran a hand over her damp hair, rubbing gently. "I don't give a shit about a lot of things, Jupiter, but I care about you. I care if you're too warm or cold." He wiped away a tear from her cheek. "I care if you skip meals and I always wonder why. I care about the sounds you make when you come." He tipped up her chin, eyes focused on the part of her lip that was injured during the fight. "And I sure as fuck care about the tiny things that make you the woman I love."

Jupiter swallowed hard, her pulse throbbing at his husky tone. "I want you for as long as I live."

A cocky grin crossed his face. "I know."

She laughed and he caught her smile under his kiss. "Love me, Kassian."

"Always."

His hands trailed to her ass and he swatted it. The singeing pain sent blood rushing between her legs and she nibbled his top lip. A low, gravelly sound escaped his throat and he tossed her onto the bed.

Jupiter landed in the comfort of pillows. Rubble hopped on the bed just as quickly with a wrapped condom in his mouth. He tore it open and slipped it on before sheathing himself in her pussy.

Arching toward him, Jupiter's lips parted, and Rubble took advantage and slid his tongue into her mouth. She lifted her hips at every thrust, tongue dancing with his. He slanted his head to the left, devouring her while he filled her to the brim. Her first orgasm hit before she could identify the humming between her legs. She shuddered around him, clenching his cock tight.

Rubble lifted her legs over his shoulders, driving in deeper when her second one crashed, momentarily deafening her. "I wonder how many times I can make you come in one night." He kissed her forehead. "Want to find out?"

Body abuzz, she nodded, head hitting the headboard. "Give me all you got."

"Challenge accepted." He pulled out so abruptly that she called out at the loss. "Don't worry. By the time I'm done, you'll be too tired to beg for more."

He meant every word. It was written on his face and in the depths of his blue and green eyes.

In one quick move, he flipped Jupiter onto her stomach and pushed into her warmth once more. He groaned when she lifted her ass so he could fully submerge into her wetness. The bed squeaked at his rough pounding and she gripped the comforter, body shaking with lust. It didn't take long before another orgasm had her crying Rubble's name like a prayer.

Despite everything the last year had brought, he was the best part of the journey. He pulled her flush with him, and she panted at the way he ran his tongue along the side of her neck, kissing and nipping.

"Had enough yet?" He kissed her cheek and slowed his pace.

Her man could go all night and they both knew it. Looping her arm around Rubble's neck, she leaned back against him, and he cupped her breasts to hold her closer. "I'll never get enough of you."

That was all he needed to hear. A contented smile didn't leave her face until well into the night that ended with her wrapped in Rubble's arms, exhaustion overtaking them both.

CHAPTER 37

RUBBLE

The side door to the shop slammed and Rubble glanced up from the ledgers. Kevlar walked through the garage, prospects calling their greetings and a few asking for advice. Rubble tossed the book to the desk and sat back. A week had come and gone since the shoot-out at the hotel. Kevlar's old lady, Nikita, managed to smooth things over with the sheriff's office. After all, the FBI had been watching Lyle Jones for some time, merely waiting for the man to slip up.

"Got a minute?" Kevlar asked, cracking open the door.

Rubble waved to the chair across from him and waited until Kevlar sat before he spoke. "I don't like the look on your face, brother. What happened?"

Kevlar scratched his forehead, pushing his beanie

up to show his military buzz was finally disappearing. "One of Jones's guys got away."

"Damn." He smoothed his beard. "Which one?"

The other man shifted in the seat. "I haven't told anyone else. Kita just found out this morning and called me."

The worry lining Kevlar's brow immediately concerned Rubble. Surely, the club could handle a single man. "Who was it?"

"Shovelhead."

The air in Rubble's lungs deflated and he cursed. "Are you sure?"

"Kita triple-checked. Apparently, Shovelhead's been bouncing from one dickhead employer to the next."

"He went to Ireland. One of our brothers there saw him, but we lost him."

Kevlar shrugged. "No surprise there."

"He never was very loyal to one club." Rubble cracked his neck, memories flooding him of the time Shovelhead was once Macha's vice president. "So, the Twelve Brothers gave him the boot and now he's freelancing."

"I think he has been for a while." He shifted again, giving away his tell.

"Spit it out, Kevlar.

"I didn't say anything because it'd stir up shit."

"Say it."

"I swear I saw Shovelhead hanging around the Greenback Cutthroats last fall." He tapped the desk with two fingers. "But he was keeping to himself, and I was only here at the onset of what happened with Doc and Isa. I never knew him to be an asshole. Well, a betraying asshole at least."

Rubble rubbed his eyes with his thumb and index finger. He'd looked high and low for the club's Judas and the schmuck was right under their noses this whole time. It made him wary of why. There was an outstanding Macha warrant on Shovelhead's head. The club didn't fuck around with those.

"Look, I'm sorry. I should've said something sooner. I thought maybe it was a misunderstanding with the club or even blackmail that turned Shovelhead."

"Unfortunately, it was greed."

Kevlar's eyes shadowed. "I'm truly sorry."

"It's all right, brother. We all wish Shovelhead made different choices." He opened the iPad on the desk and started typing a text message to the Macha MC group conversation. They'd need to discuss this, but first he needed to speak with Reaper. Shovelhead had another angle, he felt it in his bones.

"And you're positive it was Shovelhead?"

Nikita eyed him, pressing a bottle of Guinness to her lips. "For the fourth time, yes, Rubble. My IT guys verified his identity. Why're you so shocked? Eventually the outcast always wants back in."

Rubble shook his head and nursed his whiskey on the rocks. Normally, he wouldn't drink, but the subject at hand was more serious in nature that whiskey was necessary. "Not Shovelhead. He's after something else."

"What do you think it is?"

He glanced at Reaper on the other side of the bar, where he was acting as their bartender. It didn't happen often, but now and then the club president liked to take over for a while. The rest of the bar was quiet, empty save for Brewer who was taking inventory of the liquor behind the bar. The redhead kept to himself for the most part when it came to club business, but Rubble had a feeling it was better that Brewer was listening in on their conversation.

"Revenge. We blacklisted his patch, called for a warrant, and set all our allies against him. Somehow, he wound up right where he started." Rubble glanced around the room. "He's done with us. He failed once but has used the last few months to form a new plan. Macha is on his shit list."

They all took a drink as Nikita and Reaper let his

warning wash over them. Rubble had wracked his brain all day, trying to understand the situation. Nothing came to him, which was why he asked Nikita and Reaper to meet him at the bar to discuss it. He needed a little guidance from his leader before presenting this to the club in an hour.

"The presidency."

Three sets of eyes latched onto Brewer.

"Speak your mind, boyo," Reaper said, nodding to him.

Brewer set aside the clipboard and walked over to the group. "He told Isa that was why he betrayed Macha. He's been second in command for years, never once able to become head of the MC. How do we know every attack on Macha wasn't meant to take you out, Prez, and that Shovelhead wasn't behind them all?"

Nikita's brows shot up and Reaper's bottle paused at his lips.

"Could Shovelhead really be that vindictive just to get a presidency?" Reaper shook his head. "It's a patch that's cost me more than I care to admit."

Rubble thought back on the rumbles Macha had since he joined. They all seemed like normal club issues.

"What do you think, Nikita?"

Pursing her lips, Nikita narrowed her eyes. Rubble could almost see the cogs turning in her mind. If he weren't hopelessly in love with Jupiter, he'd understand how Kevlar fell for this woman twice. She was stunning, kickass, and knew more about motorcycle clubs than anyone.

"It's more than possible. MC presidents bring in the most money. They get any girl they want. They control hundreds of men. They *are* the club." She finished off her beer and licked the corner of her mouth. "I can see it."

Reaper shifted on his feet, years not the only thing wearing on him. "For as long as I can remember, Shovelhead was loyal to Macha. He never mentioned wanting the presidency." He shook his head. "Hell, if I'd known that patch was all he'd craved, I'd have never let him join. The bloodshed he caused isn't worth it."

"That's a big *if*, Prez," Rubble reminded him and everyone else. They could conjecture all day and night, but he needed proof before anything else happened. "I'm not about to put our club at risk again if none of this is accurate."

Brewer held up his hands. "Hey, I'm just going off what Dolly and I came up with."

"What do you mean?"

"Our parents died defending Macha." Brewer glanced at the framed photo above the front door. "Dolly and I always suspected someone inside the club got them killed. Nobody else knew where they were headed that day."

Rubble wracked his mind thinking about when Brewer's folks died on the way to Macha's original bakery in town. Foul play was alleged, but only bullet holes were found, no bullets. The club hadn't opened a new bakery until recently, the loss too great to face.

"You think it was Shovelhead?" Rubble asked.

Brewer nodded. "I do."

Nikita reached over the bar and grabbed a bottle of vodka. Rubble couldn't blame her. Club officers knew more than the members and sometimes it was enough to make a sober man drink. He downed the rest of his whiskey.

"We have two choices." Reaper leaned on the bar. "Fight or leave it alone." He met Brewer's eyes. "What do you say?"

"Fight," Brewer replied without missing a beat. "Dolly and I… we know Shovelhead shot our parents. I feel it in my gut, and I know Dolly does too." He balled a fist over his stomach. "Let us uncover the truth. If he's innocent, we'll accept it, but if he had anything to do with our parents' deaths…." His eyes turned dark. "May the goddess have mercy on his soul."

Rubble exchanged a glance with Reaper. He could read in between the lines. Watching out for the men was Rubble's wheelhouse. Reaper would handle the political side of things. Rubble nodded slightly.

"All right, Brewer. We'll put it to a vote tonight." Reaper clapped a hand on the redheaded man's shoulder.

"Thank you."

Rubble watched Brewer retreat. He'd been his saving grace in the gym for years and now his buddy needed Rubble to be the same for him. He'd gladly pick up the slack wherever needed for Brewer to discover the truth about his parents' deaths. Whatever happened, Macha wasn't done with Shovelhead. *Not in the least.*

CHAPTER 38

JUPITER

Snowshoe's recent festivities quickly blended into the normal hubbub of regular winter sports. Television cameras left except for the local channels. Jupiter was grateful. She and Yasmina could finally return to the bakery. Leaving was the last thing on her mind. The club installed new locks and monitors at the bakery to be on the safe side, and she didn't bat an eye at their protectiveness.

A storm rolled in the week after the Xtreme Games concluded, blanketing the sleepy town in gorgeous sheets of white easily seen through the bakery's large window. The scent of almond cookies filled the air. Despite the near whiteout conditions, customers battled the elements for pastries and sweets.

Jupiter started pulling the empty sheets out of the display case. They'd close in another ten minutes, and the two second-shift employees would come in a few hours later to prepare for the next morning. The schedule seemed to work better as each day passed.

Taking the trays to the back of the shop, she heard the bell above the door jingle. Yasmina looked up from icing the cinnamon rolls.

"I got it," Jupiter said, setting down the empties near the dishwasher. She glanced at the monitor in the back room. Seeing a short man in a hat with a fuzzy pom-pom at the top, she grinned and headed to the front.

"Hello, I'm afraid we don't have much left, but if you come in the morning, there will be fresh batches of everything." Jupiter smiled at the man who wore small glasses.

"Oh, I'm not here to buy anything, though those pecan rolls look delicious."

A tremor of worry settled in her gut. "Ah, well then, what can I help you with?" She held her breath and hoped he needed directions. It was the general question newcomers to Snowshoe popped in to ask.

"I'm looking for you, Mrs. Jones."

Her blood chilled at the name. "I'm not—"

"Oh, I know." The man nodded and held out his card. "I'm your attorney, Jupiter."

"Mr. Neffenger?" She took the extended card and relaxed when he also held up his driver's license to confirm his identity. She'd never met him personally. They'd only spoken on the phone and emailed.

"I tried calling several times. After speaking with Lyle's attorney as well as the FBI agent who paid me a visit, I now understand why you didn't answer." He pulled off the hat he was wearing, his salt-and-pepper hair sticking up in every direction. "Is there a place we can chat? We have a few pressing things to go over."

"Of course. Give me a minute." She hurried back to the kitchen and filled Yasmina in before calling Rubble.

Twenty minutes later, Mr. Neffenger, Rubble, and Jupiter sat around Macha's large table at the clubhouse.

"These are incredible carvings," her lawyer said, glancing around the room. He traced the wood engraving and smiled. "But not what we're here to talk about." He cleared his throat and passed a folder to Jupiter. "Your divorce was never finalized, Jupiter."

She cringed at the notion. "That's a bummer."

Mr. Neffenger smiled kindly. "It's actually not." He handed her another folder, this one larger and containing more paperwork. "Lyle never updated his Last Will and Testament. The only viable one is dated right after you were married." He adjusted his glasses and met her gaze. "He left everything to you, Jupiter."

Silence simmered in the room as she absorbed his words. She shook her head, trying to make sense of it all. "I'm sorry, what?"

"Every parcel of land, investment, bank account, retirement pension, and real estate asset. It all belongs to you."

Her hands shook and Rubble patted her thigh reassuringly beneath the table. "But what about the federal case? I thought they seized his assets."

"They did." Neffenger smiled coyly. "But I managed to secure sixty percent of his net worth, giving the rest to the government."

Jupiter exchanged an unsure glance with Rubble. "But what about the way he died?"

Neffenger shrugged. "As unfortunate as it was, it doesn't matter. The state and federal police tied up their cases with pretty bows and got their payouts, so they won't give you any hassle, just like we hoped."

She nodded, not sure what else to do. It all seemed too good to be true. Her problems were over. She thought back to the will. Lyle hated her with every breath in his body, but evidently he hadn't always. "Okay, what do I need to do?"

"It's been done. I took care of it all."

"For a fee, I'm sure," Rubble added, narrowing his eyes.

Neffenger chuckled. "Jupiter entrusted me with her life almost a year ago. I take that very seriously, so no, she paid her retainer, and I won't make another cent."

Jupiter's mouth gaped. "Why not?"

Leaning across the table, Neffenger patted her hand. "Because no woman should have to pay for a man's abuse."

"But—"

"None of those, my dear. I do what I can to help others. I only ask that you do the same in return."

Wiping away the tears on her cheeks, she nodded. Never in her wildest dreams did she expect kindness from this man, let alone any of them. "Of course. Thank you. Thank you so much. I don't think I could've made it this far without your help."

"You're stronger than you realize, Jupiter." He snapped his fingers and pulled another stack of paperwork from his briefcase. "I nearly forgot. This is the insurance policy Lyle purchased. Be sure to fill out the return paperwork and send them in or the company won't pay out."

Jupiter quickly scanned the documents she didn't remember anyone mentioning. The large number on the payout page made her gasp. "Three million dollars."

"Say what?" Rubble read over her shoulder and whistled.

A nagging sensation filled her gut. "Was there a policy on me?"

A strained expression crossed Neffenger's face.

"Yes, Mr. Jones had one, but I'm not sure you want to see the amount."

Rubble gestured for it to be handed over, and Jupiter's eyes bugged at the payout. "Twenty million dollars." She let out a string of curses that'd rival a sailor. "No wonder he wanted me gone so badly. I was worth more dead than alive."

"I'll let you sort out this information." Neffenger stood. "I'm in town until Friday if you have questions."

Jupiter didn't see her lawyer leave, but she heard Rubble quietly thank him before the door shut. Too many thoughts filtered through her mind. The truth hurt, but it also set her free.

"Hey, you okay?"

She turned in her seat and noticed the concern in his eyes. A man like Rubble didn't come around every lifetime. "I can't accept the money."

"I know."

"And you're okay with that?" She pointed to the paperwork. "It's a shit ton of money. Not only the insurance, but the assets. It'd set us up for life."

Rubble scooted to the edge of his chair and searched her eyes. "I don't need money to be happy, I just need you."

Her heart swelled and she pressed her lips to his. "Me too."

He rested his forehead against hers and she closed her eyes. She'd never been one to rely on a man, but he was worth it. He wouldn't leave her, let alone hurt her.

"What do you think about Macha sponsoring a shelter for women and children who were treated like I was? I can't think of a better use for the money."

Rubble tilted up her chin and lightly kissed her. "I think Macha would be proud. I know I am."

Jupiter sighed, her heart overflowing with love for the man in front of her. She tugged on his unruly beard as she kissed him back. Their pasts didn't matter anymore. Only their future did. And she planned on one hell of a long future with this Macha man.

EPILOGUE

RUBBLE

Four months. It was how long he'd known Jupiter Quinn. He didn't regret one moment of it either. He snorted. Well, except perhaps how long it took him to fall for her. *If I could go back, I'd love her sooner.*

He flipped off the lights to the garage, the larger ones flickering slightly. He made a mental note to order a new set and have the prospects install them before they burnt out. The last thing the club needed was a shop in arrears for repairs.

Locking the side door, he glanced toward Booze & Tattoos. The neon light shone through the early spring evening, but he wouldn't join his fellow brothers. Not tonight. Tonight, he had something special planned for Jupiter. A private birthday party for her. He hadn't learned when her birthday was until after the day, so he promised to make up for lost time.

Rubble trudged through the snow to the clubhouse, waving at Dolly and Brewer shooting pool with two nymphs. The brother-sister duo had yet to uncover anything damning about Shovelhead, but both were eager and wouldn't let the club down.

Glancing around the clubhouse, he couldn't help but grin. This was his family whether he liked them all the time or not. Snoopy and Legs were in a heated argument in the corner of the room, and a prospect had his arms full with two nymphs, no doubt promising to make their night unforgettable. Cueball and Hawk were at the tattoo parlor while Klink ran the bar. He missed seeing their faces but would catch up with them later.

He walked down the hall and saw Reaper trying to steal a spaghetti noodle from the pot. Queenie playfully swatted his hand away with a wooden spoon before he pulled her in for a kiss. Their no-nonsense relationship was beautiful. Nobody really knew their origin story, but only heard tidbits over the years. He'd bet good money it was a killer one.

Rounding the bend, he noticed Doc and Isa in the den, both cooing over the tiny clothes from their recent baby shower. A tightness gripped his chest at the sight. He'd never have guessed he'd want one. Hell, he probably couldn't have any, but somewhere inside, he craved a child with Jupiter's olive-green eyes and maybe even his dark hair. He put a hand to his bald head and smirked. *Well, it used to be.*

Shaking the thought aside, he climbed the first set of stairs. He passed Kevlar on the way. Nikita was hanging on his back like a kid. He didn't have to ask where they were going in such a hurry. It was scribbled all over their faces.

Finally, he made it to Jupiter's floor. She kept her room despite spending every night in his. He wouldn't pressure her. She'd move in permanently when she was ready. He'd wait. He'd waited his whole life for this woman, so he could wait a little longer.

Rubble eyed his jeans and long-sleeved blue shirt. Getting all gussied up wasn't in his repertoire, but he tried his damnedest to look acceptable. He patted the ring box in his front pocket for the hundredth time that day. *Still there.*

Turning the knob, he held his breath and stepped over the threshold. Jupiter was sitting at the desk facing the window, laptop open.

"Hey, you. How was work?" she asked, not looking up from the screen. It was all she'd done the last month. The manager of the trust Nikita founded reached out about Jupiter's story and asked her to join their cause. Since then, she'd been diligently writing out her own experience in order to help others.

"Same old stuff, different day." He leaned down

and kissed the top of her head. He'd learned to wait until she finished her thought before trying to have a conversation. Talking didn't work well when she was on a roll.

After a minute, Jupiter closed the laptop and turned the swivel chair around. "My, my, don't you look nice tonight." She wiggled her brows. "Any special reason?"

Her gaze drifted over him, and she caught her bottom lip between her teeth when she stopped at the bulge in his jeans. He couldn't help rocking a semi hard-on when she was around.

"I heard it was your birthday."

She rolled her eyes. "Like months ago."

"Yeah, but we never really got to celebrate like I want to." He took a step closer. "In the way you deserve."

"Oh really?" She smiled and he caught his breath. No matter what happened, her smile could knock him on his ass. No twelve rounds needed for her to lay him out.

"Yep. I have reservations in town at the cute little French bistro that opened last week. Yasmina mentioned you liked French food."

"God, yes. It's been forever since I had it." She leapt to her feet and hugged him, her hand grazing down the front of his jeans. "Ooh, and do I feel my present too?"

He chuckled and swatted her ass. "Later, woman. Go check your closet."

Jupiter hurried over and pulled open the door. "Oh my God." She fingered the long-sleeved royal blue dress.

"Isa made it so it should fit like a glove."

She grabbed the hanger and beamed at him. "It's gorgeous."

He nodded. She was gorgeous. "Isa picked out a pair of boots to match. I'll meet you out front in ten minutes."

Rubble paused at the door, the desire to fuck her nearly taking over when she stripped then and there. Resisting that urge, he adjusted his dick, and made his way downstairs. This woman shattered him in the best ways. He'd always love her for bringing down the walls around his heart. He fished out the box and opened it. By the end of the night, he intended to make Jupiter his woman permanently.

JUPITER

"This place looks amazing."

Jupiter looked up at Rubble and he winked. They waited in the small entryway of the restaurant. Families and singles alike filled the space. The scent of fresh bread lingered in the air, making her stomach growl. The entire place screamed French countryside and she couldn't help but yearn for a trip overseas. It'd been almost a decade since she visited her distant cousin Mason, who owned several vineyards and a stunning villa in the French countryside. She'd discuss the possibility with Rubble once they were seated.

Her phone buzzed in her clutch, reminding her that she was on a deadline for her publisher. A warm flutter filled her stomach. After inheriting millions, she'd joined in on Nikita's shelter venture, focusing on havens for women and children on the run from abusive situations. Ground would break in the spring. She couldn't wait to put the money to good use. She didn't need it for herself.

Rubble squeezed her hand, his tender touch vastly different from the strength she'd felt and seen in him. They'd only known each other a handful of months, but that was all she needed. Running was in her past. Settling down with Rubble was her future.

His mismatched eyes grazed hers and desire shot

between her thighs. He looked incredible in jeans and an untucked blue collared shirt. He'd left his cut at the clubhouse, and she couldn't help but wonder if he felt naked without it.

A waiter walked by with a bowl full of bouillabaisse and Jupiter held her breath until the scent wafted away. Over the last week, her stomach hadn't been much of a fan of seafood. She swallowed a smile, the anticipation of whatever surprise Rubble had in store for the night kept her focused on the man beside her.

"This place is busy."

Rubble glanced around and nodded. "Yeah, hopefully they didn't give away our reservation."

"Somebody anxious to eat?" She watched his cheek twitch and held back a giggle. Rubble was rarely nervous which meant something else was going on. If it were club business, he'd say so. It was one of the things she appreciated about their relationship. Since the shoot-out, they communicated openly, nothing left unknown.

"In a way."

A tall, lanky woman with brown hair piled on top of her head greeted them. "Sorry for the wait. My usual waitress called in so I'm manning the place on a skeleton crew."

"No problem." Jupiter grinned, instantly taking a liking to the woman. "Are you new to town?"

"Actually, I grew up here. I went away for college then culinary school, but there's just something about Snowshoe that pulled me back." She checked the reservation list. "Mr. Hardy, right?"

Rubble nodded and looked around the room as if someone would call him out for not using his club name.

Jupiter held out her hand. "I'm Jupiter. I'm fairly new to town."

"Delphi Windsor." The brunette shook her hand then Rubble's. "I'm a new restauranteur myself."

Jupiter sensed the beginning of a slowly blooming friendship. "I help run the bakery Heaven's Treats in town."

"No way! We should get together sometime and compare ownership woes."

"Sounds perfect to me."

Delphi's blue eyes lit up. "Great. I'll bring French press coffee. I've been craving one of your chocolate croissants all week. They're my favorite."

Rubble pulsed Jupiter's hand as they walked. Already the outing was a success. She'd hoped to find a friend in the same line of work and there was something about Delphi that Jupiter immediately liked.

Delphi led them through the busy bistro. "I believe the rest of your party has already arrived."

"What're you talking about?" Jupiter offered Rubble a perplexed glance.

Before he could answer, they stopped at a corner booth, and Jupiter's eyes widened. Sitting mere feet away was her brother.

"Hey, little sis. I hear you've been getting into trouble." Levi Quinn slid out of the booth, and it was then that Jupiter noticed a red-haired woman with sparkling gray eyes still seated.

She swallowed back the tears and rushed forward, wrapping him in the biggest hug she could muster. "I wanted to call. I really did."

Levi pulled back, his green eyes searching hers. "Damn Quinn blood makes us a bit reluctant to ask for help, doesn't it?"

"I thought I could handle it." She hugged him again, her arms barely fitting around his wide shoulders and muscular frame. His job as a police officer kept him just as fit as any of Macha's men.

"Stubborn women are my bread and butter." He chuckled. "And speaking of women—Jupiter, this is Rayna Alley, my fiancée."

"Fiancée?" Jupiter laughed and greeted the beautiful woman before they all squeezed into the booth together.

The evening passed in a blur. They were ordering hors d'oeuvres one moment, and the next she was licking the spoon from her crème brûlée. Too many years passed since she and Levi spoke, let alone saw each other. Her time in Texas disconnected her from her family, and it was a wrong she intended to right as quickly as possible.

Only after hugging Levi five more times outside the bistro did she agree to calling it a night. He and Rayna would be in town for another week, giving her plenty of time to catch up and get to know her soon-to-be sister-in-law.

Rubble clicked his remote start, letting the engine and cab warm up while they walked along the city's square. Snow fell delicately on the quiet street as the hour neared midnight.

"I used to hate snow." She glanced at her blue boots that perfectly matched her one-of-a-kind dress. "I guess a lot of shit changes over the years."

Rubble craned his neck and looked at the sky. "It does, but I'm glad. If nothing changed, I'd still be a hot-headed MMA fighter and you'd be…. I don't wanna think about where you might be." He pulled her closer, tucking her under his arm. "I always hated when Reaper used to say, 'Everything happens for a reason,' but I get it now. If he hadn't straightened me out when he did and if you hadn't escaped when you could, we wouldn't be here." He paused and met her gaze. "And I like being here with you."

Jupiter rubbed her lips together, willing him to kiss her. For a rough-and-tumble man, he had a way with words that melted her into a puddle. "Me too."

"Flying your brother out here was only half of my birthday surprise for you." He glanced around then nodded curtly to someone across the square. "I'm nowhere near as romantic as some of my brothers, but I'm trying, baby girl."

Jupiter started to respond but stopped when the whole town square lit up with white twinkle lights. She gasped, twirling around in a slow circle, taking in the beauty amid the snowflakes. When she turned back toward Rubble, she bit the inside of her cheek. Her burly biker was down on one knee in the snow.

"You changed my life, Jupiter. I was always prepared until I met you. When I saw you, my brain stopped working. All I could think about was you. All I could smell was the scent of your shampoo. All I could taste was your skin." Rubble let out a breath, the puffy cloud mingling with her own rapid breathing. "And I don't want a day to pass without waking up beside you. I want the chance to love you for the rest of my life." He opened a small black box. "If you'll let me, that is."

Jupiter had to pinch herself to make sure she wasn't

in a brûlée-induced coma. *Ow!* No, she wasn't dreaming. She was more awake than ever before and the man she adored was in front of her asking the question she never imagined she'd want to answer again.

"Be mine, Jupiter, because you're everything I need to be happy."

Staring into his one blue and one green set of eyes, she could see her future. There was excitement, adventure, and plenty of love in store with him. She couldn't ask for anything more.

"Yes, a thousand times!"

Rubble hopped to his feet and scooped her off the street, kissing her until her body ached for more. Hoots and cheers echoed through the square and they both laughed.

"Damn, I almost forgot I invited the club." He chuckled, the rumble reverberating against her chest.

"We're Macha, Rubble, the club is our family." She kissed his bottom lip. "And maybe someday, we'll add to it."

He set her down and cocked his brow. "What do you mean? Like adopting?"

"I'd love to adopt, but not yet. The timing was never right with anyone else." She placed a hand over her stomach. "I thought it was too early to know for certain, but the pregnancy test I took today was positive. I guess neither of us is flawed after all." She worried her lips together, nervous about how he'd react. They'd never discussed it because they both assumed it was impossible.

Rubble covered his mouth with both hands, eyes darting from her stomach to her face. Finally, just as his brothers surrounded them with congratulations, his face broke into a broad smile. "Macha knows what she's doing, baby girl. That much I believe with my whole heart."

"Holy shit, engaged and pregnant? Damn, girl, you're going to need a whole new wardrobe."

Jupiter grinned at Isa who looked more excited about designing clothes than attending a wedding.

"Don't worry, your kiddo will be safe with us," Nikita added, a confident nod accompanying her words.

"And as always, the club will be here for you," Queenie finished, a motherly smile on her face.

Glancing around the crowd, Jupiter couldn't decide how to react. These people, this family, brought her in when she needed help. Macha was the family Rubble deserved, and it turned out to be the one she needed too.

Jupiter met Rubble's gaze. "This next part might be scary for both of us."

"Baby girl, after the last few months, we'll crush anything that gets in our way." Rubble brushed a happy tear from her cheek. "I don't want a future without you in it."

His lips met hers and she sighed contently. He was her home and she never wanted to leave.

THE MACHA MC'S STORY IS NOT YET OVER. CHECK OUT Brewer's story, BREWER, Macha MC book four.

ACKNOWLEDGMENTS

Many thanks to my readers for encouraging me to write more of Macha MC. I am eternally grateful for your support. A big thank you to my publisher, Hot Tree Publishing, beta readers, final edit readers, and editors for making me a better writer.

ABOUT THE AUTHOR

Skye McNeil began writing at the age of seventeen and has been lost in a love affair ever since. During the day, she moonlights as a paralegal at a law firm favoring criminal law.

Skye enjoys writing romantic comedies and cozy mysteries novels that leave readers wanting more and falling in love over and over. She writes contemporary and historical novels ranging from sweet and sassy to steamy and sultry.

Her constant writing companions are two cats and Australian Shepherd. When she's not writing, Skye enjoys spending time with family, photography, volley-ball, traveling, and curling up with a cup of coffee and reading.

Website: www.skyemcneil.com
Facebook Readers Group: https://bit.ly/2we93r3

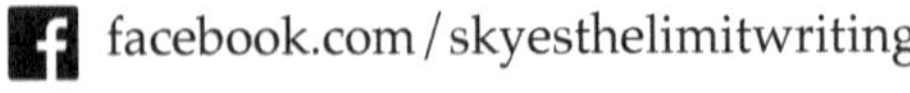

facebook.com / skyesthelimitwriting

twitter.com / skye_mcneil7

instagram.com / mcneilskye

bookbub.com / profile / skye-mcneil

ABOUT THE PUBLISHER

Hot Tree Publishing opened its doors in 2015 with an aspiration to bring quality fiction to the world of readers. With the initial focus on romance and a wide spread of romance subgenres, Hot Tree Publishing has since opened their first imprint, Tangled Tree Publishing, specializing in crime, mystery, suspense, and thriller.

Firmly seated in the industry as a leading editing provider to independent authors and small publishing houses, Hot Tree Publishing is the sister company to Hot Tree Editing, founded in 2012. Having established in-house editing and promotions, plus having a well-respected market presence, Hot Tree Publishing endeavors to be a leader in bringing quality stories to the world of readers.

Interested in discovering more amazing reads brought to you by Hot Tree Publishing? Head over to the website for information:

WWW.HOTTREEPUBLISHING.COM

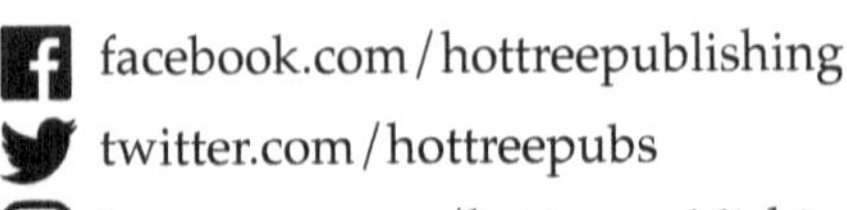

facebook.com/hottreepublishing
twitter.com/hottreepubs
instagram.com/hottreepublishing